cp smith

Restoring
Hope

Julie,
have coffee ready,
Thanks for reading,

Copyright © 2014 by C.P. Smith
First paperback edition: July 2014

Information address: cpsmith74135@gmail.com

ISBN-13: 978-1499741995
ISBN-10: 1499741995

Cover Photo dollar photo club Prochkalio

https://www.facebook.com/pages/Author-CP-Smith/739842239363610

Acknowledgements

This list is long, and I wouldn't be here without the support of so many people. To my family who supports me in everything I do, I love you and appreciate the fact you didn't throw me out of the house with all my late night writing. To my Dream Team, some of the finest ladies I've met in my life, it's an honor to call you friends. You've held my hand from the beginning and sparked my creativity. I don't know where I would be without you ladies because "the struggle is real." To my Bunco Babes, we've been together for seventeen years, and you've always made me feel like I could do anything. You ladies are my touchstone plain and simple, and I love you with all my heart. To Ellen Small, cheerleader and champion of Nic and Hope, it's truly been a pleasure. Thank you for irises and book covers ideas. To Gina Black and Casey Braun Marcotte, a mother and daughter team of Cajuns who kept my story honest and respectful of the Louisiana Cajuns I admire. *Laissez Le Bon Temps Rouler*, ladies. You rock! Thank you to all who read and reached out after "A Reason To Breathe" published. Your support and encouragement helped fuel Nic and Hope's story, and they wouldn't be here today without you.

Glossary
Cajun French words and phrases

Arréte sa petite fleur—Stop it little flower

Bébé--Baby

bon Dieu avoir pitié--good God have mercy

Bon Dieu, ma doux amour — Good God, my sweet love

Bon Dieu—Good God

C'est pas de ton affaire—that's none of your business.

Cher—term of endearment

coonass-a term for Cajun

espésces de téte dure—You hardheaded thing

grand-mére and grand-pére—grandmother and grandfather

gris-gris—voodoo spell, charm

Laissez le bon temps rouler—let the good times roll.

ma doux amour —my sweet love

Ma jolie fille, mon coeur—my pretty girl, my heart

Ma petite fille est gone—my little girl is gone

Mon 'tite fille—My little girl

mon ami—my friend

mon ange—my angel

Mon coeur je t' aime—My heart I love you

Oui, ma doux amour —Yes, my sweet love

Pas du tout—not at all

Pauve ti bete—Poor little thing

The th sound is dropped from words and replaced with d so the, there, this, that, becomes da, dere, dis, dat.

T-Hope—A "T" in front of anyone's name indicates they are tiny or small.

'tit ange—little angel

'tit boule— little balls

Tu me manques, je t'aime—you are missing from me, I love you.

For Gina and Casey "Where Y'at"

One

Rain pelted the cobblestone streets of the French Quarter, forming pools of water like little ponds as rainbows of oil danced across the surface. The day's heat, trapped in those stones, rose like a steam bath as the rain cooled the hot streets, making an already humid night, more so. There was a feeling to the night, thick and hungry, like an unseen power wielded its influence over the city. But, it was of no concern to Nic Beuve as he lit another cigarette, the last one barely extinguished. He welcomed the night; day only brought pain. Raising a glass of whisky to his mouth, he listened to the sounds of cars as they drove past, splashing water on those still out walking. The French Quarter never slept. Like a miniature New York, businesses opened early and bars stayed open late. *Laissez le bon temps rouler*—"Let the good times roll" was the Crescent Cities motto.

Throwing back the rest of his drink, Nic scanned the back of the bar looking for Henri, the bartender. The night was still young, and he was still sober. The Bayou, a neighborhood bar, owned and operated by the same Cajun family for three generations, was Nic's home away from home. Maman Rose, the current proprietor, took care of her customers and didn't water down the drinks. Dark wood paneling hosted black and white photos of the swamps around Louisiana. Pictures of moss covered trees, a Heron standing in the shallows of a slow moving Acadian river, and Cypress trees standing tall, surrounded by the black water like sentries of a forgotten time.

The musty smell of the river drifted through the door as another local walked in and sat down, as Henri came from the back with a box of beer to restock. Nic raised his empty glass indicating he needed another round, and Henri, a local Cajun with black hair and a devilish smile the ladies fought over, nodded once showing he'd seen the request. Just another night of solitude and whiskey to take away the bitter taste of loss that he couldn't seem to shake, and if he weren't careful, he'd spend the rest of his miserable life drinking away his pain, but at that moment, he didn't seem to care.

***

Hope Delaney entered through the backdoor of The Bayou, her first day on the job as a cook. She'd looked for a position that kept her out of the public eye, somewhere to hide while earning a meager living. She'd come to New Orleans hoping to blend in, or preferably, vanish. Eyes down, as she entered the back, not wanting to make eye contact with anyone, just do the work she was hired to do and then go back to the one room hole she called home.

Maman Rose had hired her the day before, and she could have kissed the woman. She'd had some money when she'd slipped into the night, enough to keep her safe for a while, but now that money was gone. Desperate, out of money, and afraid she wouldn't secure a job before her new landlord wanted another week's rent, she'd walked into The Bayou with the paper folded to the help-wanted section on a wing and a prayer. Unfortunately, she needed to be paid under the table, she couldn't risk using her name or social security number, and that was always the hitch with an employer. Maman Rose, a big, boisterous Cajun woman, with coffee colored skin and a rich Cajun accent had seen through her immediately, knew she was on the run and took Hope under her wing.

"Pauve ti bete, I don't know what's chasing you *Cher,* but Maman Rose will keep you safe," Rose had replied while looking her up and down. Hope hadn't answered the woman's questioning v eyes. *Keep your head down, don't look people in the eyes and they won't remember you. Don't stay long in one place, don't make any friends,* and *be ready to run at a moment's notice.* That had been Hope's motto for the past three months.

The air was thick with scents from the kitchen as she entered the back of the bar. Cajun spices wafted through the air like honeysuckle on a warm day back home. Each new town she'd lived in came with new and different smells. New Orleans came with the smells of magnolia flowers and spices so abundant that if you had an ounce of Cajun blood in you, you'd feel at home.

Hope didn't have a clue how to make Gumbo, Crawfish Étouffée or Shrimp Creole, but that didn't stop Rose from hiring her. Tucking her hair into a hairnet and throwing on a blue jacket Rose had given her to cook in; she entered the kitchen, and headed to the man Rose had introduced her to as Big Daddy. He stood well over six feet, and if she had to guess, close to three hundred pounds. Somewhere in his fifties from the looks of him, his caramel colored skin beaded in sweat from the heat of the kitchen and his bald head was covered with a matching blue cap to keep the sweat from running down his face.

"There she at," Big Daddy smiled as Hope waited for instructions. He looked her up and down shaking his head. *"Cher* you notin' but skin and bones you. When it slows down, Big Daddy gonna feed you yes he is."

"Big Daddy that's kind of you, but I can eat when I get home."

"Bébé, don't tell me lies. You gonna eat while I stand over you,

can't have my kitchen staff fallin' over from hunger. What dat' say bout' Big Daddy, *pauve ti bete*?" Hope nodded, knowing when she'd lose a fight, and since her last meal was stale bread that morning, she had to admit having a full stomach sounded like heaven.

Big Daddy watched as Hope acquiesced and shook his head. *Bon Dieu*, Rose was right, he thought. She looked like she hadn't eaten well in weeks, and the haunted look in her eyes told him they needed to keep an eye on this *'tit ange*. Maman Rose knew a lost soul when she saw one, and though this woman was in her late thirties, she was clearly lost.

Moving to the vegetable station, Big Daddy dumped a basket of colorful vegetables into the sink for Hope to wash and then cut. Yellow corn, plump and juicy, red peppers, big and firm, and crisp green cucumbers all would be used in the meals that night. The corn would go in the crawfish boil, a favorite at The Bayou. Local Cajuns set traps and brought them fresh crawfish daily. His regulars could go through hundreds of pounds of them in one night.

"*Cher*, I want you to start slow now. I know you don't have experience wit' Cajun cookin now, so Big Daddy ain't gonna rush you, *non*."

"Okay, Big Daddy, and thank you," Hope answered, as a small smile crossed her lips.

"*Arréte sa petite fleur*, we take care of our own, *bébé*." Nodding again, Hope moved to the sink and started washing the vegetables while worrying at her lip. How long would she be able to stay this time? A week? A month? He'd find her if she stayed too long, she knew that, he'd found her once already. Luckily, for Hope, she'd seen his man first and escaped. John was ruthless, and he always got what he wanted, and what he wanted was Hope dead, and he wouldn't stop until she was.

4

Ten years she'd endured abuse, scared if she left her husband he would kill her, scared if she didn't leave he would. And she was right, he had tried to kill her, but now he couldn't 'cause she was free, and she was determined to stay that way, or die trying.

Standing at her workstation, listening to the rhythmic slice then pound of the blade connecting with the wood of the cutting board, her mind drifted to an evening not long ago when she'd been cutting vegetables for her own dinner. She'd never eaten that meal; it had ended up on the floor of her kitchen, another victim of a violent temper. The loud crash of a pot landing on the floor broke Hope from her chilling thoughts of abuse and focused her head back on her job. She had to concentrate; she couldn't afford to lose a finger daydreaming, or in this case, waking nightmare.

Maman Rose watched Hope from behind the bar, the kitchen pass-thru giving her a view of the entire kitchen. She knew when she'd laid eyes on the woman she was running from something, or someone. Her own Chantelle had that same look when she'd come home to her Maman. A woman only looks like that when she flees for her life, and the way Hope had kept her eyes lowered, not making eye contact with anyone, not getting close, only answering with yes or no, Rose knew it had to be a man. Probably some no account fool, who thinks beating a woman till her soul is broken, and can't remember what it's like to breathe deep and feel safe, had no doubt taken a hand to her. It takes a soulless man to raise a fist to someone smaller, to control them with strength and temper, Rose thought.

"*Dieu*, just look at her. Too thin, and jumps at da' slightest noise she do." If her eyes were better, Rose was sure she could see the poor woman tremble like a dog who'd been kicked. "Da' man who'd raise his hand to dat' '*tit ange* should have bad *gris-gris* cast on his '*tit boule*," Maman Rose mumbled to herself and slightly smiled at the thought of this unknown man's balls shriveling to the size of a pea.

"*Bon Dieu*, remind me not to piss you off," Henri chuckled, watching the new woman with interest.

"Mebbe' you shouldn't hound around so much if you don't want your balls cursed," Maman Rose laughed.

She turned towards the bar and her eyes moved over her regulars. Frank, the auto repairman, who couldn't keep a wife due to the fact he couldn't stay away from bars, was seated in his regular spot enjoying a plate of Big Daddy's crawfish. As the headlights of a car passed by the window, it illuminated the end of the bar, and her eyes caught on the sight of Nic Beuve. Talk about another lost soul. His pain came from another place entirely, a place that only God and time could heal. No man should bury a child before him, but Nic had buried his only daughter a little over a year ago, and as time passed, he seemed no closer to forgiving himself for not being able to save her. No, no man or woman should bury a child; it's not the natural order of things. It breaks a person, traps them in a state of loss so deep they sometimes can't break free.

Watching Nic as he took another drink of whatever poison he needed to sleep at night, Maman Rose's lips began to curl in a smile that any wise man could see she was up to something. Fortunately, for Nic, when he raised his eyes and found her smiling, he wasn't in the mood to decipher the inner workings of a conniving old woman. If he had, he would have downed his drink, left the bar and never come back.

"I know that look," Henri announced as he watched his boss grin the grin of a woman who had a plan. Henri looked behind him at what he figured was her latest victim, and saw Nic Beuve looking puzzled as they stared at each other.

"What you got running through that evil mind of yours?"

"Maman is gonna kill two birds she is."

"Mebbe' you should leave well enough alone," Henri advised.

"And mebbe' you should get back to work and leave da' fixin' to me."

"You da' boss."

"Till da' day I die, and don't you forget," Maman Rose laughed and slapped Henri on the back.

Moving down the bar, feeling pretty darn good about her plan, Rose tossed a menu in front of Nic. His eyes dropped to the menu, and then looked back at the old woman. He didn't want to eat; it would kill a perfectly good buzz.

"Not hungry."

"*Cher*, you need to eat."

"Rosie, I need to drink."

Rose's eyes softened as she leaned into the bar, her big bosoms lying across the glossy wood. "What you need to do is forgive you," she replied in her Cajun accent, rich with French flair yet Americanized over time. Lifting the glass to his lips and swallowing more of the smoky whisky that burned his throat, but took the edge of his anger and guilt, he placed the glass down as he rose from the stool.

"*C'est pas de ton affaire*," Nic replied.

"*Mon ami*, you been comin' here for years, and mebbe' it's not my b'nez how you deal wit' your pain, but as your friend, no, I won't sit by and watch you drink till you die."

"I'm not gonna drink until I die, I've got Nicky to think about, but even if I didn't, It's my choice."

"*Cher*, you did what you had to do, and it was right what you did for Chelsea. Forgive you and move past dis' guilt."

"I'm not gonna talk about this, Rosie. I'll see you Thursday for crawfish," Nic sighed as he threw bills on the bar and turned for the door.

Picking up the menu she'd thrown on the bar and grabbing the empty glass that Nic had left, her eyes followed him as he shoved through the door. "We shall see, *mon ami*," Maman Rose whispered as she watched Nic pass the window, "We shall see."

***

A man has a lot of time to think when he doesn't sleep, but sleep would be a relief from the constant thoughts that plagued Nic's mind. The overwhelming guilt he felt for his only daughter's death meant he didn't deserve those few hours of peace. No, he didn't deserve peace with his baby gone from this world; he deserved far worse.

A parent is supposed to protect their child, keep them safe, battle their demons real or imagined until they spread their wings and fly from the nest. But, Chelsea had tried to fly too soon, and nothing he did stopped her from using drugs.

Nic lay there thinking as he did every night, wondering where he went wrong. He thought about how at fifteen, she became despondent, pulled away from him, fought with her mother and snuck out at night to meet friends. By sixteen, it was obvious she had problems that were far from normal teenage angst—then he'd found her stash of drugs and knew.

Nic stared at the ceiling, the shadows from the fan blades spinning like a carousel as he lay there thinking. They gave him something to look at while he tried for the millionth time to figure out what had gone wrong. What had he missed? Why couldn't he save his little girl?

The only person who had those answers he'd buried over a year ago along with a piece of his heart. Blonde hair, big blue eyes and a smile that would melt your heart, Chelsea was daddy's little girl—his heart and soul. Rolling to his side, her picture on his bedside table, Nic reached out and touched the frame.

"*Ma petite fille est* gone," Nic whispered to his daughter's picture. Chelsea stared back at him with smiling eyes as she laughed at the camera. He'd taken that picture on her fourteenth birthday, and by her fifteenth, she was moody and had no need for what was left of their family. He and his wife had divorced two years prior, and Chelsea and his son Nicholas spent their time between two homes. In his heart, he knew the divorce had been the catalyst for her behavior. If he could do it all again, he would have suffered through his wife's midlife crisis, and the men she brought into their bed if it would bring his daughter back. He'd worked long hours to provide what his wife needed to keep her happy, but in the end, Kat had sought attention elsewhere. No house big enough, no wardrobe large enough had kept her faithful, and he'd walked away.

"*Mon Dieu*." Nic bit out, "Look what my pride has caused."

Closing his eyes, he thought back to the last time he'd seen his daughter alive. Thin, broken, angry that he had put her into a rehab clinic for a month—she'd spat at him for leaving her there. He'd had no idea how bad her addiction was until he found her passed out in her room; a needle stuck in her arm. She'd spent three days in the hospital from that almost overdose, and then he packed her off to rehab, kicking and screaming the whole way. The last words out of her mouth had been "I hate you, Papa." He knew she didn't mean it; they'd always been close, but at that moment, he figured she did. He'd given her that and told her "I know you do *'tit ange,* but papa loves you even if you do." Then he'd kissed her forehead and tried not to look back at her anguished face, but he had, and it killed him to see her that way. "It was for the best," the doctors had said. "Private facility, one of the best in the country," they'd told him, but his angel was smart, so smart. She'd found a way out, called a friend who had drugs and then she'd taken too much. After one week at the clinic, they'd called to say she'd escaped. Six hours of searching had ended with a knock at his door from the parish police, confirming his worst fears. His baby was gone.

Breathing hard at the memories of that day, his baby's ashen face relaxed in death was forever etched in his mind. It drove a pain like a hot, sharp knife in his chest with the faintest memory. He could see her lying on that cold metal table, and he'd wanted to fold her into a blanket and wrap her in his arms like he did when she was just a babe. Nic brought his fists to his eyes and tried to rub the vision away. "Jesus, how did this happen? How the fuck did I let this happen?" he asked the room. But, just like every night he laid in the dark since his daughter's death, the only answer he ever had was the same. He'd been working when he should have been watching.

Two

Nic's eyes opened as the sun broke across his face, shining like a spotlight behind his lids. The memory that his daughter was gone from this world always took a few moments to penetrate when he first woke. In those few precious moments, all was right in his world. The knot that coiled like a snake, and was his constant companion, slowly knitted its way into his chest the instant he remembered. There were days, if not for his son that he might have gone mad with the guilt.

Looking at the clock, he knew he needed to get up, get Nicky up, and ready for school. Rolling to his side, sitting on the edge of the bed, he turned his eyes to his daughter's picture and then whispered to her sweet face, "Papa's sorry, *mon ange*, more than you'll ever know." Then he rose from the bed, exhausted as he had been for the last year and headed to wake his son.

***

"Dad, I have soccer practice after school, so you need to have mom pick me up at five," Nicky, full of energy and so much like his father in looks, reminded Nic. He was big for his twelve years, turning into a man-child already. He was tall, with black hair and dark brown eyes like his father's and their French ancestors before them. Chelsea had gotten her blonde hair from his ex-wife Katherine. She wasn't Louisiana French; she was a Southern

11

Belle from South Georgia when he'd met her in college. She'd been a beauty queen, and he'd been her prince charming. Married fifteen years before they divorced, they'd been happy once, but Kat had grown restless in New Orleans.

With her family back home in Georgia, and her friends scattered all over, she'd had a hard time adjusting to a new city. Kat was from a small town, and used to being the center of attention he'd finally deduced. Her southern charm, that Georgia Peach she'd portrayed herself as seemed too wither for some reason in the big city. Neither of them was from New Orleans, but Nic had been offered a job after graduation with one of the largest architectural firms in the city. Since Nic was from Baton Rouge, he'd traveled to the New Orleans many times, so it seemed as natural as breathing to fit in here. He'd been a year ahead of Kat, and she'd had to finish her studies before they could be married. So, Nic had moved here to New Orleans and set up house for his future wife, but they'd waited for her to graduate to plan their wedding and start their lives together.

He should have known then; the evidence was there from the beginning. Kat had made one excuse after another why the wedding needed to be delayed, but Nic was too damn busy working, to give it much thought. After a year and a half of delays, he put his foot down. "Sugar, marry me now or walk away, it's that simple." She'd married him six months later and in a huge family production, she'd moved to New Orleans, all but crying the whole way.

At twenty-four, he'd thought it was adorable his Southern Belle was that homesick. At thirty-nine, when he'd come home early to surprise Kat for missing her pot roast the night before, he'd found her in the arms of her tennis coach. It was so fuckin cliché he'd actually laughed, and what had surprised him more—he hadn't beaten the shit out of the guy—he simply wasn't that upset.

After the initial shock of moving and being newly married wore off, Kat had gotten restless quick. Since Nic came from old money and plenty of it, she'd gone about spending it on whatever made her happy. The strong-willed, southern girl, who seemed to hold the world in the palm of her hands, turned into a spoiled wife of leisure. When the kids came, she'd wanted a nanny to help raise them, he'd said no. She'd wanted a housekeeper and cook because her outside obligations took up her time, again he'd said no. Hell, to his estimation, if she could have hired a hooker to sleep with him, she'd have asked for that too.

After growing up in a home where his father adored his mother, Nic had wanted the same for his life. A woman who would stand by him, fight with him, crave his touch above all others, but mostly, love him unconditionally. He'd realized too late that Kat wasn't that woman. She was so self-centered she did absolutely whatever she wanted—damn the consequences and Nic. So, when she'd done what she'd done, and friends came forward with tales of other men, he was done and filed for divorce.

Nick sighed, not looking forward to calling Kat to remind her of the schedule change. Since their divorce, and then the loss of their daughter, Kat had been in reconciliation mode and used every opportunity she could too spend time with him. He knew the loss of their daughter was his fault, but to his estimation hers too. If she'd put their family first instead of her own selfish needs, their marriage might have turned out differently.

Pausing before phoning her, Nic needed to steel his temper before talking to her. His fuse was short these days, and no one lit it quicker than his ex-wife did. Looking at the clock, he knew he was out of time, so he picked up his phone and dialed.

"Hey there, sugar," Kat purred when she answered.

"Nicky has soccer practice until five today."

Though Nic had more than enough money to pay his ex-wife's

alimony, he still worked long hours several days a week. Since Hurricane Katrina, his expertise in historic renovations was in high demand and his schedule was full. He tried to work from home more days than not, but meetings with clients dictated he spend several days a week in the office. So, Kat agreed to pick Nicky up from school on the days he was in his office and took him home with her until he got off work. Her recent change in attitude also meant that if a job ran over, he could switch days with her easily instead of losing a single day with his son. Nic wished she'd been this fucking accommodating in their marriage then maybe things would have turned out differently.

"All right, I'll just pick him up at five and maybe the three of us can have a family dinner together just like old times. How does that sound, Nic?"

"I got plans, Kat, but thanks for asking," Nic replied abruptly and then listened as his ex-wife huffed down the line. He had no doubt, if he were standing in the same room with her, he would have seen her stomp that little foot of hers in frustration. Kat was tenacious when she wanted something, but what she wanted was never gonna happen. Their family back together was impossible, for one crucial reason.

"What you got planned, Nic?"

"Takin' my boy to eat crawfish at Bayou."

"I'd love a plate of crawfish," Kat hinted.

"I'm sure you would, Kat, but this is my time with Nicky. You can take him on your own time."

"You're just darn stubborn, that's what you are," Kat whined but Nic just ignored her as he always did when she got like this.

"I gotta go, Kat. Thanks for picking Nicky up, I'll see you at six."

"But—" Nic didn't hear her final words, he'd already moved on to what was next.

"Right, that's settled. Did you get your bag for soccer? How about your books for school?"

"Packed and ready," Nicky mumbled around a mouthful of toast.

"Then let's hit the road."

Both Nicholas Beuve's, one tall, dark and broken, one growing tall, dark and full of life, headed out the door of the condo Nic owned. Nic looked at his son, all arms and legs, and could see the man he would become. He hoped with time the sad expression he saw on his son's face whenever he looked towards his sister's room, would vanish. But, until that time, when he was with him, Nic would make damn sure his world was filled with love and attention. He would not make the same mistake he made with his '*tit ange.* He would be there for his son and teach him to be a man, but most of all, to talk to him about anything that was bothering him before he turned to drugs to ease the pain. He realized the hypocrisy of his thoughts and scoffed at himself. How was he gonna teach his son how to handle pain and disappointment when he knew with certainty, on his nights without Nicky, he'd be found with a drink in his hand? He was doing exactly what he'd tell his son not to do—drown your sorrows and hide your pain from the ones you love.

***

Peering out the window of her run down, one room, rat infested, pay by the week apartment, Hope checked and double-checked to make sure no one was sitting in a car watching her building. Rose had scheduled her to work the kitchen, and she wanted to leave in plenty of time so she could walk slowly and see if anyone followed her. Whenever she left whatever place she was staying, she always brought her most important items with her in case she caught sight of a tail. She needed to be able to run at a moment's notice, so she kept a bag packed with a change of clothes inside. Any cash she'd scraped together before she left was now gone, but when she'd had it, she kept it close as well and other than a few books she had for reading, she kept the bag light for a quick getaway.

All was clear, no cars outside with passengers watching, no shadowy figures hiding in doorways waiting for her, so she grabbed her bag and the blue cook's coat she wore at The Bayou and headed for the door.

Her apartment was in the French Quarter and within walking distance of The Bayou. The building was old, set in between two homes boasting beautiful architecture with French, Creole and American design. The houses were painted in stunning colors that reminded her of the spices she used cooking at The Bayou. Old homes with cast iron balconies and walled in gardens that were an architectural gift from the Spanish, a tour guide had said when she first came to the city, and she wondered who lived in them. Were they happy families or single people just starting their lives?

She'd taken time to wander the city since arriving in New Orleans, feeling secure when she'd first arrived that she hadn't been followed. She'd decided Bourbon Street was her favorite. There were bars, fortunetellers, gift shops and glamorous hotels all on the same street. The whole area gave her a sense of wonder and excitement, and the thousands of tourists who came daily helped her feel anonymous. A person could get lost here, never to be found, she'd thought. It was a perfect place for someone like her who needed to hide.

She walked past a bakery that had just received a shipment of flour and was pumping the light powder down a large hose into the basement of the bakery. The air around the shop was littered with a billowing cloud of white. She walked through it, not caring if it got in her hair, her blonde locks would cover it. But for some reason she wanted that pure powder that created something tangible, a form of sustenance, to coat her, like the white of it or the purity of it might wash away the dirt that always seemed to be just under the surface of her skin.

Making her way down Frenchman's Street, the heart of the bar district, Hope entered The Bayou through the front door and went behind the bar and into the kitchen. She saw Big Daddy inspecting a bag of crawfish and waved to him as she went past. She'd worked here for two days, and Big Daddy had made sure on both nights, she had eaten before she went home. Between the food and sleep she was getting, the dark circles she'd been living with for weeks were clearing up, and she was starting to look like herself again.

"T-Hope! Where y'at?" Maman Rose called as Hope tucked her bag into her locker. The Bayou, located in an older building, had been renovated sometime in the 60's by Rose's father. He'd built an employee area for breaks and a few lockers to store coats and purses. Plaster walls over the old brick kept the heat from the kitchen out when the door was closed, giving the employees a bit of a break from the heat. Hope opened the door and looked for the older woman whose bright eyes and loving heart were going a long way to making her feel safe. Finding Rose at the entrance to restaurant and bar, Hope walked to the woman while she buttoned up her coat.

"Sorry, I was putting my stuff away."

"No problem, *Cher*, I just wanna let you know we short on da' floor tonight. I need you to take orders."

"Me? But I've never been a waitress before."

"Dat' no matter, I train you myself. Everyone come on crawfish night; we need hands on deck we do."

Hope paused before answering. Her eyes grew wider at the

thought of being in the public eye where anyone could see her.

"I promise no one will touch you here," Maman Rose said on a whisper and Hope believed her. Besides, how could she refuse the woman who had been so kind to her? She couldn't, so she nodded her head and looked down at her blue jacket.

"You want me to change?"

Rose tossed a Bayou T-shirt at her mumbling, "Dat' figure will look good in my shirt."

Hope held up the brown shirt; it had a black and white picture of the bar on the front, with a neon-green sign proudly saying, "The Bayou, shoes or shirt not required." Hope smiled. She loved the shirt and the laid back friendly bar it portrayed.

Big Daddy, who'd been watching the exchange, walked over to Maman Rose as Hope headed to the back to change. With a puzzled face, he told Rose "We not short tonight old woman."

"*Pas du tout*," she replied, looking for all the world like she had a secret.

"Then why?"

"Because, my Cajun friend, love conquers all."

He watched Rose saunter back into the bar and stood there wondering what in the hell that woman was going on about. Love may conquer all, but it doesn't get his crawfish boiled. He needed to be short in the kitchen like he needed a hole in his boiling pot.

He heard the kitchen door open again and Rose yelled out in her loud Cajun accent. "*Cher*, put some makeup on while you at it, you make more tips you."

"Okay, Rose," T-Hope shouted back and Big Daddy just stood there shaking his head. *Dieu*, that woman, she has a love-match on her mind all right, and if the guy she's got her eye on for '*tit ange* had any clue what he was in for, he'd give in now and call a priest. That woman doesn't stop until a ring is on the finger, Big Daddy thought. "*Bon Dieu, avoir pitié!*" Big Daddy hooted.

Three

The Bayou is known for its crawfish. Big Daddy didn't boil them too long; it was more like a hot soak, slow, allowing the meat to absorb the Cajun spices and then he'd pull them out just as they sank to the bottom of his big pot. He loved cooking those feisty crawfish, full of attitude, ready to latch onto a finger if he got too close. Opening an onion bag full of the pissed off critters, he dumped them into his oversized sink and started rinsing them, getting them ready for the boil.

While he washed them, Hope walked out of the employee break room, her blonde hair down and makeup on her angel face for the first time since he'd met her. Rose wasn't kidding when she said Hope would look good in the bar's T-shirt, and from what Big Daddy could see, it was a size too small, as well. Nevertheless, she wore it well, and if he weren't at least fifteen years older than she was, he'd have a mind to come calling on her himself. Big Daddy grinned as she walked out of the kitchen and into the bar, ready for her night of slinging beer and crawfish, and if Rose had her way, a little love-match on the side.

The Bayou was full to the brim when Hope walked in looking for Rose. Searching the room Hope noticed the wait-staff that evening consisted of three women. Barb, a round woman in her late forties with bright red hair and an infectious laugh, Susie, a twenty something brunette that put the "s" in sexy with her cut off T-shirts and short shorts; and finally Abby.

Hope wasn't sure what her age was; she had to be in her late thirties, as well. Their lockers were next to each other and on the nights Hope had worked, they'd spoken briefly. Abby was tall, unlike her, and had medium blonde hair that fell to her shoulders. She was all legs, and Hope thought she looked like a runway model. Her husband came in at night to drive her home. Hope had watched as they left, and wondered what it was like to have a man who loved you and took care of you, instead of controlled you, and watched over you like a prized possession. Abby had reached out to her in the break room, engaging Hope in conversation, and she'd liked her instantly. If she didn't know, deep-down to her very bones that she'd have to leave someday soon, she would have wanted to get to know her better, maybe even become good friends.

Hope saw Rose standing next to a table, talking to a man with black hair that looked almost blue in the light, and a boy who looked older than his face said he was. She moved towards the table, stopping a few feet away to wait on Rose as she finished her conversation. She watched as Rose laughed with the man at something funny the boy had said, and you could see the pride in the man, for whom, Hope thought, had to be his son. The word "mini-me" came to her as she looked between the two, both with dark hair and olive skin. The boy's eyes twinkled with mischief, and she just knew he was smart. The man, sharply dressed in a dark suit, though he'd taken his jacket off leaving him in a crisp white shirt with the sleeves rolled up, was in profile. She could tell he was handsome in that European way the French had. Not so handsome that he was too pretty, but with a rugged sensual look about him. He had a strong jaw, thick manly eyebrows and sensual lips. His body looked toned; she could see his biceps tugging at the sleeves of his shirt, and his legs looked in shape, as well. He looked tall; he was big and brawny and a familiar reaction to someone that imposing set her nerves on edge.

Rose turned around, looked back and smiled big when she saw T-Hope had cleaned up real nice. She'd been guarding the table with Nic and his son, so the other waitresses wouldn't grab the table. Nic was a sexy man that women, young and old, were drawn to, so whenever he came in with his son to fill his belly with crawfish, they would fight over who got to serve him.

"Dere' my girl," Rose told Nic. "I'm training her, so you go easy on her you hear me, Nicky?"

Nic turned his head to take in the new waitress and saw a curvy woman with long blonde hair the color of snow. Her skin was pale, the color of ivory, her eyes a light blue that reminded him of the clearest and the bluest sky he'd ever seen. The word angelic seemed to fit her, and if she'd sprouted wings, he wouldn't have been surprised. Something like arousal hit him square in the chest, took him off guard when he looked at her. Then he smiled that smile he had, the one that stopped women in their tracks, when her eyes glanced at his. She lowered hers quickly when their eyes met, not quite looking at him. Then she looked to Rose for instruction, like a timid mouse, and something about that called to him, as well. He was used to women being bold, flirtatious with him. He knew women considered him a good-looking man, but after being married to a woman who readily cheated on him, he'd lost his taste for outgoing, flirtatious women. Watching her closely, he noticed she seemed almost scared to be standing there waiting to serve them. Apprehension was written all over her face.

"Come here, T-Hope meet Nic and his boy Nicky," Rose, demanded. Nic watched as the woman hesitated then came forward, rubbing her hands on her jeans nervously.

"Nice to meet you," Hope mumbled still not meeting his eyes, and he wondered how she would ever make it as a waitress if she couldn't even look at him.

"T-Hope just moved here. She knows no one but dis' bar. No Maman, no Papa, just me and Big Daddy, shame you know?"

"Did you want to look at the menu?" Hope broke in, hoping to draw the attention away from her and back on Nic and his son. The sooner she got their orders, the sooner she could move away from this man. His height and build reminded her of her husband, and try as she might, she couldn't stop her heart from racing.

"Nicky and I will start with five pounds of crawfish and two cokes, please," Nick replied feeling her nervousness coming off her like waves on the ocean.

"Got it, I'll be right back," Hope answered and then turned faster than a jackrabbit and hauled herself back to the kitchen.

"Dat' girl is timid, but don't let dat' fool you, she a fighter dat' one." Nic drew his brows together hoping Rose was right, but he couldn't see that shy woman lasting long in a profession that required interaction.

"If she puts up with you, she'll have to be strong," Nic laughed.

"She much stronger than puttin' up wit' da' likes of me, I 'guarontee," Rose pushed, making sure that Nic knew that Hope was strong, that when the time was right he could count on her to bear the burden of his broken heart. Any woman who was brave enough to leave whatever situation Hope was running from had to be strong, and Rose knew, deep to her core, it had been an abusive man. One she feared that was still looking for her.

Hope returned promptly with their order, placed a large bowl of steaming crawfish with plump yellow corn and potatoes full of Cajun spices on the table, and then went to retrieve two plates and two cokes from the waitress station she'd seen the others use. As soon as she got close to the table, and looked at Nic, she felt her heart start racing again.

"Can I get you anything else?" Hope asked the back wall,

again, not looking in his eyes. It bothered Nic she wouldn't, and he waited for her to look at him before answering. When he didn't reply, her gaze moved to his and when their eyes officially met for the first time she inhaled quickly, and her reaction caused his lips to twitch and a slow grin crept across his mouth.

"This will do for now, sugar," Nic drawled out, a natural reaction to this frightened mouse. She was so tiny, so blonde and so damn sweet looking it was automatic to think of her as sweet as sugar. Nic had a southern drawl, but more sophisticated and uniquely manly with his deep baritone voice that women of the south swooned over. As he watched a blush run up her throat, his grin became brighter as the color of her cheeks turned a sexy shade of pink.

"I'll let you eat then," Hope blurted out in embarrassment, knowing full well her face gave away that this man unnerved her. Needing to escape, she turned quickly and headed back to the kitchen as Nic stared after her, the sway of her hips locking his eyes in place.

"When you need more crawfish, you let T-Hope know, 'kay Nic," Rose jumped in as she watched Hope scurry away and then turned without waiting for his answer to chase after her.

Turning his head back to his son, they both dug into the big bowl of crawfish. Nic watched as Nicky devoured what he thought was the best crawfish this side of the Mississippi. Pulling the shell apart, until the white, tender meat showed itself, he grabbed it and popped it into his mouth.

"That T-Hope is pretty," Nicky replied around a mouth full of food.

"Saw that did you," Nic smiled, and then leaned forward and ruffled Nicky's hair.

"Kinda hard to miss, she's got curves in all the right places." Nic stopped chewing, and wondered when he'd missed his son turning from a boy to man.

"What do you know about curves?"

"Not that much, but like I said, hers were hard to miss."

Looks like it's time for "the talk" Nic thought, but he had to admit, Nicky wasn't wrong, Hope did have curves you couldn't miss.

A few tables over, several men who apparently had been drinking too much and consuming their weight in crawfish, seemed to be growing louder by the minute. Nicky turned his head and watched them for a moment and then turned back grinning.

"I love coming here, all the crawfish you can eat, and I get to see ass—I mean drunks make fools of themselves." Nic shook his head chuckling. Yeah, he'd definitely missed the moment when his son had taken that step into manhood.

Grabbing a piece of corn, Nic's eyes caught on Hope as she came out of the kitchen with another large bowl filled with bright red crawfish and his eyes stayed on her as she placed them on a table near the belligerent diners. One of the men caught a look at her in that tight Tee and said something to her. She ducked her head ignoring them, and Nic watched as her face paled. Considering how ivory her skin was, he figured whatever the man said must have been bad to cause a reaction like that. Hope shook her head when he said something else, and when she tried to leave the man grabbed her arm and pulled her into his lap. She went stock-still, and the look on her face turned his stomach sour. Without a thought, he stood up and walked over to the table.

"You've had your fun now let her up," Nic rumbled low in his throat. Hope kept her eyes to the floor, and Nic watched as she started to tremble. Reaching out to help her up, she jerked when his hand came into view of her face and bucked back; looking up, fear in her eyes.

"We're just having fun man, chill," the drunk slurred.

"Give me your hand, sugar," Nic told Hope, his voice gentle, not wanting to spook her again. Hope finally looked at him and without hesitation put her hand in his outstretched one, grabbing on tight.

"The lady wants up, now let her up," Nic repeated. He was pissed Hope could tell, but he wasn't the only one. She was angry with herself for reacting the way she did to some asshole. This "good old boy" might have been a nice person when sober, no, scratch that, Hope knew better. Alcohol brought out the bastard quicker than flies on manure, as Big Daddy would say. Taking a deep breath, determined not to let another man make her feel small, she leaned forward suddenly breaking the drunken fools hold on her and stood as Nic pulled her up and then pushed her behind him. Nic leaned into the drunk and with an icy voice told him, "You keep your hands to yourself, and we got no problems, you hear me?" One of his friends put a hand on his shoulder saying, "Be cool, Jason." Jason, being drunk, shrugged off the hand and stood, but only reached the top of Nic's chin. Apparently being drunk also made Jason think he was bigger than he was, 'cause he didn't notice Nic outweighed him by a good thirty pounds, and most of that was muscle, Hope figured.

Nic stood his ground staring down on drunken Jason, jaw tight, eyes hard, and hands on his hips looking formidable against any man. Jason's friend mumbled, "It's your funeral" and stayed in his seat, not backing up his friend. Though, Jason must not have been as stupid as she thought, 'cause after a moment of staring Nic down, what was left of his brain cells started firing. He causally brushed of the threat with an "If she don't want men to touch; she shouldn't wear her shirts like that," and then fell back in his seat and picked up his beer.

Hope was looking down at her shirt when Nic grabbed her arm, turned her around, and started walking away. Without thinking, she mumbled, "What's wrong with my shirt?"

"By my estimation, not a damn thing," Nic muttered and she realized she had voiced that out loud. Hope looked over her shoulder at him and when she caught Nic's eyes, he winked at her. Hope couldn't help it herself, it was an involuntary response, she smiled slightly and then rolled her eyes.

Nic chuckled at her response and then watched as she realized what she'd done and color returned to her face. *Dieu, she was cute when she blushed.*

"I, um, thank you for, I, uh, need to go check on the kitchen, but thank you for, well, thank you," Hope spit out on a rush of words, tumbling over them, breathy, and completely mortified that she was tongue tied in front of this man. The minute she'd laid eyes on him, he'd made her nervous. The second she'd looked into his eyes she'd felt rocked to her core. His eyes, dark brown and soulful, so brown they were almost black, but with sadness in them that she recognized. She knew that look; saw it each day in the mirror staring back at her. Not wanting to embarrass herself further, she turned quickly and went back into the kitchen.

As she walked to the door, Nic felt something inside him tighten, but this time it wasn't pain thinking of his daughter, it was a yearning for something beautiful. It had been too long since he'd had anything in his life that made him smile, other than his son, and that bit of loneliness he carried with him from Chelsea's loss didn't seem as sharp at that moment, watching Hope flee. Unfortunately, he didn't have time for a woman, he needed to keep his focus on his son, so he walked back to his table to finish his meal and keep the lines of communication open with Nicky.

Maman Rose stood at the back of the bar tallying receipts as she kept one eye on the floor and one eye on her newest love match. She was feeling pretty smug with herself when she watched Nic standup and defend T-Hope's honor, and then the looks they gave each other when the other wasn't looking. Yes, with a little well placed pushing she was sure it was only a matter of time before she could pat herself on the back at another job well done. "*Laissez le bon temps rouler.*" Let the good times roll indeed, she thought.

Four

Night had fallen in Nevada; the temperature dropping by degrees until a person could finally tolerate being outside without soaking his shirt through from sweat. Not that John Cummings would have noticed, he was too busy staring at a picture of Jessica Hope Delaney Cummings. She'd snuck off in the middle of the night like a thief, but she wasn't a thief she was worse, and she would pay for that. He should have kept a closer eye on her, should have put one of his boys on her 24/7, but he'd been busy managing his trucking empire, seeing to other matters that kept the books in the black.

He'd spent years building his empire, he and his brother, and then Hope had entered their lives changing everything. She was like an angel with her light blonde hair and cherub face, but looks could be deceiving. He learned that all too well and she had to die for her betrayal to the family. She should have known her place, should have understood not to push a man, and she should have kept her mouth shut and not argued, forcing the beatings she endured. All of it was her fault, all of it, and she would pay with her life when he found her.

His eyes focused on the light shimmering in her hair as he lifted a highball glass of whiskey to his mouth. She was, in his opinion, one of the most beautiful women he'd ever known, and if he were honest, he'd been a little in love with her. She was supposed to be a trophy wife; someone who looked good walking into a room, but in the end she'd become an obsession, one with disastrous results.

John heard a knock at his office door but ignored it; he was too busy wondering where she was hiding to care. After a moment or two more, the knock returned and he threw back his drink, replaced the photo of Hope and then turned to the door, barking out "Enter."

As his assistant entered, her skintight dress wetting his appetite like it always did, he motioned for her to come to him. As Viv walked around the desk and stopped in front of him, he reached out and circled her nipple with his finger then watched as her head fell back at his touch.

"On your knees, I want my cock in your mouth," he ordered, and like the well-trained whore that she was, she kneeled in front of him, and released his hard shaft from his pants. She opened that hot, pink mouth of hers and took him all the way to the back of her throat. John groaned, leaned his head back on his Italian leather chair and enjoyed her mouth, as she sucked him deep, swallowing all that he gave her when he pumped his seed down her throat. When he finished, she stood and started to lift her skirt. John reached out and grabbed her arm, wrenched sideways, twisting it until she whimpered, growling, "Out, I need to think." Like the smart whore she was, she lowered her eyes and then turned and left him alone to his thoughts of Hope.

He hadn't heard from his private detective in two days, and he'd lost her trail in Houston over two weeks ago. She'd disappeared, never returned to her crappy apartment, and she'd left nothing behind that would tell them where she'd gone. But, that wouldn't stop him. He'd look under every rock until he found her and then she would pay. Oh, she would pay, and he'd be the one to exact the punishment when they found her. "You can run, but you can't hide, not for long, Hope."

***

"Ride me darlin, yeah, that's it, give it to Teddy the way he likes it."

Before she did something she'd regret, like march next door and pound on the door, Hope threw the pillow over her head and tried to drown out the noise coming through the wall. It was going on two in the morning, the pounding from the headboard had woken her, and for a brief panic-stricken moment, she'd thought it was her door, and John had found her. This living in constant fear was exhausting, but no less exhausting as the constant fear she lived in while under her husband's roof. Ten years she'd lived in fear, and the thought of having to live the rest of her life this way was daunting.

When she'd met her husband while working at a boutique in Reno, Nevada, he'd been charming, swept her off her feet, and then married her within six months of their meeting. As a child, she'd dreamt of having a family of her own, not being alone, and she figured her desire for that had blocked out the warning signs. He always wanted to know where she was, would be angry if he couldn't reach her. But, after a childhood in social services bouncing around from foster home to foster home, the lure of a man who wanted her and the family *she* desperately wanted, Hope had ignored his possessive nature and married him.

The first time he'd hit her they'd only been married six months. He worked a lot, and she'd complained she never saw him when he came home late one night with alcohol on his breath. Then she'd found lipstick on his collar, and she'd confronted him with the same results, only this time he hadn't been drinking. When she'd tried to leave him he'd become enraged and attacked again saying she was his, she could never leave and if she did, he would kill her. The crazy look in his eyes as he straddled her, spittle dripping from his mouth like a rabid dog as he threatened her, told her she should believe his threat.

She'd towed the line, kept the house perfect and became the dutiful wife like he wanted, never questioning him again. However, that hadn't stopped the beatings. One particular beating ended the life of their child, a child she'd feared to bring into that house, but wanted desperately when she found out she was pregnant. Hope's throat closed at the memory and tears formed in her eyes when she remembered her baby boy would have been five this year.

Hope never allowed herself to get pregnant again; she knew it was selfish to bring a child into this world with a father who was abusive, and one, Hope had suspected, didn't want to share with his wife. He'd confirmed what she'd feared when he felt like being a loving husband one night, and confided he'd worried the baby would take her love from him. With sinking dread, she'd remembered his anger when she'd said no to sex; she was six months pregnant and tired. He'd lost it, then he'd beaten her and she'd lost her little boy.

The memory of that painful night came back to Hope, and she buried her head deeper into the pillow and cried. She'd never seen her son; her husband had insisted he be taken away when she'd delivered him stillborn, told her it would be too traumatic and then had her baby boy cremated. She never forgave herself for his death, never thought about having children again after that, just got her shots every three months and accepted her childless life.

In what seemed like forever, she heard the final thud and groans on the other side of the wall, and figured the deed was done. Hope heard laughing and giggling by the unknown couple, and for some reason, that disturbed her more than the sex she'd just been privy to. She covered her head to block out the sound, but the vision of a happy couple laying between crumpled sheets, clinging to each other in their post sex glow, wouldn't leave her. For a brief moment, she traded places with the woman, and when she envisioned herself looking up into the eyes of this unknown lover, she saw almost black eyes looking back at her. Nic's face came to her at that moment, and an involuntary blush ran up her face heating her, as her heart beat out a rapid pace with thoughts of the man.

When Nic had stood up for her, he'd made her feel safe for the first time in years. His overall package was sex personified, and even though she'd felt embarrassed in his presence, she'd been attracted to his virility. His strength had scared her at first, then it had called out to her on a primitive level, and she knew she needed to steer clear of him for several reasons. But, mostly, to guard herself against any attachments. It wasn't fair to any man; woman or child to become close to them, and it would make it harder to leave when the moment came, and there was one thing she knew with certainty, she would have to run eventually. John wouldn't stop looking for her, not as long as there was breath left in his body. He didn't give up; never backed down, not in the ten years she'd known him.

Breaking her thoughts from Nic, and done giving John anymore headspace, Hope reached for her iPod, turned it on shuffle and the first song that played was "This Ain't Goodbye" by Train. She closed her eyes and chuckled with a heavy heart; it seemed like all she had done her whole life was say goodbye. To her parents, to her son, even her dreams of a family who loved her, and now to any chance she had at a normal life as long as John was alive.

***

Nic closed the door on Nicky's room after he'd checked him to make sure he was safe; this was something he'd done nightly when his son stayed with him since Chelsea's death. He needed to reassure himself, know that he was in his bed and not out running around like his sister had done. Needing a drink, he walked into the kitchen of his three-bedroom condo in a remodeled historic building in the French Quarter he'd bought. He'd designed it himself, but only occupied the top floor, he still needed to finish the first floor condo and rent it out. He loved the French Quarter, its roots deep with his own French ancestry. They called to him, these old buildings, with their brick and mortar, steeped deep in architectural influences of the French, Spanish, Cajun and American's. His view looked down on Royal Street, just around the corner from Frenchman's street and only a three-block walk to the Bayou. He'd discovered The Bayou when he'd first moved to New Orleans. He'd gone out with a coworker one night and the old bar with its dark wood and Bayou theme he'd grown up around had felt like a piece of home. Rose had taken a liking to him right off, and her brand of Cajun cooking, love and acceptance had reminded him of a Creole woman who'd been a family friend. Being young, and in a new city, any semblance of home was welcome as he built his life here. Over the years, he'd taken his family there, and Rose had become close to his kids. When Chelsea died, she'd been like a mother bear looking out for him once his own family had returned to Baton Rouge, and the process of dealing with his loss began.

Nic looked around the condo at the old brick walls that were left untouched and incorporated with his design. He loved this condo; it suited him, more so than that gilded museum of the past that Kat had created when they were married. He loved old furniture and the history that went with them, but he preferred rugged pieces, hand-honed furniture rich in Creole and Cajun history. New Orleans was the perfect place for him as an architect, and after Hurricane Rita, his love for remodeling spaces and building conversions put him in high demand by those who could afford to remodel. His mind drifted to his ex-wife while thinking about the differences in their homes, and the all too familiar feelings of contempt he had for her resurfaced.

Kat's blonde hair, the color of corn silk, morphed into hair that shimmered like snow on a sunny day and her face turned into Hope's frightened one when that asshole had manhandled her. It still made him angry when he thought about it. No woman should be that scared by a man's touch, and it bothered Nic to think about why she'd had that visceral of a reaction to being pawed at by a man. Most women would have been pissed and given a man like that what-for. That her natural reaction had been one of fear told him she'd had reason in the past to be afraid, and that made the anger he'd held onto like a slow-simmer heat back up.

He sighed; he didn't need to be thinking about this woman, he needed to stay focused on his son, but for some reason he couldn't shutdown his train of thoughts. Even when he tried to steer them in a different direction, something would take him back to their evening at the bar and those sky-blue eyes full of fear. Running his hands through his hair, and noting the time was well past two, he walked down the hall and climbed in his king size bed. Hands behind his head, he stared at the ceiling, the shadows of the fans blades keeping him company again as he continued to think about Hope. What he didn't do as he fell asleep was turn his thoughts to his daughter for the first time in over a year. If he'd been aware of it, he might have taken a deep breath, and realized the knife in his chest wasn't there for the first time in that same year, as well.

***

The bustle of Bourbon Street at mid-day might be annoying to some, but to Hope it gave her a sense of anonymity, just another faceless person in the crowd wandering the streets of the French Quarter killing time. With the tips she'd made the night before, Hope decided to visit some of the offbeat stores in the area. She wouldn't buy much, needing to save her money, but she wanted to find a little treasure to remind her of this place when she left. She had about an hour to kill before work and was making her way down the crowded street when a woman stepped in front of her. Dressed in layers of gossamer fabric in vibrant colors, her long, dark hair in contrast with those bright colors gleamed in the sun, and the whole look gave her a gypsy feel.

"Your soul is in turmoil," she replied looking Hope from top to bottom.

"Pardon?"

"I felt you from a block away it pulled me from my shop."

"I'm sorry?" Hope replied, thinking the woman was upset but confused by this conversation all the same.

"Come, I will read you for free," the gypsy woman continued and then grabbed her hand and pulled her into her store. The store was dark with similar gossamer fabric draped around sectioning off the front from the back and in the center, was a display of crystals and candles with the prices displayed. There were candles lit on mantels and tables scattered throughout the store, and incense burning in dishes; a kinda woodsy smell that made Hope relax. There was nothing much to her store, just a table and chairs in the back with a stack of tarot cards waiting to be shuffled.

"I *really* don't need a reading," Hope tried to explain to the woman.

"If anyone ever needed a reading it is you, now sit, I won't charge you the spirits are yelling at me to read you. Now, what is your name?"

"Um, Hope, my name is Hope."

"I am Madame LeFarr. Sit, sit, I need to stop the shouting in my head."

Hope sat abruptly in the chair, forced down by Madame LeFarr. She could feel her heart beating quicker, afraid that the cards, though she didn't believe they could tell someone their future, would somehow tell her sordid tale.

Madame LeFarr shuffled the cards while staring at Hope, reading her with her eyes, looking for whatever caused the sadness is this woman. She'd been drawn to the door, almost shoved out of it and into this woman's path. Very seldom did the spirits push her so hard to read for someone, and her own curiosity as to this woman's problems, and the need for the spirits to intercede, was making her own heart pound. Cutting the cards in half, she focused her mind on this woman so the cards could answer her questions. After she'd centered her thoughts, she took a deep breath and starting dealing out the cards.

"The Hierophant, the Fool, the Devil, the Ace of Cups and the Ten of Swords," Madame LeFarr announced as she placed the card down in front of Hope. "The cards tell me you have met a mentor or teacher of some sort, someone who is showing you the way." Hope couldn't help but think of Maman Rose.

"The Fool card tells me you are starting over, and the Devil card tells you that no one has any power over you if you don't let them." Hope's heartbeat picked up as the cards seemed to be telling her tale, but they were wrong in one aspect, someone could wield power over you whether you wanted them to or not.

"And the last two? What do they tell you?" Hope found herself asking.

"The Ace of cups usually stands for love. I would say there is a relationship in your future. One, if given time and attention, could move from a slow moving stream to a river flowing so fast and hard it will take your breath away. But, take heed, the Ten of Swords in my experience signals danger. The cards are telling you something, and you must be vigilant. I get the feeling you're a magnet for trouble, that an unknown force is tracking you, always in the recesses of your life causing havoc."

Hope rose abruptly, shaken by the reading, not wanting to acknowledge there was any truth to the cards. She smiled weakly at the woman saying, "Thank you for your time," and without a backward glance ran from the store and into Nic Beuve as he walked past the shop on his way to lunch.

Nic, being plowed into from the side, grabbed onto whatever had hit him. Looking down, he saw sky-blue eyes staring back at him in shock. Hope's mouth moved as if she was trying to say something, but the words wouldn't come.

"You okay, sugar?" Nic asked concerned.

"I'm so sorry! I wasn't looking where I was going," Hope stuttered, shocked she ran into the last person she needed to be close to at that moment. Nic's face had come to her when Madame LeFarr had spoken of love, and to run into Nic after that disconcerting reading, just made the whole reading seem genuine.

His arm at her waist seemed to grow tighter as he moved her out of the doorway of the store. His eyes moved to the sign above, and she could feel her cheeks grow hot with embarrassment. He'd think she's stupid for being in that store.

"Gettin' your palms read, sugar?" Nic asked. There was amusement in his voice just like she knew there would be.

"Um, no, just checking out the stores in the area before heading to work."

Hope stepped back from his touch needing to distance herself; the masculine smell of his cologne was too appealing. "It was good seeing you again. Have a good day," Hope rushed out and then turned quickly not waiting for his reply.

Nic stood there with a confused look on his face as he watched Hope walk away from him. He didn't need any distractions in his life, but something about the woman spoke to him, and the more he was around her, the harder it was for him to ignore her. When he turned to leave, he caught sight of a woman in the tarot card window looking in the direction Hope had just gone. Her face was full of sorrow as she watched Hope disappear down the street and then her eyes moved to his. They stood there staring at each and a small chill ran down his spine as she smiled sadly at him, nodded once and then turned from the window and left. Nic stood there a moment longer and then looked back the way Hope had gone. Making a decision, he didn't understand, he put a nightcap at The Bayou on his agenda for the evening. He didn't normally go to the bar on the nights his son was with him, but Nicky's soccer practice got out later tonight, so after his daily run to Café du Monde for beignets, he intended to break his pattern.

Five

The musky, manly scent of Nic's cologne lingered on Hope, his dark, soulful eyes rambling around in her mind's eye. In another place, another time, if she were another person, she might have been tempted, but it was out of the question now. Heading to The Bayou early, she figured she could hang out in the break room until her shift started. The encounter with the Madame LeFarr left her shaken; exploring more shops had lost its appeal. Entering through the back, Hope headed to the break room and hung up her purse in her locker then pulled out a book she'd been trying to read; a romantic suspense with a sheriff and a reporter based out of Colorado. Why couldn't her husband have been like the sheriff in this book? Possessive but loving, she knew this man wouldn't lay a hand on his wife; he was a real man, one who protected the heroine and fought for her. That was what Hope had been looking for when she met him, and his possessiveness made her think he was that type of man. One who protects you, keeps you safe, and loves you unconditionally. She should have known men like that are only in romance novels.

Turning the page and laughing out loud at the ridiculous situations the heroine got herself in, she was smiling when Abby walked into the room.

"Good book?" Abby asked as she put her own purse in her locker.

"Yeah, the hero and heroine argue a lot but their conversations are hilarious."

"Sounds good. You workin' the floor again tonight or in the kitchen?"

"Oh, um, that was just for one night to help out, I'll be in the kitchen tonight."

"You got lucky last night waiting on Nic and his son. They've been coming here for years; easy customers and big Nic isn't hard on the eyes, either," she laughed. Hope nodded but didn't reply and soon felt Abby's eyes on her. She looked up at the woman, and it seemed like she wanted to ask her something.

"Is everything ok with you?" Abby finally blurted out.

"Sorry?"

"You just seem, I don't know, sad."

"Oh," was all the reply Hope had for her. What did she say? She was sad, tired—lonely.

"Sorry, I shouldn't pry. But, if you ever want to talk, I'm here, okay. I won't judge you; we girls have to stick together, ya know?"

"That's sweet, but I'm fine, really. I like to keep to myself; I'm just shy." Hope looked back at her book hoping to end the conversation, but Abby seemed inclined to talk.

"Did you like working the front of the bar last night?"

"Sure, it was different but I prefer the kitchen. Less chance of being grabbed by a man," Hope laughed.

"You'd make more money out front. With your looks and that figure, the tips you'd make in an evening would make up the difference in pay."

"That's good to know, but I'm happy back here."

"Well, if you change your mind, let me know, I'll put in a good word with Rose and we can share days if you want."

It shocked Hope that Abby would be willing to share hours with her when she probably needed them herself. She knew Abby had three kids to feed, and that was even more reason for Hope to like her and not ask for work out front. Abby needed the money more than she did.

The conversation lulled, as Abby turned to get her apron for the night, when Rose entered the break room as Hope watched Abby getting ready to go on shift. She stood there flipping through the schedule, talking to herself and shaking her head. The big woman always made Hope smile; she had a presence that brightened a room when she entered.

"We got too many on tonight. Don't know what I was tinkin' when I made dis' schedule," Rose complained. Abby turned suddenly, a huge smile on her face and jumped into the conversation.

"Hope and I can take the night off if you need to cut some people. I'd love a night off, and I already have Eric at home with the kids. What do you say Hope, wanna get a drink with me instead of working in that hot kitchen?" Before Hope could answer, Rose smiled nodding her head, agreeing with the plan.

"Sure she do, you both get outta here and have some fun while you still young."

"Oh, that's ok, I can just go—"

"No—" both women shouted at the same time, looking back and forth at each other. Hope could swear there was almost panic in their voice.

"But—"

"It settled it is. You and Abby will go and have a good time yes you will."

"But—"

"Let's blow this place, Hope, grab your purse before she changes her mind," Abby joined in, closing her locker, her purse in hand moving towards Hope.

"But—" Hope tried to get out again, but neither would let her talk.

"While I'm tinkin' about it, you didn't get tipped out last night, you run off too quickly," Rose informed Hope and then pulled out a wad of bills handing it to her. Staring at the money, she was confused, she was sure she'd gotten all her tips the night before. Turning to Rose, Hope tried to tell Rose she'd made a mistake.

"This isn't—"

"You done good last night, *tit ange*, take your tips and go have fun." Before she could protest, Abby grabbed Hope's purse, handed it to her and started pushing her towards the door. Trying, but failing to explain she would just go home, Hope was surprised at how quickly she'd lost control. Her mouth opened and closed, trying to find words to excuse herself from a night out on the town, but no one would listen. *How the hell did this happen?* Hope wondered as she dragged her feet.

"You girls have fun, have a drink for Maman, you hear?" Hope heard Rose say as Abby pushed her out the backdoor and into the alley.

Abby folded her arm through Hope's and started walking them towards the street, pulling Hope with her as her feet protested. Going out on the town didn't seem smart, but she hated to let Abby down, mothers needed a night out every once in a while, she figured. Keeping her mouth shut, Hope decided one drink wouldn't hurt; she'd just keep her eyes peeled for anyone suspicious. Though, in the crowds of the French Quarter, she felt safe from detection.

As they headed down Frenchman's street, they kept passing bar after bar. In no hurry to stop it seemed, Abby kept walking and talking about her kids and husband. She explained that she loved them, but they drove her nuts most days, so a night away from them would be just the ticket. What she didn't do Hope noticed, was stop at a bar. Not knowing the area well, Hope kept quiet and kept listening, laughing and responding in the appropriate places and before she knew it, they were on Decatur Street, and Jackson Square was in view.

She'd toured the square once since arriving but hadn't had much time to take in the area extensively. Jackson Square was a large park, known for the artist and musicians who shared their craft for tourists. Artists drew their portraits and the musicians performed for tips. It sat directly across from the historic St. Louis Cathedral, with a large statue of Andrew Jackson, the namesake for the park, in the center.

It was early evening when they arrived, and a Jazz band had set up in the center of the square next to Jackson's statue. They were playing bluesy tunes while tourists listened, and artists drew, but Abby kept Hope walking past the park until they crossed the street and headed straight to Café du Monde. This café was renowned for their *café au lait* and its French-style beignets. With its green and white striped awning covering the patio seating, and just cattycorner from Jackson Square, it was the perfect location to people watch. When they made their way through, Hope could see it was full to the brim with customers taking a break and enjoying the heady coffee and sweet beignets.

Abby pushed through the crowds of people looking around the patio for a table. After a moment more of searching, she moved them the edge of the patio that overlooked the square and found a table close to the street. The table had a great view of the square and all the tourists milling around, allowed them to people watch while they had their coffee. Though, Hope was surprised Abby had chosen a coffee house instead of a bar, but she wasn't going complain, this was more her speed. She didn't need to be drinking; she needed to keep her wits about her at all times.

Once they had placed their orders, unfortunately for Hope, Abby wasted no time in grilling her for answers.

"So, tell me about yourself, Hope," Abby asked as they waited for their coffee. Hope had rehearsed her answer thousands of times, and the story she told people to protect them and herself about her past, rolled off her tongue with practiced ease.

"I just moved here from Arkansas, recently divorced, I wanted to start over in a new city."

"Arkansas? You don't have an accent."

"I'm not from there, we moved for my husband's work."

"Where did you grow up?"

"Here and there, I was an army brat."

"Why didn't you move closer to your parents?"

"My parents are deceased, car accident." Abby's eyes widened then she gave Hope a small sad smile, as she reached across the table and grabbed her hand. She felt bad about the deceit, but told herself it was for the best. She wouldn't be here long, anyway.

"I'm sorry that must be hard. No kids then?"

"No, my husband was, um, sterile."

"Well, you're still young enough; women have babies all the time in their forties; you should find yourself a good man and have one before it's too late." Ignoring the knot, she always got when she thought about what she'd lost; Hope smiled and nodded in agreement. Luckily, for Hope, the coffee and fresh beignets came before Abby could dig deeper into her past.

The coffee was sublime; the beignets smothered in powdered sugar and so good, Hope thought about buying some just to have at her apartment. After consuming their treat, they moved across the street to view the artists who had set up around the outside of the square. Several were very good and one man was wasting his talent sitting there in the square. He should be painting somewhere with a setting sun and offering up his work to a gallery somewhere.

"You know, Hope, I meant what I said. If you ever need to talk,

I'm a good listener," Abby began, taking Hope by surprise.

"Thanks, I appreciate that."

"But you won't?"

"I didn't say that."

"It was implied . . . Look, Rose and I have both noticed how quiet you are. We're your friends, and I hope you know that you can trust us to keep any secrets you have." Hope knew that Rose was worried about her, she could see it in her eyes when she caught Rose watching her, but she had no idea that Abby had noticed, as well.

"I know I don't talk much about myself, but there really isn't much to tell, that's all."

"Uh, huh. Well, keep in mind the offer is there, I mean it."

"Okay, thanks, but I'm fine, really," Hope replied, hoping Abby would change the subject.

As they wandered the front of the park, Abby's attention seemed to be on the people, as if she was looking for someone. Hope was just about to ask if her husband was coming to join them when she heard the sound of a horse snorting air through its nose. She loved horses, dreamt of owning one as a little girl, but she'd never ridden. Turning, she saw a walnut colored horse and large carriage with the driver standing on the street corner. The driver offered rides around the French Quarter at a leisurely pace, the sign said, so she walked over to the horse and rubbed its nose, clucking her tongue at the horse. As she stepped down off the curb to get closer to the animal, a nearby car backfired, startling the great beast. The horse jerked its head back, knocking Hope in the chest and sending her to the ground just as the horse reared up. She threw her arms across her head to protect it; had no doubt the animal would come down on top of her. Hope heard Abby scream "Oh, my god," just as strong arms suddenly grabbed her at the waist, pulled her off the ground and onto the sidewalk. Shaken, positive she was going to be trampled by a horse, Hope turned to say thank you and found the same dark, soulful eyes looking down on her for the second time in one day.

"You all right?" Nic asked, checking her from head to toe.

"I, I think so."

"You think so or you know so?"

"I'm fine, really," Hope replied as her bottom lip started to quiver. Taking a deep breath to settle her nerves, she tried to smile at Nic.

"Why don't you sit down," Nic told Hope as he watched her shake. His heart had about stopped when he turned the corner heading for Café du Monde for his nightly coffee. Hope had been standing rubbing the horse's head when it knocked her to the ground. He'd started running towards her as the horse reared up, startled by a backfire, and pulled her into his arms just as the horse landed in the spot she had occupied. Twice in two days he'd come to her rescue, and he got the feeling she wasn't exactly new to these precarious situations.

Turning Hope in his arms, he walked her to a bench and had her sit. Abby came over with a bottle of water she'd bought from a vendor and handed it to her. Both he and Abby stood over her as she took a drink, her hand shaking as she raised the bottle to her lips and drank deep.

"You better now, sugar?" Nic whispered to her as he kneeled down in front of her. Hope wouldn't hold his eyes, just like last night, but she nodded.

"Well, that was enough excitement for one evening I think," Abby laughed.

"I'll second that," Hope agreed. "In fact, I think I'll head home and take a calming bath if it's all the same to you, Abby?" Hope didn't want to be there, not with Nic, he rattled her. She felt off balance around him and just wanted to slink back to her apartment.

"Ok, we can call it an evening. I'll call my husband and have him come pick us up."

"No, I can walk. It's not that far from here," Hope insisted, needing to get away as soon as possible.

"I'll walk you home," Nic told her and she started shaking her head no.

"NO! No, I'm fine you enjoy your evening."

"I'm not lettin' you walk alone; my momma would be cross with me if she knew I allowed a lady to walk home unescorted."

"But— "

"You want us to wait for your husband to arrive?" Nic asked Abby as he helped Hope to her feet.

"No, it's fine; we don't live far from here, and I think I'll get some beignets for the kids, you guys run along," Abby smiled and then winked at Hope like they had a secret.

"You ready?" Nic asked.

"Really, I can walk home by myself," Hope explained but no one listened.

Nic smiled at her, took her arm and folded it into his as he started moving toward the edge of the park. Hope looked back at Abby, who was smiling, watching them leave and then she gave Hope two thumbs up. *What on earth?*

"Which way?" Nic asked, pulling Hope away from thoughts of Abby's bazaar behavior.

"Um, Royal Cross apartments," she answered not thinking.

"You live at the Cross apartments? Jesus, that place is a dump, is it even safe?"

"I think so."

"Does it have a deadbolt?"

"Of course."

"Fire exit, smoke alarms?"

"Yes, but—"

"You need to find a new place to live, sugar—"

"Look, it doesn't matter. It's what I can afford," Hope broke in but let slip she was short on cash. *What was it about this guy that she couldn't keep her mouth shut?* Hope was done; she couldn't take another minute in this man's company, or she'd start spilling secrets to him. He didn't know her, and she needed to keep it that way for his own safety. Determined to keep her distance, she pulled her arm from his and stepped back as Nic turned a confused look to her.

"I appreciate your concern, but I'm only here for a little while until I get on my feet, then I'm moving on. So you needn't worry about my living conditions, in fact, you can just forget about walking me home, I don't need your help." She turned to leave, but Nic grabbed her arm stopping her.

"I said I'd walk you home and considering where you live, I'm doin' it," Nic bit out, trying to keep his anger in check.

"Well, here's the thing, Mr. Beuve." Hope leaned in looking him square in the eyes, "I don't want or need your help."

"Are you always this reckless?"

"Are you always this daft?"

"Daft?" Nic growled.

"You clearly have the impression I'm seeking your attention, but I can assure you that I'm not. If I never saw you again, you wouldn't cross my mind." The word liar ran through her head because Nic was a man not easily forgotten and she knew it.

"Is that so?" Nic chuckled.

"It is, now, if you'll excuse me, I have better things to do than stand here arguing with you. Enjoy your evening, Mr. Beuve, maybe I'll see you at the bar sometime." With that, Hope turned on her heels, walked down the sidewalk, and disappeared from

Nic's sight.

Instead of being pissed, Nic was intrigued even more. Though he was sure of one thing, she hadn't lied when she said she wasn't seeking his attention. Hope was clearly hiding something, and her behavior told him what she was hiding was bad. She'd recoiled at a hand raised towards her face and a drunken man made her shake like a scolded dog. Yet, she seemed to have a core of strength she called on when she needed it. She was a mystery wrapped up in a mystery he didn't have time for, but her reaction to him, and the drunk, had his mind working overtime, and the thought of her hiding, for whatever reason, set his protective instincts into overdrive.

Setting out after Hope, Nic kept his distance until he saw her enter her building safely. He watched from the street until he saw the second floor apartment in the front turn on a light, illuminating the street with its glow. A dark figure peaked through the blinds but didn't move—watching the street—searching for someone. Nic's jaw tightened and he felt his hands curl into fists. She was alone, scared, and hiding.

Not while you're around to protect her, Nic thought as he pulled out his phone from his back pocket and dialed the number he knew by heart. When the rich Cajun accent answered, Nic got down to business. "Rosie, we need to talk."

Six

The Bayou was in full swing when Nic entered. Cajun music was blasting from the sound system and there were diners at every table. The sound of silverware hitting plates rang out as they consumed their meals, but Nic ignored it all. Rose was waiting for him behind the bar, so he pulled up a seat, nodded once at Henri for his usual drink and watched as Rose made her way down to him with an intrigued look on her face. After Henri had placed his shot of whiskey in front of him, Rose leaned in for their talk.

"What's this about, *Cher*?"

"Hope," Nic responded and he watched the old woman's mouth twitch into a smile.

"She a fine looking woman, no?"

"She's a woman in hiding."

"She dat' too."

"What's her story?"

"Come to me dis' week looking scared, hungry and beat down. I give her a job and dat' it, I knows notin' but dat.'"

"She hasn't told you anything?" Nic asked surprised. Women as a general rule loved to gossip, he was sure Hope had told Rose her troubles.

"Some troubles cannot be spoken, *Cher*, *you* know dat' bettah' dan' anyone." Pausing to take a deep breath at the reminder of what he'd lost, Nic nodded in agreement, some things were hard to talk about.

"I know you well enough to know you've got an opinion on the matter. What's your take?" Nic asked moving the conversation from him and back to Hope.

"She runnin' from her past, from a man who used his fist I sure a dat.' A woman don't look da' way she looked unless it been bad dat' much I can tell you." Nic felt his jaw tighten when Rose said fist. The thought that any man would raise a hand to a woman made his blood boil, but when you took in how small and fragile Hope was he saw red.

"What you tinkin,' Nic?"

"I'm thinkin' she needs to stop runnin' and let people help her."

"She won't listen. Dat' girl got one foot out da' door anytime she here. She got to have a reason to stay and fight, *pas de bétises.*"

Thinking about Hope's curves and those sky-blue eyes, Nic wanted to say he'd give her a reason to stay, but he knew he couldn't make that promise. He had to focus on Nicky, not get involved with a woman.

"Then make her feel like she's wanted here, give her a reason to stay, Rose. Invite her to your house; spend time with her out of the bar, anything that will build a connection."

"I will do what I can, *mon ami*, but notin' will keep dat' woman here but love. She scared for her life she is."

"If you think that someone should be me then get it out of your head," Nic sighed.

"I not tinkin' about you. You too wrapped up in your own pain to give T-Hope what she need. I tink' Henri could use a good woman and he need to stop his wild ways he do." Rose smiled then looked over her shoulder at Henri. The man in question was a tomcat; bed everything that came into the bar that was a willing participant. Nic looked at the man, all playboy and not a lick of common sense that he could see. Then the thought of Henri looking out for Hope didn't set well in Nic's gut and a surge of jealousy flared when he thought of Henri touching her. *Shit.*

"Why don't we concentrate on keeping her safe instead of fixing her up with the neighborhood manwhore," Nic ground out.

"How you gonna do dat? She won't let anyone help her. I say a man who falls for her is what she need. He'd protect what is his, no?"

"Yeah, if he's any kind of man he protects what's his," Nic agreed and then thought of how he hadn't protected the one thing in his life he should have protected the most.

Nic didn't agree with Rose, he knew Hope needed to feel safe before she could get her life back on track, and she needed people in her life she trusted, not to be set up on blind dates. In Nic's opinion, getting her out of that rat-infested building was the first order of business they should concentrate on, not her love life.

"You got bettah' idea, Nic, I all ears," Rose broke in after he'd been silent thinking.

"She's livin' at the Cross on Royal," Nic informed Rose and then watched as she inhaled sharply with disgust. "She's not safe there; she needs to move, period. She let slip it was all she could afford, so we need to find a place that we can control the rent. Do you know anyone with an extra room?"

Rose thought for a moment and then a smile crossed her face. There was a reason she always succeeded when it came to affairs of the heart—she was devious.

"I know da' perfect place for *tit ange.*"

"And that would be?"

"Wit' you."

"Excuse me?" Nic barked out. He couldn't have the one woman who's piqued his interest in three years living in his daughter's room.

"You got dat' downstairs condo you workin' on, yes?"

Rose watched as Nic thought about that and then smiled as she watched the inner workings of his mind. He was more than just worried about Hope being alone and she knew it. She saw the way his eyes had followed Hope around the bar the night before. He was interested in her as a woman, but too caught up in his own grief to see it, or his guilt about Chelsea wouldn't allow him to act on it. She knew Nic, knew what kinda man he was, knew when something was his he'd move heaven and earth to take care of it, even if that person didn't deserve it. His no account wife came to Rose as she waited for Nic to sort out his head. He'd worked his ass off for her, taken care of what was his, and she'd thrown it all away because she was a selfish cow. Nic deserved better than Kat, and Rose was gonna see to it he got better.

"Well?" Rose finally asked when he said nothing.

"Yeah, that would work," Nic agreed, and couldn't believe he hadn't thought of it himself. She needed someone to look after her whether she wanted it or not, and with Hope downstairs, he could keep an eye on her and be there if something happened.

"Good, how you gonna convince her to move?"

Nic shrugged, threw back the shot that Henri had brought him, then stood. "I'm not gonna ask, I'm gonna tell her she's moving."

"Oodoggies, dat' what I like, a man who takes charge."

Nic shook his head at the old woman and grinned. If he didn't know better, he'd think she was trying to set him up with Hope the way she pushed him. Nic paused on that thought before leaving and turned back to Rose setting her straight.

"I'm only helpin' her out. Don't get any ideas," Nic warned.

"*Mon ami*, only idea I have in my head is dat' everyone I care 'bout live life good." Nic gave her a look that said he doubted that, but gave her a kiss on the cheek before he left.

Rose remained at the bar as Nic walked out, then she looked

out over the old restaurant and saw families enjoying themselves, eating Big Daddy's cookin' and feeling life was good. She smiled when she thought about how far she'd come in getting' Nic and Hope one-step closer to what they needed to heal. People pay good money to have doctors tell them what they are feeling, but she figured they could save themselves some money if they'd just remember that the answers to all life's troubles begins and ends with love. Love of family, love for a good man or woman, that's all anyone really needs. With love, anything is possible.

***

"What did I tell you about keeping your mouth shut?"

"I can't just sit here while—"

"You will do as you're told," John bellowed.

"You're filth and I won't let either of you get away—"

"You will keep your mouth shut, or you're dead do you understand?" John yanked Hope's head back by her hair and then backhanded her across the face. The force of the blow sent her flying to the floor like a ragdoll forgotten by a child. As she lay stunned on the ground a foot connected with her ribs, and she felt the snap echo throughout her body. Hope gasped, trying to catch a breath through the fire that burned in her chest, as she stared at her husband and his brother. The pain was minor, compared to the pain in her heart, just knowing this was her family. Not done with her, John grabbed her by the back of the head, fisting her hair taut as pain shot through her scalp, then pulling his fist back he mumbled, "You brought this on yourself."

Gasping for air, Hope sat up and looked around her sorry excuse for an apartment. She tried to clear her head from the reoccurring dream. The view didn't help much; it was one-room with a small grimy kitchenette. The bed was old, the mattress older. She'd bought a plastic mattress cover to seal in whatever lived on the surface, and a used pair of sheets at the local Goodwill. No TV, one lamp, dirty cream-colored walls and a single dresser for her clothes. The bathroom had disgusted her and she'd scrubbed it for two days to get it clean enough to use but this dump of an apartment was all she had in the world and her new form of hell.

John invaded her dreams each night and he invaded her headspace when she was awake. She couldn't escape him mentally even if she'd escaped him physically, and it was exhausting her. Something had to give.

Rising from the bed, Hope walked to the bathroom and began her daily routine. In her former life, she'd had to be up at the crack of dawn to cook breakfast for her husband. Now, out of spite for all the years she'd been a prisoner in her own home, she slept in. It was pushing nine o'clock and she didn't have to be anywhere for hours, so she decided to get dressed and walk down to the bakery on the corner and enjoy a cup of bold French coffee and a pastry.

She tugged on a pair of her favorite jeans, a low cut V-neck t-shirt in soft lavender that reminded her of an Easter egg and her Nike Free Runs. Then she left her apartment and descended the stairs two-at-a-time thinking about the coffee that awaited her and the powdered sugar goodness of a beignet. When she opened the door to the apartment building and stepped outside, she came face to chest with Nic Beuve. He was leaning on the wall outside, as if he'd been waiting for her to come down. Dressed in dark jeans that hugged his thighs and a black T-shirt that announced he was "Coonass born and bred," Hope sucked in a breath at the sight of him and tried to control her breathing. Nic Beuve, plain and simple, is the sexiest man she'd ever encountered, and she needed to be in his presence like she needed a hole in her head.

"Get packed, sugar," Nic said by way of greeting.

"What?"

"Pack your things. You're movin' in with me."

"Sorry?" Nic moved from the wall, grabbed her hand and pulled her back through the door of her apartment building, dragging her up the stairs.

"I got a place a few blocks from here. It's eighty percent done, so no one is livin' in it. You need a safer place to live and now you got it, so get packed."

"I can't move—"

"You can and you will, no arguments," Nic ordered and kept dragging her up the steps.

"But—"

Nic stopped on the stairs and leaned down until he caught her eyes, and she had no chance to look away, saying, "Sugar, you like livin' with rats?"

"No, of course not,"

"Then pack your bags."

"This isn't a good idea."

"What's not a good idea is you livin' in this piece of shit apartment building, it's not safe and you know it."

"Then I'll look for another place."

"No need, like I said, you're movin' in with me. You'll have the whole floor to yourself."

"But, I barely know you."

"Goes both ways, Hope, I barely know you." He had her there, and more to the point, she was probably more dangerous to him and his son than he was to her.

"Mr. Beuve—"

"Nic," he corrected.

"Nic, I appreciate the offer but it's out of the question."

"Hope, it's not. I've got security on the building; no one can get in or out without the code, so you'd be safe day and night."

Hope bit her lips together trying to figure out how to get out of this without telling him Nicky and he weren't safe with her around. Finding no way around it, she went with the truth.

"Nic," Hope whispered, afraid to look him in the eyes, "My life is such that it wouldn't be safe to be around me."

"I got that yesterday," Nic replied.

"Then you'll understand when I say I can't move in."

"Hope, the condos are separate from each other, just like apartments. School will be out in less than a month, and Nicky is headed to my parents for the summer to be spoiled rotten. I've got two more weeks with him before that happens."

"It's not just your son who shouldn't be around me."

"I'm a big boy; I can take care of myself."

"I can't take that risk," Hope replied and tried to move away from him.

"You gonna run your whole life?" Nic bit out.

"If I have to."

"You have friends here who are willing to help."

"Then I guess it's time to move on. I can't have friends; I can't take the chance anyone gets hurt."

Nic bit his tongue to keep from shouting at her. She was determined to play the martyr. The thought of her leaving, scared and alone, possibly in danger, pissed him off. She needed help; she needed people around her who cared. Taking in her small frame, the thought of anyone hurting Hope sent his heart racing and he was done playing around. As she turned to walk away from him, he grabbed her hand and pulled her back to him.

"I'm not lettin' you go it alone another day. You're done running and that's final, now pack your bags."

"Nic—" He cut her off, growling his words, "Pack your fuckin bags." Hope's eyes grew wide at his order and then she narrowed her eyes at him.

"NO, I'm not moving," Hope shouted, and it felt good to yell. She put years of pent up feelings into it for all the times she had to hold her tongue or get slapped for opening it. When Nic smiled at her and then threw his head back and laughed she didn't' know what to make of it. In fact, he laughed a little longer than she thought was necessary, but she had to admit it was a tension breaker. When he pulled himself together, he threw his arm around her neck and led her down the hall to her apartment door.

"I like your spunk, sugar, but make no mistake, you're not runnin' anymore, so pack your bags you're coming with me."

Seven

Manhandled her, that's what he'd done. Told her what was gonna happen, and she'd just let him. Hope was pacing the living room of the condo Nic had taken her to, and she didn't know whether to sigh in relief or catch the first train out of New Orleans. To say that her new living conditions were for the better was an understatement. She didn't need this much space, three bedrooms and two baths, it was remodeled for a family. Nic said he was almost done with it but from what she could see there wasn't much to do. It had brick walls, hand-honed wood floors, and top of the line appliances in stainless steel that went well with the marbled black counter tops. There was a couch in the living room, a TV, a coffee table and an end table, and a single bed in one of the bedrooms. He didn't say much about where he'd gotten the furnishings, just that he'd had the extra furniture in storage and moved it in for her.

What she was trying to wrap her head around was the why of it. Why would Nic go to this much trouble for a stranger? Rose, Abby, Nic, even Big Daddy, all seemed to be concerned about her. Her first reaction was to be suspicious of them. She'd grown up in foster care and then married a man who thought communication began and ended with a fist. She'd never really had anyone care what happened to her, and she didn't know how to feel about it. She knew there were good people in the world, the kind that would help a friend or neighbor. She supposed she'd just been lucky and stumbled upon a group of people who looked out for someone in need and she felt guilty. The problem was, she felt like she was using them. What little she knew of Nic and Rose, even Abby and Big Daddy, they were good people, all of them, and the crux of the matter was, she didn't deserve their loyalty.

Panic welled up in her, and she started pacing again. If she were any kind of friend, any kind of decent person, she'd leave right now, but for the life of her, she couldn't seem to do it. *You're tired of running Hope, and you know it. Just a few more weeks, enough to save up some money*, she thought. Maybe God would let her stay a few more weeks.

With nothing else to do, and no energy to do it, she decided to take a bath in one of the exceptionally clean, *thank you, God,* bathrooms. The master bedroom had a walk-in shower and a big antique tub and the thought of sinking deep into warm water and falling asleep sounded like heaven. Entering the bathroom, she found shampoo, conditioner and bubble bath on the shelf of the stonewalled bathtub. Nic had done the tub surround in slate with small river rocks running through a third of the way down around the three walls as a border. The darkness of the rock set off the bright white tub as the focal point, and the antique faucets and claw feet on the tub mixed the old and the new seamlessly together.

There were towels on a warming rack just to the side of the bathtub and Hope let out a breath. She'd forgotten to pack her towels when Nic had rushed her to get her stuff. Leaning in and lowering the tub stopper to fill it with water, she then turned on the faucet, poured bubble bath into the streaming water, and the smell of jasmine filled the air as she stripped out of her clothes. Pulling her hair out of its ponytail, she remembered her brush was in her purse and her purse was on the counter in the kitchen.

Grabbing one of the warm towels, she wrapped it around her body and headed down the hall. As she reached her purse, she heard a key in the front door and whipped around just as Nic entered the condo, bags in hand.

Hope froze in place, as Nic took in the sight of long blonde hair, shapely legs that looked smooth as silk, and a towel that barely covered Hope's more than generous breasts. Neither said anything, just stood there staring at each other like a deer caught in the headlights of a car. Hope watched as Nic scanned her body, his eyes growing darker, hungrier. He took a step towards her, and she came out of her frozen state squeaking out "I'm so sorry. I was taking a bath," as she ran back down the hallway disappearing into the master bedroom.

Nic stood there for a long moment, his breath coming in deep and hard trying to force down his reaction. It had been too fucking long since he'd had a woman and seeing Hope standing there like that lit a fire in him.

Moving to the kitchen and unpacking the food he'd brought her, he pulled out the coffee pot and went to work making a pot all while the vision of Hope was seared into his brain. He pulled cups from the cabinet and then paused, he could hear the water in the tub splashing, and he groaned. In his mind's eye, bubbles ran down her chest, clinging to what he was sure were light pink nipples. Taking a deep breath, he pulled a plate down and loaded it with beignets from the bakery down the street. He heard the sound of the tub draining and another vision of Hope standing naked, water running down her body as she grabbed a towel to dry off, and he closed his eyes and clenched his fist.

Nic turned when the coffee maker gurgled the last of the water through the filter and grabbed two cups, filling them. He pulled milk from the fridge, got sugar, put it in a bowl, and then placed them on the counter. Then he leaned back against the countertop, lowered his head, closed his eyes, and tried to will away the erection his thoughts had created.

The smell of jasmine had hit him before Hope did, and he wanted to say, "Fuck it," grab her head and kiss her until she moaned in his mouth. But, he knew he shouldn't, couldn't. He needed to focus on Nicky, not on his own needs, and Hope was ready to bolt at the slightest provocation; she needed his help more than he needed her legs wrapped around his back.

Taking a deep breath, he turned his head as she walked in dressed in a loose T-shirt and shorts, and big socks covering her feet; she almost looked like a kid standing there. Before she could open her mouth to speak, Nic beat her to it and apologized.

"I should have knocked before I entered, sorry, it won't happen again." Hope barely met his eyes. She was mortified at having been caught in just a towel.

"It's fine," she laughed nervously.

Nic grinned a crooked grin, then, not being able to help himself mumbled "I'm not complaining, sugar, I just don't want you uncomfortable your first day here."

Hope rolled her eyes at his answer and he smiled. She looked at the counter and saw the sugar coated beignets and licked her lips. Nic's eyes zeroed in on them and for a second wondered what she tasted like. Breaking his stare, he cleared his throat moving to the cups of coffee he'd poured.

"You take milk or sugar in your coffee?"

"Both, two sugars. You didn't have to do this, Nic, I was going to go out in a little while and get some lunch."

"I was hungry, figured we both could use some food, it's no big deal."

"Yes, it is, and I'll repay you. I saw those bags from the grocery store."

"Keep your money, just a friend helping out a friend."

"I can't let you buy me groceries, Nic."

"You gonna be stubborn about this, too?"

"Definitely," Hope answered.

Nic grinned and shook his head; he didn't doubt for a minute she'd put up a fight.

"Then you can invite me for dinner when you cook the food and we'll be even." Hope stared at Nic, and for the life of her couldn't find a reason to say no. Nodding her head she reached across the counter and grabbed a beignet, bit into it, smearing white powdered sugar on her nose and then closed her eyes moaning at the taste.

Nic watched as she chewed, savoring the sweet pastry, and he tried to remember the last time he'd enjoyed anything as much as the site of Hope devouring a French pastry.

***

"Order up," Hope called through the kitchen pass-thru and then rang the bell for good measure. Business had been brisk that night at The Bayou; tons of tourists came in after a day of sightseeing. Rose stuck her head in the opening just as Hope was about to turn, grinning.

"How you doin' T-Hope."

"I'm good, Rose. How about you?"

"I always good, *Cher*. Any'ting new wit' you?"

Hope started to say yes, but the look in Rose's eyes said she already knew. *Crazy old woman probably put Nic up to it.*

"Nothing new, Rose," Hope answered and then watched the old woman's face fall in disappointment. Hope almost laughed at the sight and figured it served her right. Nic's place was beyond wonderful, but she didn't want to get too comfortable there. It's temporary she kept telling herself.

"I see. Well, I bettah' get dis' to da' customer," Rose groused and then grabbed the plate of Cajun fish, her lips puckered in frustration and when she was out of sight, Hope did laugh.

"What you do?" Big Daddy asked. He'd been watching the interaction between Rose and T-Hope and he could tell that something didn't agree with the old woman.

"Teaching her a lesson," Hope laughed.

"Fill Big Daddy in. Dat' woman sticks her nose in everah'ones b'nez. Be good to see her get some."

"Oh, I got moved today against my will and I think she's behind it."

"Where you move?"

"Nic Beuve's downstairs condo."

"You don't say?"

"Yep, and I got caught with my knickers down by him too, it was so embarrassing."

"*Cher*, trust me, da' man won't care if you walk around naked. Trust Big Daddy, you all dat' and more."

"Yeah, yeah, get back to work," Hope laughed but a part of her wondered if Nic really did like what he saw. Not that it mattered she had to keep reminding herself. Nic was a nice guy, a great guy from what she saw, and there could never be anything between them. He deserved better, deserved someone whose past wasn't tainted and dirty. Shaking her head at her schoolgirl crush, one that could never be acted upon, Hope got back to work filling orders.

Later that evening Rose entered the kitchen clucking her tongue with a look of triumph on her face.

"Notin' new, huh?"

"Whatever, did you call him just to find out?" Hope asked, surprised Rose would go to that much trouble.

"No need, he come to da' bar. Just told me himself you moved in wit' him."

"I was strong-armed, Rose."

"It don't mattah,' you in a safe place now, dat' what mattah,'" she preened on, happy with herself. "You should go out and say hi."

"I'm busy."

"It slow now, go, be nice to da' man. You not the only one wit' troubles."

Hope stopped wiping down her workstation and turned towards Rose gauging her honesty. She stood there with both hands on her hips staring back at Hope, her stern face saying she was telling the truth.

"What trouble does he have?" Hope found herself asking.

"He lost his *tit ange* a year ago. Dat' girl was da' light of his life, but he couldn't save her and he blames himself."

"He lost his daughter?" Hope whispered her eyes already moving to the door behind Rose.

"*Oui.*"

"How?"

"Chelsea was smart but did not handle her parent's divorce well. Got mixed up wit' bad kids and took drugs."

"Oh, my God."

"Nic put her in rehab and she took off, used too much and she is wit' God now. He blames himself for da' drugs because of divorce."

"Oh, my God," she repeated again and without thinking threw her rag down and moved to the door, pushing through it and looking around until she saw Nic. He was seated at the bar, a shot of amber colored alcohol in front of him, his eyes staring out the window, lost in thought. As she walked towards him, he caught her approach, turned his eyes to her and with a smile said, "You like torturing Rose."

"Guilty," she laughed.

"What tipped you off?"

"She looked like a dog salivating over a bone . . . So; she put you up to it?"

"More or less, but I didn't hesitate when she mentioned it, so don't get any ideas I don't want you there."

"Okay, fair enough. Have you eaten?"

"Nope, was busy. I'll get around to it," he answered, and then threw back his shot. Looking around the restaurant, she didn't see Nicky, not that she thought he'd slide up to the bar and do shots while his son was with him.

"Where's Nicky?"

"With his mother, she gets him this next week."

"That must be hard. Guess you miss seeing him when he's gone?"

"Yeah, you could say that. Been divorced three years, still haven't gotten used to not seein' him and his sis—" Nic stopped, but Hope knew what he was going to say.

"Rose told me, I hope you don't mind that I know."

"Not much Rose won't talk about, don't worry about it." Nic sighed, feeling older than his forty-two years all of a sudden.

"I think you're right about that," Hope chuckled then leaned in, and with sincerity said, "Just so you know I'm a good listener. I'm sure you have plenty of people to talk to, but I wouldn't mind at all, you know, if you needed an ear."

A piece of blonde hair had escaped from her ridiculous hairnet, and Nic fought himself to keep from pushing it behind her ear. She was so damn pretty, so damn sweet; nothing like Kat. He was tempted, more than tempted, and he was about to ask her if she needed a ride home since he'd come in his car, when he heard "Dad," from behind him. Turning on the stool, he looked behind him and saw Nicky and Kat walking into The Bayou.

"What are you doin' here?"

"Practice ran late and mom said we should come here and see if you wanted to eat with us."

"How'd you know I was here?" Nic asked.

"Now, sugar, I know you better than anyone. Always have, always will," Kat purred, running one of her hand up and down his arm. Kat was in a tight dress of deep burgundy with a low cut V-neck to show off all her charms. She wore black strappy sandals with three inch heels that made her legs look longer and showed off the hours she put in at the gym. Her blonde hair was down, curled slightly; volume put in at the crown and had that "just had sex" look about it. She was dressed to impress, and any other man would have been hard at the sight of her, but Nic wasn't any other man.

"Kat, nice to see you," Nic deadpanned.

"Always a pleasure seeing you, honey."

"Hey, T-Hope," Nicky called behind Nic and they all turned to see Hope standing there watching them.

"Hi, Nicky, nice to see you again," Hope called out, feeling like a third wheel. "I'll just get back to the kitchen; you all enjoy your meal."

"Hope," Nic called out stopping her. When she turned to him, he smiled, saying "Thanks. I'll be here until you get off, come find me and we can ride home together."

Nic saw her eyes go wide then she looked over his shoulder. Ducking her head, she nodded and then turned on her heels and went back into the kitchen.

"What do you mean ride home together?" Kat gritted out.

"Hope is renting the downstairs condo."

"Is she now? Well isn't she fortunate to have such an accommodating landlord." Nic ignored her. He could see her claws coming out, so he motioned them forward and out of hearing distance of Hope. As they moved towards the table for a meal he'd rather not have, he looked back at the bar and saw Rose standing there looking fit to be tied. Nic rolled his eyes at the old woman 'cause he could read her thoughts. She hated Kat and if Nicky weren't here, he was sure she'd have marched over and thrown Kat out with her own two hands. Rose marched back into the kitchen, and a few moments later as they were all seated, Big Daddy came out with a smile on his face and said, "What can I cook for my two fav'rit boys?" Kat arched a perfectly plucked eyebrow at Big Daddy for the slight and Nic bit his lips to keep from laughing. Rose may not throw her out, but no way in hell was she serving Kat. Tired, and not caring if it pissed her off, for the second time that day Nic couldn't help himself, he threw his head back and laughed.

Eight

The sound of a bell ringing woke Hope. Opening her eyes to the morning light, she shut them immediately and groaned. She'd closed the night before and didn't get to bed until after midnight, and from the angle of the sun, it couldn't be more than eight in the morning. The bell sound came again, and she wrinkled her brow. It sounded like the doorbell. A moment of fear crawled up her throat as she slipped from the bed and moved to the window to look out front. Standing with a phone at his ear, Nic was waiting at the front door looking freshly showered; a light tan suit dressed his large frame. He must have noticed the movement at the window because he turned his head towards her and grinned, raising a hand in greeting. Half asleep still, she stumbled down the hall to the front door and unlocked it, pulled it open and looked up at Nic. His almost black eyes gave her a cursory once-over, and she realized all she had on was a large T-shirt. Stepping behind the door to cover herself, she saw Nic's grin grow wider.

"Sorry to wake you, sugar, but Rose is on the phone and needs to speak to you."

Not saying a word, she stuck out her hand for the phone, and Nic chuckled as he handed it over to her.

"Hello?" Hope finally spoke in the phone.

"No work today havin' a partay' at my house."

"You're closing the bar?"

"No, why you tink' dat'?"

"You just said I didn't have to work today."

"Dat' 'cause you comin' to my house for da' partay.'"

"Rose I don't think—"

"Abby and I gonna take you shoppin' be ready at ten we gonna pick you up."

"Rose, I don't need to go shopping."

"Pretty girl like you need sometin' pretty to wear to my house, no arguments, we'll be dere' at ten."

"But—"

"TEN!" Rose bit out, and then hung up the phone.

"Rose's shindigs are legendary," Nic broke in as Hope stood there wondering how she kept being roped into things.

"How does this keep happening to me?" Hope whispered, not really paying attention to Nic.

"She's Rose," Nic explained as if that was all that needed to be said.

"Hurricane Rose is more like it," Hope mumbled.

"Now you're getting' it," Nic grinned and Hope kinda lost herself in his smile. His olive skin set off his straight, white teeth, and the effect was bewitching. Clearing her throat to cover the fact she'd been staring, she looked at the clock on the wall and noticed it was eight-thirty.

"Shit, there gonna be here in an hour and a half."

"Then you better hop to it. Rose hates to wait," Nic laughed and winked at her as he started to turn. For some reason only known to God, she blurted out "Are you going tonight?"

"Wouldn't miss it, besides, I'm your ride."

"What?"

"Rose informed me when she called that I was escorting you to this shindig."

"She told you to escort me?"

"Yep."

"Is she trying to set us up?" Nic grinned bigger his face sexier with his full smile.

"Absolutely," he replied then gave a one-finger salute and turned to leave.

"It won't work," Hope blurted out and he turned back around, his lips twitching at her outburst.

"Nope," he answered back as he kept walking backwards and then he winked again, turned on his heels and headed to his car.

Hope watched from the door as he got into his black Mercedes with the black leather interior she'd been in every night this week. They'd fallen into a routine since she moved in; he'd bring beignets on the mornings he worked at home, and they'd have coffee on the patio, surrounded by all the white irises in his garden. Then he'd stop by the bar for a nightcap before she got off work and drive her home. Only problem was, he'd done so much for her in the past couple of weeks, and spent so much time with her almost every day; she could feel her walls breaking down every time he smiled at her. It was obvious to her at this point if she let her guard down and Nic made an advance; she'd have a hard time holding him off and that was dangerous for Nic.

When John came looking for her, and she knew he would, she had to be ready to run. Not only would emotional entanglements make it hard to leave, she'd be putting all those she'd grown to care about in harm's way. John was ruthless and would stop at nothing to get what he wanted, and what he wanted was Hope dead and anyone in his way would pay the price.

Looking around the condo, she thought about leaving now, instead of waiting. She didn't have enough money to leave yet, and she knew it, but could she risk staying and becoming more attached? The more time she spent with Nic, be it in the car or his popping in with beignets, she could tell he was attracted to her, as well. If she could just keep her distance and had a little more time to save money, she could thank them all for their help, promise to keep in contact and then leave town before anyone got hurt.

The clock chimed nine breaking her from her thoughts, and she realized she'd been standing there thinking way too long and needed to make a decision. Pack now and leave, or stay a little while longer and risk losing her heart to the man. Thinking about spending the day shopping and then an evening with Nic, she hesitated about leaving. Just once, she'd like to forget about her past and look forward to something. Right or wrong, selfish or not, she wanted to be normal for just one day. *One more week, just one more week and then you'll leave.*

***

Hope stared at her reflection in the mirror. Her long, light blonde hair was down, flowing around her in soft curls. The aquamarine halter-top that Rose had insisted was perfect for a hot night in New Orleans seemed a bit too revealing. Her back was bare down to the dimples above her curvaceous butt, and the front was cut sharp, at an angle from the sides up to the collar around her neck. No cleavage at least, but when she turned back and looked at how low the back fell she felt naked. She had a new pair of jeans in a dark, indigo blue that hugged her curves like a second skin, and a new pair of wedge sandals in tan leather. Silver bangles on her wrists, large silver hoops at her ears and a new tan leather clutch that matched her shoes. She looked dressed to kill from head to toe, and the price for this look about killed her. Rose being Rose had insisted on paying, said it was her treat and she wouldn't take no for an answer. She'd been right when she called Rose a Hurricane; she blew in, took over, and left you speechless with her aftermath.

cp smith

Taking a deep breath, she surveyed her face and worried if she'd gone overboard. She'd gone a little dramatic with her eye makeup. The smoky shadow brought out the blue of her eyes and light pink gloss finished off her face, she'd thought. But, she looked ready for a date, and that's what concerned her. She was a little excited, well, more than a little, it had been a while since she'd looked forward to anything this much. A night out eating good food, listening to music and spending time with people she really liked seemed too good to be true, and as she stared at her reflection, she questioned her sanity. *What are you doing Hope?* Having one night of fun before she left the people she'd come to care about, whether she believed herself or not.

Looking at her watch she knew she was out of time, Nic would ring the bell any moment and then there'd be no turning back. She looked in the mirror one more time, and she liked what she saw, then told herself one night of fun wouldn't hurt anyone. She'd keep Nic at arm's length, and she could plan where she'd go tomorrow. Maybe up north, a cabin in the mountains, she could grow her own food and live off the land and never be heard from again. Chuckling and shaking her head at the thought of living like Grizzly Adams, she heard the doorbell ring, and she panicked for a second. *It's just one night, relax!*

When Hope opened the door, Nic stopped breathing. She'd gone from an angel to a seductress all in one day. Seeing her that morning with her hair wild, no makeup on and that huge T-shirt had sent his thoughts to a place they shouldn't. In his bed. He'd spent the better part of the day trying to ignore how she'd looked. Seeing her now in those tight jeans, that sexy as hell top with her hair down; begging him to wrap his hand in it and tug her to his lips he knew he was losing ground. Taking a much-needed breath, he filled his lungs and then, as casually as he could, asked if she was ready to leave.

73

"You ready to go, sugar?"

"Ready as I'll ever be," she smiled.

Hope exited the condo, turned and locked the door, and Nic moaned, *Mon Dieu*. The silky skin of her back, all of it, was calling him to run his tongue down her spine. He wanted to tell her to grab something to cover herself, 'cause the thought of another man seeing her sexy back made his hands fist, but he didn't.

Nic tightened his jaw to reign in his attraction and replied, "Then let's go sugar." Hope turned back to him and without any thought in the matter; he grabbed her hand and held it as he walked her to his car. He was surprised she didn't' pull her hand away from his, but he noticed a little spasm as their hands touched for the first time. Helping her into the car, he mumbled "Buckle it," once she was settled, and then waited to see that she'd done it before closing the door and rounding the car. This was going to be a long fucking night he decided as he climbed in and started his car.

Rose's house wasn't far from the French Quarter; it had been in her family for years and just like her father before her, she'd raised her children there with her husband Roscoe. It was two-story, antebellum, plantation style home with a huge front porch that wrapped around on both sides. Whitewashed with black shutters, it reminded Hope of "Tara," the famous house in the movie "Gone with the Wind." She heard loud music coming from the backyard, and there were people hanging around shooting the breeze when Nic parked the car. He'd insisted she wait for him to come to her side and open the door, and after he had helped her out, and they started to move toward the house, she felt Nic's hand on her back guiding her. A tingle shot up her spine at his touch, and she stiffened a bit. If Nic noticed he didn't react to it, he just kept leading her to the side of the house. There were twinkle lights everywhere, in the trees, the shrubs and intertwined in the trellis of the homemade stage, where three men and two women were in full swing playing a soulful Cajun song called Evangeline. An older woman with long, dark brown hair dressed in jeans, dark T-shirt and boots, sang in a rich Cajun accent about a woman standing on the banks of the Mississippi looking for her lover who was a gambling man. The song, mournful and full of longing spoke about a man married to the life of a riverboat gambler on the Mississippi Queen.

Everyone was dressed casual, even Nic. He'd worn jeans and another black T-shirt with motorcycle boots that made the already sexy man, even more so. Even though she was in jeans, she felt over-dressed, and wondered why Rose had insisted she wear this to the party. When she felt Nic's hand on her back never leaving it, as if he was covering her skin, Hope finally got it and shook her head. Hurricane Rose had struck again she was sure of it.

Taking in the huge yard, she saw tables and chairs scattered around with candles in the center of each. A long table with food of every kind laid out at the side, with big wooden tubs filled with beer. Big Daddy was manning a huge pot with crawfish Hope had no doubt, and Rose was talking with a guest next to a man that made her look small.

"Is that Rose's husband?" Hope leaned in and asked Nic. He turned to where she was pointing and saw Roscoe, all six foot five and two hundred and fifty pounds of him, standing next to Rosie. The man adored his wife, would kill anyone who did her harm, and at sixty-five, after years of working oil rigs, he hadn't lost his edge.

"Yeah, that's Roscoe."

"How come he doesn't come to the bar?"

"Spends his day's fishin,' some of the fish you cook at the bar he caught," Nic explained.

Rose looked their direction as Nic was speaking and hollered, "Dere' she is . . . *Cher*, look at you. Ain't she da' prettiest ting' dis' side of Mississippi, Nic?"

Rose had broken away from her friends as she spoke and grabbed Roscoe's hand dragging him with her. When she'd gotten close enough, Rose grabbed Hope by the shoulders and gave her a big bear hug.

"T-Hope, meet my Roscoe."

Hope smiled at the huge man, and he looked down at her and whistled. Then he grabbed her and crushed her to his body, squeezing the life out of her. He replied "Rosie you weren't lying, this one looks like an angel fell down from heaven."

Trying to breathe enough to say thank you, Roscoe finally pushed her back from him, and when he let go, she fell back a bit. Nic put his arm around her to steady her, and Rose smiled big when she saw it.

"It's nice to meet you finally, Roscoe," Hope replied, still in awe of the big man's size.

"Heard nothin' but good things about you darlin,' good things indeed," Roscoe smiled and Hope was surprised he didn't have a Cajun accent, as well. There was a crash behind them, and as Hope turned to look she heard Rose yell, "Boy, I told you dis' was Maman's party, get back in da' house wit' your brothah's." She saw a young boy, maybe eight, with a plate of food running for the back door of the house laughing, and he bound up the steps with his plate of contraband food.

"Roscoe baby, go see what da' hooligans are doin' to my house." Roscoe rolled his eyes, kissed his wife's cheek, and headed to the back door to check on the hooligans, chuckling as he went. No doubt, he knew their grandchildren were indeed causing havoc inside.

"Go get you some food and drink, it a partay' live it up T-Hope,"

Rose commanded and then pushed both Nic and her towards the table of food.

The crawfish was tender, the beer ice cold and it quenched her thirst, but when Hope and Nic sat to eat, the conversation was sparse. He tried to engage her about her past, but the less anyone knew about her, the better. The conversation finally moved to Nicky, and Nic was animated when he talked about his son. They laughed over his antics, and how he seemed to be noticing girls, and Hope advised him if a twelve-year-old girl was giving Nicky the cold shoulder, it meant she liked him.

Soon the band picked up the tempo with a snappy tune lead by a fiddler player who was snapping bowstrings left and right. Hope's foot bounced to the melody as she watched couples dancing the two-step. Rose suddenly appeared behind her, talking to Nic in her big booming voice, ordering Nic, and it was nothing short of an order, when she shouted "What kinda man sit dere' when he can see *tit ange* wanna dance. Get your sorry butt up and lead my girl 'round da' dance floor."

"Oh, no, I'm fine, I don't really dance that well." Nic grinned when he heard this and ignored her. He pulled her from her seat, dragged her to the dance floor, pulled her tight against him, and started to move.

"Just follow me, sugar," Nic purred, his accent dripping with southern charm.

"Just so you know, I have two left feet," Hope replied, sure she would embarrass herself.

Nic moved slowly with her as she watched her feet trying to learn the basic moves of the two-step. She soon had it down, and he picked up the pacing, leading her around the dance floor. One moment she was watching her feet, the next he was spinning her out, and then bringing her back to him, slamming Hope into his chest. Letting go for the first time in what seemed like years, she threw her head back and laughed as he tried to show her more technical moves. He threw her hands over his shoulders, and his own hands moved slowly down her side until he reached her hips, moving them seductively. Hope gave him a look of "watch it mister" and Nic just grinned and then wiggled his eyebrows up in down like a Lothario getting ready to attack. Moving her hips in a circular motion, she gasped when she encountered evidence he liked what he saw, and she stumbled back, her own arousal for the man with soulful eyes was getting out of control.

"I need water," Hope breathed out, feeling her traitorous cheeks flame with heat, and passion she couldn't give into.

Walking to their table, occupied by other friends of Rose's and people Hope recognized from the bar, she grabbed her beer and took a long deep drink. She prayed it would calm her emotions before she made a huge mistake.

As a slower song began to play, Hope felt a tap on her shoulder and turned to see Henri standing there smiling down on her.

"I believe this dance belongs to me," Henri crooned, as he looked her over, his eyes lingering on her back longer than Nic thought was necessary. Not caring if she'd just left his arms, running from the force of their mutual attraction, he grabbed her hand not wanting this man anywhere near her.

"Sorry, she already promised this dance to me."

Drawing Hope away, he scowled at Henri and then led Hope back to the makeshift dance floor once again. As one of the musicians belted out a song about the Mississippi, a slow bluesy song that sounded familiar to Nic, a man slowly picked his guitar as the rest joined in. They created a symphony of sounds that mellowed Hope out as he pulled her close and wrapped his arm around her back, then grabbed her right hand and curled it into his chest as they began to sway to the slow song. He felt Hope's breathing increase as she laid her head on his chest, and as tiny as she was, she fit him perfectly.

They didn't speak as the words of longing flowed through the air. They just kept moving and swaying. She pulled her head back and looked up at him, and he watched as she licked her lips unconsciously, invitingly, and without reservation Nic started to lower his head to taste those pink lips. As he angled his head to brush her lips, an intake of her breath and the wide-eyed look on her face stopped him.

"Don't worry, sugar, I won't bite," Nic whispered forgetting his vow not to get involved with this woman. But she'd been charming, though a little quiet until he got her on the dance floor, and then what he figured was the real Hope opened up to him. She was nothing short of irresistible and he wanted her. He was about to break his promise to himself and taste those cupid lips, when Hope pulled back, ducked her eyes and whispered "Nic, I can't, I, I just can't I'm sorry."

He felt his jaw tighten when he realized he'd pushed her too far, but more importantly, he realized he'd lost his head. He had to keep his focus on Nicky, not his own needs. Taking a deep breath to control his raging hormones, he realized from his reaction to her, that it was just as well she had stopped him. He wasn't sure if he'd kissed her he'd ever be able to stop.

Nodding he understood, he stepped back, took her hand and led her off the dance floor asking, "You ready to leave?"

"Yeah, let me get my purse," Hope replied afraid to look at him.

Watching Hope walk to the table, he felt something inside him tighten. He wanted her more than any woman he'd wanted in a while, maybe more than he'd wanted Kat when they'd first met. But, his priority was Nicky, and the idea he could find any measure of happiness with this woman when his Chelsea was gone didn't seem right.

With new resolve, he didn't take her hand or wrap an arm around her waist as they said their goodbyes and left. The car ride was quiet; the walk to her door brief. When he climbed into bed, he tried not to think about Hope as he tossed and turned, sleep eluding him like it had every night since Chelsea died. Only this time his regret and longing were for a pair of eyes the color of the sky, and hips a man could hold onto as he buried himself deep, exhausting himself in the ecstasy of her body. Then, slip into sleep, tangled in her warmth, and the knowledge that she was his.

Nine

Maman Rose paced, and Big Daddy watched as the old woman talked to herself. It had been building for a week now, her agitation. He'd seen T-Hope and Nic enjoy their time at the party the same as her. They'd eaten and laughed with each other, but then something changed on the dance floor. Near as he could tell T-Hope had put a stop to whatever had been brewing between them all night. Then they'd left suddenly, and the way Nic had been watching her all night, if they had been holding hands he'd have laid money down they'd have ended up in bed, but they hadn't. Barely talking, both deep in thought, they'd left like strangers just sharing a ride.

The past week Hope has been too quiet. Doing her job but not interacting, just pulling away from everyone. She'd been working there three weeks, and some of her walls had come down as she'd joked with him, with Rose and all the staff. Now she was back to business as usual, and he had a bad feeling she had more than one foot out the door ready to leave.

"Dis' won't do," Rose mumbled to herself, concerned that she'd lost control.

"Rosie what you mumblin' 'bout?"

"Nic's ain't been here in a week old man and Hope act like she do when she first come."

"Den' work your magic, *espésces de téte dure.*"

"*Mon Dieu,* what you tink' I doin' here? Hush you."

Rose paced her mind scheming. She needed a way to get them in the same room 'cause she had no doubt that they were avoiding each other even while living a floor apart. Looking around the room for any inspiration, she actually considered causing a grease fire when T-Hope was on duty so Nic could rush in and save Hope like a white knight. Chuckling at her foolish thoughts, her eyes landed on the softball league schedule.

"Big Daddy?" Rose shouted excited.

"Standin' right here old woman why you shout?"

"Tell me you got a softball game soon."

"*Oui,* tomorrow at one, why?"

"'Cause Maman got idea yes she do."

***

Seven days, seven fucking days he'd avoided her, tried not to think about her one floor below him. He'd also tried not to watch her leave from his second floor window, as he worked on designs for some wealthy couple that wanted to gut a historic home, destroying everything that made it unique. Now Hope was walking towards the softball diamond, wearing a T-shirt and shorts that fit her like a glove. Nic wanted to moan at the sight of her.

She'd covered her hair with a baseball cap and wore sunglasses, like she was in disguise, and part of him thought that was exactly the point. One of these days she needed to tell someone what she was hiding from or who.

Big Daddy had called, said they needed a catcher for their softball game and would he fill in. It didn't once occur to him that Hope would come. He'd brought Nicky; he loved to watch Nic play. It was Kat's day, but she was more than happy to let him go, said she would stop by and watch, as well, make a family day of it. He hadn't commented it was easier to let her do what she wanted. He had no intention of ever going there again, he'd told her that in no uncertain terms. But, she was so full of her own perceived allure she figured she could bide her time, and he'd give in. Watching Hope walk towards him dressed down in shorts and a tee, he had a new definition for allure. Forget skintight dresses and spiked heels, this all-American girl look worked just fine.

He knew the minute Hope saw him sitting on the bench—she hesitated. He watched as she turned her head and said something to Big Daddy and when the man looked his direction, he knew she'd asked what he was doing here. He tried not to let that bother him, he had his own reasons for staying away, and she'd had her reasons for stopping the kiss—but that didn't stop him from wanting her.

As she got closer, Nicky saw her and shouted, "Hey, T-Hope come sit by us." She smiled at Nicky, and he watched as she reluctantly made her way over to the two of them.

"Hi, Nicky."

"Hiya, T-Hope. You playin'?" Nicky asked.

"Well, they were short players and Big Daddy wouldn't take no for an answer, so, yeah, I guess I am."

"Cool. What position?" Nicky asked as he scooted Nic over so she could sit next to him. Nic was beginning to think his son had a crush on her as he watched him puff out his chest.

"Well, I used to play pitcher with my friends when I was a kid."

"You were a pitcher?" Nicky asked, sounding like he was shocked.

"Hey, girls can pitch," Hope defended and then nudged shoulders with his son. Nic waited to see if she would say hi to him and after a moment or two of silence; she looked up at him finally and with a small smile said, "Hey, Nic."

83

Those two words washed over him, the breathy quality to it like she couldn't breathe for saying his name. His reaction was immediate; his lip twitched at the sound of his name coming from her lips and then he grinned. Not a "nice to see you" grin, but a grin that could call a woman to him from twenty feet away. He watched as her eyes went to his smile and then she looked away. *They were quite a pair*, Nic thought. Both attracted, but neither one of them willing to do anything about it for their own reasons.

Big Daddy walked over and started shouting positions at the team. When he called Nic and Hope's names one went to the pitcher's mound and the other to home plate. Nic grabbed his mitt and ball so they could warm up her arm, and they both stood.

"Show me what you got, sugar," he whispered in her ear as they made their way to the field. Hope grabbed the ball from him, crossed her arms and for women everywhere said, "You doubt a woman can pitch?"

"Oh, no, sugar, I think you're capable of doin' just about anything you set your mind to."

Hope rolled her eyes like she seemed to do whenever he was around and then chuckled "Whatever," as she walked to the pitcher's mound. Henri came over from first base to say something to her and when he was done, felt the need to slap her on that sweet ass. No doubt, he thought since she was playing ball with the boys, it was appropriate. Nic narrowed his eyes at the man and watched as he walked back to first base, grinning. For a brief moment he wished he were on the opposing team, so he could hit a line drive right into Henri's skull.

"Ready?" Hope shouted, and Nic turned his attention back to his job. Securing the catcher's mask over his face and kneeling down, he brought his glove up, and readied himself for her first pitch.

To say he was surprised when she threw a perfect strike was

no lie. When she threw five more, he was impressed. She looked fragile, angelic, as if a hard wind would blow her away. But, watching her he could see she was made of tougher stuff, hadn't been coddled as a child or raised to be a debutant like Kat had been. As the game began he enjoyed watching Hope as she waited for his signals, her eyes intent on him as each batter came to the box. The longer they played, he watched her become bolder with the batters, taunting them as she struck each one out. It was then he realized she wasn't timid or shy, she was guarded, had a wall around her so no one could get in. He'd been attracted to shy Hope, but this Hope, the one who forgot to put her shields up, who high fived her teammates when an inning was over, this Hope was sexy as hell.

It was the bottom of the fifth; the score was tied and the batter was taunting Hope.

"Come on angel face, show me what you got."

Hope cracked her neck from side to side, feeling alive for the first time in a long time. She'd forgotten how much she loved to play. Had forgotten all the times she and the other kids would grab whatever they could find for bases, and if they didn't have a real bat and ball, they'd improvise. She'd been a good pitcher, really good. She remembered how the kids fought over who got to be on her team, and she realized there was good with the bad of her childhood.

Caught daydreaming, Nic, shouted, "Strike him out, sugar," and she pulled her thoughts from the past and focused on the batter. He was big; he was strong, and he'd hit a line drive his last at bat. Watching Nic for a call, he signaled inside, and she nodded. Leaning, knees bent, she wound-up and let the ball fly, putting all her weight into it. The batter misjudged and swung. Strike one. Nic threw the ball back to her smiling and shouted, "There ya go ace."

Out of the corner of her eye, she saw a woman with long blonde hair dressed as if she was going to a garden party instead of a day at the park. The closer she got, Hope realized it was Kat, Nic's ex-wife. She tried to keep her eyes off the woman as she swung her hips in an attempt to have every man's eyes on her. She saw Nic turn his head towards her, his face unreadable and she wondered if he was still in love with her. Jealousy reared its ugly head, and she envisioned her next pitch slamming into Nic's head as he watched his ex-wife approach. From a place she didn't want to examine closely, she didn't wait for Nic to set his stance and let the pitch fly before he was ready, before she was ready. Unfortunately, when it reached home plate the batter caught a piece of it with the end of his bat and sent it driving right at her.

She tried to duck, but the ball caught her in the back of the head, clipping her, not a direct hit. She went down, saw stars, and lay there as the sound of pounding feet came towards her. She heard Nic's panicked voice shout, "Hope," as he made his way towards her, and she rolled to her back, opened her eyes and then shut them again. She was pretty sure she saw double unless Big Daddy had grown two heads.

Nic reached Hope the same time as the rest of the team, and started shoving people away so he could get to her. When the ball collided with her head his heart about stopped. She was lying in the grass; her knees bent and a hand over her eyes when he reached her. Relieved to see she wasn't knocked out, he kneeled down, put his mouth to her ear and whispered, "That's not how you stop a ball, baby."

She opened her eyes to look at him and moaned, "There are two of you."

"That's it, game over, we're going to the hospital," Nic ordered and then picked her up, cradled her in his arms and carried her towards the bench.

"Dad, is she okay?" Nicky shouted; concern written across his face.

"She'll have a goose egg by nightfall if not sooner," he told his son.

He was surprised Hope didn't fight him when he carried her; she'd laid her head on his shoulder and kept her eyes shut. When he reached the bench, he laid her down and put a towel under her head.

"You hanging in there, sugar?" Nic asked her cupping her face and running his thumb back and forth across her cheek.

"Still two of you, lucky me," Hope whispered trying to breathe through her headache. She pulled the hat off her head, and then pulled the ponytail holder from her hair. The pressure from being pulled back all day wasn't helping, and when her hair was free, she felt relief. The ball had hit her in the same spot as her ponytail, and she figured she owed not being knocked clean out to her fashion sense. She opened her eyes, and watched as Nic and Nicky gathered their things. She felt bad Nic had to cut the game short, but she wasn't going to argue about seeing a doctor; she knew head injuries could be serious. As she waited, Kat moved to them both, running her hand through her son's hair, smiling at him, and then she put her hand to Nic's arm stopping him.

"Sugar, you're all hot, why don't we go someplace cool and grab a bite to eat."

"Can't," Nic replied gruffly and Hope watched his jaw get tight.

"Don't say can't, you'll disappoint Nicky," Kat pouted and if Hope could have rolled her eyes without hurting more she would have. *Does this woman really think pouting works on men?*

"I'm not hungry, besides, Hope got hurt and we need to take her to the doctor," Nicky jumped in to keep his parents from fighting. Blue eyes, almost as blue as her own turned to Hope, and she watched as the woman turned cold as ice.

"I see, well, we wouldn't want anything to happen to your favorite waitress." The word waitress came out as an insult, as if waiting tables was beneath her.

Nic barked "Kat," and Kat turned her eyes to him, softening her face. "Yeah, sugar?" she purred and Nic leaned in and hissed, "Take your claws and go home." Nic then walked around her, came to Hope with his bag thrown over his shoulder, bent down and without saying a word picked her up again and started heading for his car. Nicky hollered, "I'm coming with you," then grabbed his bag and followed his father.

Kat stood there watching as her husband and son walked briskly to his car. She realized they'd both forgotten all about her for some blonde bimbo who didn't know when to duck. Narrowing her eyes at the three of them, she made a note to herself to find out more about the harlot who seemed to have *her* husband's attention.

***

The waiting room was crowded, but that was no surprise, so Nic found two seats in the corner for him and Nicky to sit while they waited for Hope. Luckily for their stomachs, the hospital was equipped with a variety of vending machines selling everything from coffee, pop and milk to tuna sandwiches and salad, so they both grabbed a snack while they waited. Nic watched as one person after another came out from the back, wishing he could be inside to hear what the doctor said. The waiting game didn't set well with a man like Nic; he liked to be in charge of the situation, not at the mercy of others.

After several hours of waiting, snacks consumed and the

choice of magazines exhausted, he realized Nicky had gone quiet. When he turned to his son, he caught him staring and turned his eyes to see a teenage girl with blonde hair the color of Chelsea's and his chest tightened for a moment.

"You okay, Nicky?" he questioned; knowing the resemblance to his sister wouldn't go unnoticed.

"Yeah, I miss her ya know? We fought a lot, but I loved her."

"I know you did, bud."

"I just wish . . . I should have said something sooner," Nicky whispered, and he watched his son's lip quiver.

"Said what?"

"I knew, I mean I did, but I didn't . . . I found her pot, but she told me it was oregano. I didn't know any better, so I believed her."

"Nicky it wasn't your job to look out for your sister, it was mine. You didn't do anything wrong," Nic assured him; troubled that his son carried any guilt about his sister's death. *The blame belongs with you.*

"You don't understand; she was using before you and Mom split up," Nicky explained. He looked like he had the weight of the world on his shoulders and Nic wrapped an arm around his son and leaned in.

"What are you talking about?"

"I've heard you and Mom argue about whose fault it is that she started using. Dad, it wasn't because of you or Mom, she started using before Mom cheated on you."

Nic closed his eyes; he didn't think his son knew why they'd divorced. He'd always told them that sometimes people grow apart 'cause he didn't want to place blame, have his kids look at their mother differently.

"Nicky, I should have been home more, it's my fault not—"

"No, Dad, I asked her why she did drugs. She told me because it's fun; all the cool kids do it. Her friend Wendy told me they did them to fit in."

Nic sat in shock. *Did Chelsea take drugs because they were cool?* He looked at his son, tall for his age, good-looking and he wondered if Nicky felt the need to be cool.

"Drugs don't make you cool, Nicky, they—"

"Drugs killed my sister," Nicky spit out, "You don't have to worry, Dad, I'd rather be a nerd gettin' beat up every day than try that stuff." Relief swept through Nic; his son was a shit liar, and he saw nothing but truth and anger from him.

"Why didn't you tell me before?" Nic asked and watched as his son's face blanched. Taking a deep breath, Nicky looked at his shoes. "Cause Chelsea and I had a pact never to rat the other out. It was the last secret I had of hers," Nicky told him, stumbling over his words, trying to be the man he was turning into much faster than Nic wanted. So, he let him be, knowing his son wouldn't want comfort right now, he'd want to put on a brave face.

Mon Dieu, had his tit ange done drugs to fit in?

Clearing his throat, and trying to act like he wasn't emotional about what he'd just told his father, Nicky straightened, and looked at the door to the ER. As he stared, Hope emerged from the back, an icepack on the back of her head, and Nicky thought not for the first time she was hot. But, she was too old for him, like, way too old, so he figured she'd be perfect for his dad, and if he wasn't mistaken, and he didn't think he was, his dad was already interested in her. Why else would they have spent three hours at the hospital on a Saturday?

Ten

Leaning back against the headrest in Nic's car, Hope tried not to think about why she'd pitched that ball before she and Nic were ready. Examining her actions would do her no good, whatever her reasons for reacting recklessly towards Nic staring at his ex-wife, it didn't matter—she was leaving in a week. She'd spent the last week, since Nic had tried to kiss her, telling herself it was just a crush on a nice guy. That with space and time her feelings for him would change. Obviously, her reaction to Nic staring at his ex-wife meant she was just fooling herself. All week she'd avoided him, and kept to herself at the bar to make leaving easier for everyone. Then Big Daddy had begged her to play today, given her the day off for the game, and she'd stupidly agreed.

Playing softball, a sport she loved, and hanging with Nic and his son had broken through the wall she'd tried to piece back together this week, and her feelings for Nic were now front and center again. She needed to leave soon, before the walls came tumbling down making it impossible for her to leave.

Drifting back to her surroundings, it occurred to her that the car was quiet. Nic seemed lost in thought as he drove and when she glanced at Nicky in the backseat, he had his head resting in his hand staring out the window at the passing cars. Looking back and forth between the two, she got the feeling that something had happened while she was examined.

Within a few minutes, Nic pulled his car into a neighborhood with houses that could only be described as mansions. Two and three-story homes with large yards, custom landscaping and expensive vehicles parked out front. He slowed to a stop in front of a two-story gem with a red tile roof that looked like it belonged in Hollywood. It seemed a mixture of craftsman and Spanish influence, with dormers across the front with lights burning bright. It had a large front porch the length of the house, with rock covered columns that led to a large wood door with divided light windows on both sides. It was off white in color and looked to be covered in stucco. There was a Mercedes parked in the driveway, and when he put the car into park, the front door opened and Kat walked out onto the front porch.

Nic didn't say a word, just opened his door and got out. Nicky turned and grabbed his bag and just before he got out; he looked back at her and with a smile that didn't reach his eyes said, "Glad you're ok, T-Hope." Then he opened his door and got out as she tried to say goodbye.

Seeing both Nic and Nicky like this bothered her. The more she watched them as they walked to the house; she was convinced something was wrong.

Nic stopped short when he got to the front porch, said something to Nicky, and he nodded his head and then ran inside the house. He started talking, and she could tell by Kat's reaction it was upsetting. Nic kept going as Kat threw her hands over her mouth and within moments launched herself into Nic's arms crying. Hope felt her throat tighten watching them; whatever was going on she was sure it had to do with their daughter.

Nic didn't hesitate to hold his ex-wife, she may have cheated on him, but she adored their children and was devastated when Chelsea died. She sobbed into his neck as he held her; finding out your daughter died because she wanted to be popular was hard to wrap your mind around. There were tragedies in life, senseless killings, car accidents that took fathers and mothers, drunks who were selfish and got behind the wheel, but this? *Dieu*, he didn't think he'd ever come to terms with this.

Rubbing his hand up and down her back, she finally pulled back and wiped her eyes free of the makeup that ran under them. She looked up at him, and her bottom lip quivered. It was the first time in a long time he saw the girl he'd fallen in love with. She'd changed so much from that girl from Georgia who'd had dreams of family, hearth and home. Leaning in, he kissed her forehead to give her comfort and then turned to go.

"Aren't' you staying?" Kat asked confused.

"No, Kat, I gotta get Hope back to her place so she can rest."

"Why on earth is she still with you?" She hissed.

"Hospital was full, took longer than expected to see a doctor."

"Nic, she's just some waitress, you should have had that Big Daddy guy take her, for goodness sakes."

"Jesus you're somethin else. Hope is a friend and I'm not gonna argue with you, not tonight of all nights, woman. You're emotional, and I've got no patience for bullshit."

He watched her narrow her eyes and then she snapped out "What kind of friend?" as she looked over his shoulder at the street. Before he could answer her, she marched past him heading for his car. Nic tried to grab her arm, but she pulled free, moving quickly on those damn high-heeled shoes she always wore.

"Kat, get back in the house," Nic ordered as he caught up with his ex.

"This is *my* family," Kat shrieked through the window at Hope.

"Jesus, woman, are you insane?" Nic ground out. Kat wheeled around and got in his face, and Hope felt the color drain from her own as she watched Nic's face grow hard. A dangerous looking anger she'd seen before in another man crossed his face, and

93

she braced herself for what would come next.

"Haven't *I* lost enough? Haven't we *both* lost enough?" Kat screamed.

"Get. In. The. House." Nic repeated his jaw tight, but he didn't put a hand on her.

"Why? So you can leave with that slut and forget you have a family that needs you?" Nic's head fell back looking at the heavens. He closed his eyes and took a deep breath, but still he didn't put a hand on his wife. Hope realized she was panting, holding onto the handle of the passenger door ready to bolt once he started swinging. When she saw Nic tip his head back and take a deep breath to calm himself, it finally sank in that he wasn't going to hit Kat. *How fucked up was she that she automatically assumed Nic would put a hand on his ex-wife?*

Hope turned her eyes from the fight and looked out the side window trying to stop shaking. She heard him say, "Nicky's watching out the window, you need to get inside." Kat replied, "Nic, we need you," in a voice that sounded like a lost child, and Hope closed her eyes at that sound of her desperation and wished she could slink away and leave.

"Yeah? Nic bit out, "Well your family needed *you* when you were off fuckin' every guy in town."

She heard Kat gasp and then the sound of heels running away pulled Hope from the window, and she turned in time to see the front door slam shut. Nic stood there looking at the house and then bent his head to stare at the ground, hands on his hips, a look of exhaustion on his face. He stayed there a moment longer, just breathing in and out trying to control his anger. Raising his head, he turned to the car and took the few steps needed to reach it, opened the door, folded his large frame and then climbed in.

Hope kept her eyes down, her hands folded in her lap, and waited as he sat there staring out the windshield.

"She took drugs to fit in," he finally whispered.

"Who?" Hope asked, but she had a bad feeling she knew the answer.

"Chelsea, my daughter, she started using drugs so she could be popular." Hope's breath caught and without thinking, she reached out and grabbed his hand.

"Nic—"

"My *tit ange* is dead because she wanted to be cool," Nic mumbled and his hand tightened around hers.

"I'm so sorry, Nic."

"Yeah, so am I," he sighed. "I'm sorry I didn't see it sooner because I worked too damn much. I'm sorry that I didn't teach her that drugs don't make you cool. And I'm sorry I left her in a rehabilitation clinic; that her last days were filled with thoughts that I didn't care enough to make her better myself," he bit out his face blank as his dead eyes looked at her. "I better get you home so you can rest," he mumbled and then let go of her hand and started the car.

Nic was quiet the whole way to his condo; his jaw was tight, fingers flexing on the steering wheel and Hope tried to think of words to ease his pain. Her own loss was heartbreaking, and even though she never held her son, she would have given anything to have him here with her. But Nic's grief hadn't come full circle yet, he blamed himself as all parents do. She should have left when she found out she was pregnant, but didn't out of fear. Nic blamed himself because he thought he should have done something different, and she understood that. She knew there was nothing she could say that would change his mind because it *is* a parent's job to protect their child from everything. Yet, no matter how good a parent you are, sometimes, bad things just happen to good people. Period. No rhyme or reason for it, they just happen.

When they pulled in front of his condo, and he turned off the car, Hope turned to him and in a gentle voice told him, "I'm not going to tell you you're wrong for feeling the way you do. You lost your daughter, and that is beyond any pain a man or woman should have to bear. I'm sorry for your pain, and I wish I'd gotten a chance to meet your daughter."

"You would have liked her. She had a hell of a sense of humor, was always playing practical jokes on her brother and me."

"What did she look like?"

"Blonde, like her mother, same eyes, she was beautiful, perfect really." Hope smiled and thought she probably was perfect having both Kat and Nic for parents. Kat may have been a shrew, but she was a beautiful woman nonetheless.

"I'm sure she was lovely, Nic," she replied and then grabbed the handle of her door to open it. Nic touched her on the arm and Hope turned back to him and watched as he scanned her face.

"How's your head?"

"Better, I'll be fine. Thank you for, well, for taking care of me, I guess."

"Least I can do for the star pitcher," Nic grinned.

"Yeah, well, I think my pitching days are over."

"Big Daddy will be sorry to hear that, nothin' he likes better than kicking ass in the bar league," Nic laughed and then it hit him it was the first time he'd laughed since Nicky had told him about Chelsea and he stared back at the reason why.

Hope had given him permission to grieve, didn't try to tell him he'd get over it and move on some day. She wasn't afraid to ask him about Chelsea, as if the mention of her name would send him over the edge. She didn't say she knew how he felt or compared his loss to her grandmother's death. She'd just said your feelings are justified; I'm sorry you're hurting, and those small considerations had calmed him down and helped him move past his anger. Looking at Hope, he felt the knot in his chest break loose, and a burning in his chest started to rise.

"You okay, Nic?" she asked. He'd been laughing one second and then deep in thought the next.

"No," he replied looking back at her, searching her face again. His own face grew intensely, and she watched as something like determination grew in his eyes.

"Hope?"

"Yeah, Nic?" Hope replied puzzled by his demeanor.

"Just so you know, I'm gonna kiss you now. You're gonna protest, and I'm tellin' you right fuckin' now it'll do no good."

Hope's eyes grew wide as Nic's hand snaked out and grabbed her around the neck pulling her forward towards his mouth. She gasped, tried to say, "Wait," but Nic told her "We've been dancing around this for a month and I'm not waitin' another minute, so shut it and kiss me."

Hope lost all reason when he growled at her, it sent a primal shiver down her spine, and her ability to fight him off was gone. She said, "Okay," as Nic leaned in, brushed his lips once, twice, three times gently over hers and when she inhaled sharply from the feel of his lips on hers; he slammed his mouth over hers, silencing her moan as his tongue invaded her mouth. This kiss was like no other she'd experienced, it was hot, demanding, and it spoke of his virility. He buried both hands in her hair, tugged gently to angle her head so he could devour her mouth and then tangled his tongue with hers, fighting for dominance. She felt a warm sensation in her chest that radiated down between her legs and she moaned again. Nic ran his hands down her back, grabbed her at the waist, and pulled her across the console and into his lap, never breaking the kiss, but deepening it so he could drown in her sweet lips.

Moments later, he broke the kiss and stared at her both

97

breathing in perfect unison, like some erotic beat that only they could hear. His eyes lowered to the rise and fall of her breasts, and he heard her breathing increase. Nic looked back at her mouth and saw it was red and swollen from his kiss. Wanting more, he leaned in and nipped her lower lip, then swept his tongue across it to ease the bite he left behind.

"I'm about two seconds from ripping your clothes off," Nic told her to break the mood. He didn't want to take her in his car. He wanted her in bed where he had room to move, room to lick her body from toe to ear.

"I can't," she whispered.

"You can, but not tonight while your head is injured," he told her leaning in again, flicking his tongue across her lips. "And when I take you it will be slow and exhausting. I want you rested," Nic explained against her lips and her response was immediate, "Oh, God."

Nic smiled and shook his head "Oh, no, baby, there is no God involved. Just you, me, and the things I'm gonna do to that sweet body of yours." He punctuated his answer by placing both hands on the side of her face, lowering her mouth to his, and kissed her once again until his own desire was quenched enough he could let her go.

Once he'd had his fill of her; Nic opened his door and helped Hope out. Turning her towards her door, they walked hand-in-hand, neither talking the whole way. At her door, he used his key to open it and turned off the alarm. When Hope entered she was still dazed, and he liked that look on her best of all. Needing more of her sweet lips, Nic grabbed her at the waist and pulled her to him. Her hands slammed into his chest as he leaned down and took her mouth again, backing her into the wall. He couldn't get close enough, wanted her wrapped around him, but he needed to go slow. So this time he moved his hand under her shirt, finding one of her breasts, and then he rubbed his thumb across the taut peak. Hope moaned low in her throat, and melted into him as his thumb flicked her nipple. Her own hands went up the back of his shirt, running her nails down his back, and Nic growled in approval. He then moved to her neck and bit down, giving her a taste of things to come, and Hope gasped in pleasure. Satisfied he had her attention, that she knew exactly what to expect from him, he moved to her ear, nibbled the lobe and whispered "I'm gonna leave now, *ma doux amour.* You have sweet dreams, baby."

Without another word, Nic slowly removed his hand from her breast, his fingers brushing lightly down her side as he stared into her sky-blue eyes. Hope shivered at his touch but held his eyes, her expression one of shock and amazement. He took her hand, raised it to his mouth, and his tongue darted out to taste the sweet skin before he walked her to the door. Once there, Nic was all business as he opened it, leaned in and kissed her gently then walked out, looked back at her and ordered, "Lock it and set the alarm." He waited for her to close the door, grinning at her dazed expression. Hope nodded, said nothing, then shut the door, and set the alarm all while in a trance like state. She stood there a moment her thoughts racing, and then leaned back, slid down the door, brought a hand to her mouth and whispered "Oh, my God."

Eleven

Pacing her living room, surrounded by priceless antiques that she'd once thought were so damn important she'd taken a trip to France just to buy, Kat needed a plan. No way was she gonna let some cheap floozy come between her and Nic reconciling. She knew if he'd just forgive her for her silly transgressions they could be a family again. However, that two-bit harlot with her bright eyes and pert little nose could put a snag in her plans she just knew it.

She needed information, needed to find something she could use against the woman and send her packing. Her momma taught her to fight fire with fire, and if the look on Nic's face when she got hurt were any indicator of his feelings, she'd need an inferno. She knew she couldn't ask Nic, and that old woman Rose hated her, so that was out of the question. Still pacing, she thought about Big Daddy a moment; he was a man, maybe she could bat her eyes at him and sweet-talk the information out of him? Continuing to pace she realized that wouldn't work either, she couldn't get close enough to him without Rose seeing, and that old Cajun was like a mother bear when it came to people she cared about.

Wandering into the kitchen where Nicky was, still plotting, she paused when she saw his face, and she forgot about the blonde for a moment. She could tell he was upset. Confiding in Nic about Chelsea had taken a toll on her precious boy, and she hated that he'd carried that burden with him. He was so much like his father, handsome, smart, and extremely loyal. Running her fingers through his hair and then leaning in, kissing his head, drinking in his smell, she felt her throat close a bit. She had been so busy chasing men, looking for her youth, that she'd missed the signs that Chelsea was using drugs. It never occurred to her that her perfect princess would do something like that. She'd raised her to be a lady, debutant balls, Saturdays at tearooms learning the fine art of manners all young women should have. Her own momma had done the same for her, she was just passing on those traditions all southern women do. Apparently, she should have been talking to Chelsea, finding out more about her daughter instead of assuming she was fine. Looking at Nicky, she wondered if she should talk to him, maybe ask if he's doing okay, and make sure he didn't need to talk.

"You doin' okay, my sweet boy?"

"Yeah, it was good to finally tell Chelsea's secret."

"Is there, uh, anything you need to talk about?" Kat didn't know how to talk to her son, but she figured she'd better learn.

"Naw, I'm good. I already told Dad that I won't use drugs, not after what happened to Chelsea."

Kat stared at her son, thought about him telling Chelsea's secret, and it occurred to her it was at the hospital while they waited on that woman. Of course, Kat being Kat, her mind moved from concern for her son to how to win her husband back.

"Nicky?"

"Yeah?"

"Your friend . . . that sweet woman who got hit in the head is she from around here?"

***

101

Nic sat at his desk staring out the window. His mind was on sweet lips and blues eyes he could get lost in. His chest was tight, but not from loss for once. The tightness stemmed from emerging feelings he'd tried to ignore, tried to suppress in his waking hours but fell victim to in his dreams. He'd left Hope a few hours ago speechless, flustered and aroused. His lip twitched when he thought of how dazed she'd been standing there with swollen lips, her hair a mess from his hands running through it. She'd been more devil than angel at that moment, and he could feel himself grow hard at the memory of her lips.

His reluctance to get involved with Hope had vanished; the barrier he'd put between them had fallen with a resounding thud. His instinct to kiss her, touch her, bury himself in her was too strong to ignore, and he gave into it. Now that he had, he felt a calm like he hadn't felt in a year.

He had no doubt she was downstairs trying to figure out a way to keep him at arm's length. Now that he'd tasted her, had her in his arms, felt her heart beating in sync with his own and had returned his kiss as if only he could give her the air in her lungs, there was no turning back.

He looked at the clock on his desk and saw it was after midnight. Sitting next to the clock were two pictures, one of Nicky and one of Chelsea. He reached forward, grabbed the frame with Chelsea's picture and traced his finger along her face. Her smiling eye's stared back at him. She was happy then, just a girl who wanted to be popular, but she'd gone about it the wrong way. He'd always thought they were close, thought he'd taught her self-worth. He couldn't comprehend that his *tit ange* would use drugs to be popular. To escape some sort of pain he could almost understand, but this? "*Ma jolie fille, mon coeur,* why?" he whispered, but like always he got no answer.

Replacing the picture, he stood from his desk and walked to

the window looking out at the street below. Rain was falling, the lights of passing cars reflecting off the water. He leaned against the windowsill and looked towards the cloud-covered sky. No stars or moon could be seen, just gray clouds illuminated by distant lightning. He caught movement on the sidewalk below and squinted his eyes searching the darkness. He heard Hope's door close and then watched as she struggled with her bags heading for the gate. "Fuck," Nic hissed then turned, knocked his desk as he passed, and his kid's pictures fell over as he ran for the front door.

Struggling to drag her bag through the gate, Hope didn't hear Nic before he was right behind her. She jumped when he grabbed her arm and swung her around, his dark eyes angry.

"Going somewhere?" he ground out.

Gone was the man who had kissed her senseless, and in his place was a man who looked almost dangerous.

"I have to go," was all she could say. She couldn't tell him the truth; she wasn't sure she knew the truth.

"You're not going anywhere, not now, not ever."

"Nic, I have to."

Reaching down he pulled a bag from her hand, grabbed her arm and started walking her back to the condo, but he veered right towards the stairs that led to his upstairs unit. Hope panicked and pulled back locking her legs.

"No, I have to go," she shouted just as they reached the rock wall that partitioned off his stairs and the garden from the street.

With rain streaming down his face, Nic dropped her bag and wheeled around, getting closer, and barked out, "You made a promise to me, and you're not breaking it."

"What promise?" she whispered, watching, as he got closer still, leaning in intimidating her.

"The promise of something beautiful at the end of the day, the promise of you," he whispered. "I've been in a fuckin' nightmare for over a year and you stumbled into my life and turned me on my head. You gave me sweet; you gave me sass, and you gave me a fuckin' headache from wanting you and tonight you gave me you, I'm holding you to that."

He raised his hands to her face, and both thumbs caressed her cheeks. Hope closed her eyes at the pain she saw in his eyes and tried to steel her nerves. She started shaking her head no, her bottom lip trembling with emotions, "Please," she whispered, "Please let me go."

"Baby, I'd rather cut off my right hand than let you walk out that gate."

Nic leaned down to kiss her, but Hope stepped back, blanking her face, setting the lie in place so he'd believe her.

"I'm sorry, Nic, but the attraction is one-sided. You've been wonderful to me; everyone has, but it's time to move on before it gets messy."

Staring at her, his face unreadable, he gently shook his head in disbelief and then bent to pick up her bag, and then replied, "You're a shit liar." She couldn't reply without crying, so with her stony expression in place she put out her hand to take her bag.

With Hope's bag in his hand, Nic raised it up, tossed the bag further away, then grabbed both her arms, and spun her behind the covered patio blocking them from prying eyes.

Hope gasped, dropped her other bag and put her hands on his chest to shove him off, but he leaned in pinning her to the wall of his garden.

"What are you doing?" Hope shouted and then struggled to get free. Panic rose up her throat, memories of violent hands on her creeping in.

"Explaining something to you," he rumbled in a low graveled voice and then leaned his whole body into her."

"Just say it," she begged, needing to get away, far away.

Nic didn't say a word; he grabbed her face and slammed his mouth over hers as she inhaled in surprise. His hard body kept her pinned as he kissed her, stoking the fire that had been simmering below the surface since he left. She tried to resist, knew she had too or she'd never leave, but he was relentless. He was making a point, proving her the liar she was and with her shields down, she gave up the fight. She wrapped her arms around his neck and gave in cursing her weakness for this man.

Nic groaned in satisfaction when she gave into their lust. He couldn't get close enough, wanted to sink himself into her, hold her to him, and keep her from leaving. He deepened the kiss, moaning as he reached the warm recesses, tasting her, claiming her, making her moan in return. His hands moved from her head to her T-shirt and with no regrets, he tore his mouth from hers, grabbed the hem and ripped it up and over her head.

She stood in the rain, water glistening against her pale skin, the swell of her breasts spilling over her tan lace bra and he'd never seen anything so beautiful. She was panting; her eyes filled with hunger as he raised his hand, pulled down her bra and cupped her breast, the weight of it hardening his cock even more. "So fuckin beautiful," he whispered.

As he rubbed his thumb across her pebbled nipple, her head fell back, a soft whimper spilling from her lips. Leaning down, he drew her nipple into his mouth and bit down.

"Nic," Hope gasped her legs about to buckle from the feel of his mouth. Sucking her nipple deep, he then released it and then flicked his tongue across it once more. He returned to her mouth, biting, sucking—claiming her lips. Then from the depths of his throat, he growled as his need for her body escalated to a savage level.

"You're not going anywhere," he groaned when Hope's hand

grabbed his cock through his sleep pants, rubbing down the length of it as it swelled to the point of pain. Rubbing himself against her hand, he moved his own to the shorts she wore, flicked the button open, and with both hands pushed them down while never leaving her lips. He removed her hand, pulled his pants from his hips and then lifted her up, and wrapped her legs around his waist. He looked between them as he slid her down on his aching cock, hissing in pleasure as her heat surrounded him, sucked him in, made him burn.

"Bon Dieu, ma doux amour," Nic gritted out, breathing deep to keep from exploding. She was tight, almost too tight for his large size. Her velvet, hot skin caressed him, drew him deep into her, and he surged forward, pulled back and then slammed her back down again, both moaning when he seated himself all the way in.

Too much, it was too much, too many feelings spiraling in Hope at the same time, and she couldn't hold back. She held onto Nic's neck as he pounded her, built her to the coming crescendo at a speed she'd never known. "Oh, God," she cried out, feeling her climax building to a pinpoint clarity.

"Jesus, I can't get enough of you," Nic growled and then watched as he pulled her up his length and then sunk her deep again. He brought a hand to her apex, found her throbbing clit, rolled it and then watched the beauty that was Hope exploded on him, milking him with her climax. "Jesus, you're fuckin beautiful when you come," Nic whispered as her eyes slid closed, her mouth half open in ecstasy. The desire on her face, the tightening of her core all sent him over the edge, and he spilled his seed deep inside her, grunting his pleasure as he fully claimed her body.

His body jerked as he slowed his strokes, and Nic moved to her neck nipping and biting as he found her ear. Then he let her know, in no uncertain terms, "You're mine now, you don't fuckin' run from me again."

"Nic—"

"I protect what's mine, whoever is after you, they won't touch you," Nic told her still buried inside her sweet warmth.

He didn't wait for an answer, he wouldn't accept anything less than she was his, so as far as he was concerned the subject was closed. He lifted her off, put her on her feet, pulled his own pants up and then assisted Hope as she pulled on her own. When she was done, Nic picked her up, carried her up his stairs and into his home, and then walked down the hall to his bed, and laid her on it.

Crawling onto the bed, and then pulling her into his arms, Hope laid her head on Nic's chest while she panicked.

"You ok?" Nic asked.

"No," Hope answered honestly.

"I lost my head and didn't think about birth control."

"I'm covered if that's what you're worried about." Nic sighed and changed the subject, feeling her pull away from him.

"Talk to me, tell me why you felt you had to leave," he asked, running his hand through her hair.

"I was scared."

"What about?"

"My past, my future, not wanting to hurt any of you."

"Then let me help you."

"It's not that simple," Hope explained, but the truth was she didn't want him to know, knew if he knew the truth he would turn her away and now that she'd slept with him, opened herself up to him she didn't think she could bear to walk away.

"You need to trust me, Hope."

"I do, I'm trying to protect you."

"Sugar, that's my job now. You living your life alone ends now. I've lived the past year with what happens when people keep secrets and don't talk. You need to trust me to take care of you. I promise nothin' will happen to you, but *you* need to promise to be honest with me." Hope wasn't sure she could keep that promise. Not sure she could ever tell him the truth.

"Hope?"

"I'll tell you just not tonight, okay?" Nic sighed, and squeezed her tighter against him, trying to give her the security she obviously needed.

Rubbing her head on his chest, trying to avoid his questions, she realized they were wet from the rain; she still had her shoes on, and his bed was now wet. "Nic, I think we messed up your bed."

Knowing when to push and when to hold back, Nic knew she was changing the subject for now, so he rolled Hope to her back, kissed her lips and then wiggled his eyebrows, chuckling "Oh, angel, it's gonna get worse."

Twelve

Hope landed on her back; cold fear replaced the pain she felt. He would kill her this time she knew it. Trying to get her feet under her, she scooted backward, her eyes on the knife on the kitchen counter. She'd been cutting vegetables for a salad and made the mistake of saying he was late when he walked through the door. She should have learned by now not to antagonize him, but what was left of the woman she once was held on tight, and every now and then, she'd bite back. "You don't tell me when to be home," he roared then pulled the tie from his collar. He stood over her as she tried to crawl away, tried to escape his fucked up mind. Snatching her hair, stopping her as she reached for the knife, fingers slipping on the granite countertop, he wrapped his tie around her neck and twisted….

Gasping for air, her hand at her throat, Hope sat up, looking around the bedroom. She was alone in Nic's bed, the sun shining through the blinds. Her dream, an old friend; one she pulled around her like a coat of armor, so she'd never forget that day. She'd left within a few days of the night and had been looking over her shoulder ever since.

Shaking off the dream, she looked around. The room was masculine, brown walls, old weathered furniture that looked like it came from a rummage sale, but you could tell they were expensive pieces, historic pieces of a time long past. There were black sheets and comforter on the bed, and black and white photos on the wall of Nic's kids. Looking at the pictures, her gaze caught on one of Chelsea smiling. Wanting a closer look at his daughter, she rolled and found a white iris on his pillow with a note under it. Smiling at the delicate flower that filled Nic's garden, she loved their purity, how white they were. When she'd first moved in, and they had their coffee in the garden, Nic had told her they were the symbol of France, of the fleur de lis, they meant wisdom, hope and the promise of love. Last night when he'd made love to her in the garden, they'd surrounded them with their scent, mixing with the rain and heat; it was a powerful memory of fresh flowers, sex and passion.

Lifting the flower to her nose, she breathed in its scent as she picked up the note from his pillow.

"Gone for coffee and beignets, Nic."

Smiling, she crawled out of bed and threw on a discarded T-shirt. Moving to the pictures of Nicky and Chelsea, she gazed at each one, the happy smiles on their faces, Chelsea at different ages, beautiful in all of them. Blonde hair, light, blue eyes like Kat's, Nic was right—she was perfect. Hope's chest tightened thinking how hard it must have been for all of them to lose her. For the pain they go through daily still, trying to cope with the loss as they go about their lives. Running a finger down the contour of Chelsea's face she was startled when warm, hard arms surrounded her.

"Like I said, she was perfect," Nic whispered in her ear, resting his chin on her shoulder as they both stared at the photo of his daughter's angelic face.

"She was beautiful, Nic, is beautiful. I wish I knew what to say to make it easier for you."

"Sugar, there isn't anything you can say that will help, it just takes time."

Turning in his arms, Hope looked at Nic and saw he wasn't in pain, just resolved to the fact that his road to healing would take him on a winding one. Nic leaned in, kissed her gently and then smiled against her lips. Moving backward, still holding Hope in his arms, when his legs hit the bed he fell back taking her with him.

Laughing as she fell, when she collided with his chest she smiled, still amazed that last night she'd been on her way out of town, prepared never to return, and with one kiss, her resolve to leave washed away in the rain.

"Did you bring me beignets?" she asked raising her eyebrows, this was serious business—those sugarcoated pastries had become an addiction.

"Sugar, I've seen the way you look when you eat them. I wouldn't deny you or me the satisfaction."

"And just how do I look?"

Lifting his head, running his nose against her neck, he nipped her ear and then whispered, "Like you're gonna come from the sheer taste of them."

"That," she gasped, enjoying his tongue as it flicked out, teasing her, "Would be accurate."

Nic rolled Hope to her back and worked his way down her neck and back. He whispered, "Close your eyes," so she did, waiting to see what happened next. Moments later, the smell of pastry and powdered sugar engulfed her, and she opened her mouth when the sweet treat hit her lips. Moaning as she bit down, she opened her eyes and watched Nic as he watched her. His attention was on her reaction, so she moaned again giving him more of a show.

"Just so you know," Nic explained, getting hard just watching her. "I have to be at work in forty-five minutes, so I'm hauling your ass to the shower. You give me a show like that I'm not waiting to pay you back."

Hope smiled, licked her lips, and he watched that too, growing harder. Then she leaned up and said, "I'll do your back if you do mine."

One minute she was on her back, the next she was in the air thrown over his shoulder. Hope laughed; Nic smacked her sweet ass, and for the next thirty minutes, Nic gave Hope another reason to forget about ever leaving.

***

"What?" Hope asked Rose. The old woman was standing there staring at her.

"You tell me what," Rose demanded.

"Tell you what?"

"Dat' what I'm sayin,' what?"

"What's going on?" Abby asked Rose when she entered the kitchen and found Rose standing over Hope.

"Dat' what I want to know," Rose replied.

"What?" Hope asked again, still confused by the whole conversation.

"You standin' dere' wit' your head in da' clouds."

"She does look kinda of dreamy," Abby joined in and Hope just stared at the women.

"She got a look dat' say—" Rose stopped mid-sentence and then smiled the smile of a woman who knew when a woman had been thoroughly loved by a man. And not just any man, a man who knew how to make a woman feel good, a man who knew his way around the body, and Rose began nodding and mumbling "Mm hmm, he done good. Fill you up wit' hope he do, make you dream."

"It worked?" Abby replied, but Hope was too busy thinking about what Rose had said to catch her meaning. *Had Nic filled her with hope, helped her to dream again?* It had been so long since she'd had anything to dream about except staying alive, she'd missed the moment when her thoughts turned to more than just survival. How had that happened in one night? She'd been lonely for so long, trapped inside a hell that she'd forgotten how to dream. But Rose was right. As she stood there cooking she *was* dreaming about the future, one that included all of them.

"You gonna tell Maman it *not* work? She got da' look of someone wit' purpose, wit' a reason to fight instead of run."

Hope looked back and forth between the two women and finally tuned into what they were saying. "You two plotted against me didn't you?"

No, *Cher*, plotted for you," Rose smiled then put bother hands on Hope's face and leaned in, kissing her forehead. "Plotted for da' both of you," then she turned on her heels feeling like she'd won the lottery and patted herself on the back at another job well done.

Hope watched as Rose left the kitchen and then turned to Abby, "So, you were forced into service were you?"

"Please, I saw how he looked at you when you served him. And when he came to your rescue? Have mercy, I almost took a picture and updated my Facebook status. That was like something out of a romance novel."

"He was being a gentleman."

"He was protecting what was his."

"Abby, he'd just met me."

"Hope, clue in, Nic's a man's man, he took one look at you and decided you were it. He may not have known it at that moment, but his caveman did," Abby laughed.

Hope smiled at the mention of Nic being a caveman and thought back to him throwing her over his shoulder.

"Okay, the caveman bit I believe," she admitted feeling good to just laugh with a friend. It was all so normal, something she hadn't had in a very long time.

"Grunts does he?" Abby asked.

"Grunts, growls, manhandles," Hope answered looking around to make sure no one was listening.

"Sounds like a good time to me," Abby laughed and then she leaned in, "You deserve this; he deserves this, take care of it. A man like Nic, sugar—you won't know a day of unhappiness if you take care it, let him take care of you." Nodding her head, she smiled at Abby and then waved as her friend went back into the restaurant. *Take care of it, huh?* She might need help in that department; she had no clue how to take care of a relationship.

She was biting her lip deep in thoughts about the how's of taking care of a relationship when Big Daddy shouted from across the kitchen.

"*Bébé*, you give da' man what he needs, let him take care of you and you give him da' truth. Dat' recipe for *amour*." Hope smiled at Big Daddy and then ducked her head when she thought about the lie she'd knew she'd have to tell. *No way would a man like Nic want her if he knew the truth.*

Her chest tightened when she thought about John hurting any of the people she cared about, and she thought again about running to keep them safe. Her chest tightened further at the idea, and she became nauseous just thinking about it. One month, that's all it took. How had it happened so fast? One minute she was passing through and the next minute she'd fallen in love. Hope froze when she realized she loved Nic. But, it was true; she felt it deep in her bones. His moving her in, the morning coffees, the rides from work, all of it had paved the way for what happened last night, and now she was in so deep she didn't want to surface.

Feeling sweat break out across her forehead, she wiped it away with a towel. She looked back at Big Daddy, and he burst out laughing, "Don't look so scared, *Cher*, love never killed anyone." Closing her eyes, she shook off his words and prayed to God that he was right. 'Cause if he was wrong she knew it would be her who died fighting to protect it.

The night was busy, the traffic steady so Hope didn't have time to worry about what would happen next, only what meal needed to be prepared. Mid-way through the evening Rose handed Hope a ticket. When she looked at it, instead of a number indicating a menu selection, there was a message. As she read the words, she started giggling.

"Angel, fix me something fiery like you."

Hope looked up at Rose and saw the old woman smiling her know-it-all smile, and she rolled her eyes at her. Grabbing a bowl, she ladled up a steaming bowl of gumbo filled with spicy sausage, shrimp and crabmeat. She added Big Daddy's special cornbread and a big slab of bread pudding, drizzling a warm buttery caramel topping over it. She took off her blue chef's coat, pulled off her hairnet so she didn't look unappealing, and then picked up the tray she'd set the food on and headed to the floor.

She backed into the door, pushing it open with her bottom and then turned as it opened wide. She saw Nic at the end of the bar; a seat she was coming to figure out was his spot and headed towards him. He was lifting a bottle of beer to his lips when he saw her coming, then paused before the bottle reached his lips and his grin appeared. His gaze moved down her and then back up as she got closer, and when she reached him and put his plates in front of him, he reached out, grabbed her at her neck and brought her in for a kiss. It wasn't sweet; it was claiming, toe curling and when he released her, she took a step back and blinked several times. In a daze, she looked at him and saw his smug look; his eyes turned to her right, and he said, "Henri, another beer?"

Hope turned and saw Henri standing there with his arms crossed, watching Nic's little show. He had no expression on his face and then he grinned, raised his hands in surrender, and mumbled, "Message received loud and clear big guy." Nic nodded once and then turned back to Hope.

"Did you just throw down?"

"Sure did, sugar."

"That's kinda hot just so you know," Hope replied and leaned on the counter. Nic grinned, leaned in and kissed her sweetly this time, and then she watched as he picked up his spoon, winked at her and then spooned the spicy gumbo up ready to eat it. They both heard, "Dad," shouted from behind him, and Nic turned around and found Nicky and Kat both standing at the entrance again. Nic looked back at Hope, and she knew he didn't want to eat with his ex-wife, but wouldn't say no to his son. She grabbed his hand and squeezed it to let him know he should go and then it hit her. If Nic could throw down why couldn't she? When he turned to speak to Nicky, she stopped him. He looked back at her with a questioning look, and she grabbed his face and kissed him for all she was worth.

Nic's hand came up and held her mouth to his, consumed by her kiss and felt her own possessiveness. He recognized what she was doing and wasn't about to stop her. He stroked her tongue, gave her what she needed, letting her know she had nothing to worry about from his ex-wife, and then slowly ended the kiss, trailing two more quickly across her lips when he finished. Then, he placed his forehead on hers and stared back at her, giving her even more. Giving Hope him.

"Will I see you later?" Hope whispered, hoping he'd say yes.

"Angel, I've had a glimpse of heaven and tasted paradise, if you think I'd be any place else you'd be wrong."

"Okay, see you later," Hope replied and smiled brightly at him.

Just for an instant, he thought he could drown in those eyes; they'd turned the color of the bluest ocean after his kiss and the result left him wanting. Releasing her, he kissed her nose and said "Later, angel," as he stepped back.

Turning to greet the smiling face of his son and the eyes of a woman who looked like she would explode at any moment, but wouldn't in a crowded room, so Nic smiled at his son.

"Does this mean you're more than friends?" Nicky questioned.

Nic didn't say anything back to Nicky. He needed to put a stop to any ideas Kat had about running her mouth off about Hope in front of his son. He grabbed Kat by the arm and walked her away from Nicky's ears then leaned down, making sure he had her eyes. He tilted his head to the right and with a serious tone said, "Are we gonna have problems or can you act like an adult for once?"

Kat narrowed her eyes at him, looked over his shoulder at Hope as she pushed through the door of the kitchen and shot lasers of heat at the retreating woman. She smiled tightly, and then through gritted teeth said, "We just thought you might like to eat together, but I can see you have plans."

"Got no plans till Hope gets off shift, you wanna eat together we can eat together, but I'll warn you now, not one word out of your mouth about Hope. Nicky likes her, and it wouldn't go over well if you bad mouth her."

"Then we'll agree not to talk about your," she paused to look for the right word and decided on, "Slut." He knew she had to get a word in before Nicky joined them she couldn't help herself. She wasn't wired to keep her mouth shut. But, no way in hell would he let that slide. He leaned in and bit out on a growl, "I'd watch who you call names, Kat. I'm not the type of man who'll stand for it, and you know it." Nic then turned and walked away after his parting shot and curled his arm around his son's neck. She wants to eat, he'll eat. He'd do anything for Nicky. Including keeping peace with his mother.

Thirteen

With the kitchen finally clean and the prep work for the next day's business complete, Hope was ready to head home and kick back with Nic. They'd been a couple for more than a week now, and she still got excited thinking about seeing him each night when she got off work. She'd get butterflies in her stomach when it was time to leave and realized she felt like a schoolgirl with her first crush, and Nic was like the captain of the football team.

Looking back on her time being courted by her husband, she realized she hadn't felt the same about him. The blaring difference in attitude and feelings was obvious now she had something to compare it to. She'd known then he was dangerous, but she'd chalked up her nervous stomach to butterflies and ignored her own subconscious. After years of being alone, shuffled from one foster home to another and no money for college, at eighteen, she'd set out on her own. She'd worked retail at a high-end boutique and tried to better herself taking classes at night. Then the Cummings brothers had walked into the store where she worked, looking for a gift and all of that changed. Her husband's perverse fascination with her, his possessiveness that she now saw as unhealthy had felt good after being alone. Now when she looked back, she remembered wringing her hands in nervous energy whenever he came to pick her up. At the time she'd worried he would find her lacking, but now she knew it was because she saw the darkness just under the surface. With Nic, she just felt connected, wanted, maybe even loved a little.

The past week and a half had been nothing short of amazing. They'd spent every night in each other's arms until it was time for Nicky to stay with Nic. Then they'd spent each night she was off work hanging out with him playing games or helping him with homework. She'd cooked for them; they'd cooked for her and each night when she'd closed her eyes, whether it was in Nic's bed or her own, she'd felt a contentment she'd never known in her life.

Grabbing her purse to leave, Hope waved at Abby and Henri as they finished their work for the evening. When she opened the front door of the bar, she found Nic leaning against his car like he'd done every night this week. Arms crossed over his chest; legs crossed at the ankles, looking down at the pavement in quiet reflection; Hope's breath caught when she took in all that was Nic. He was in jeans, his black biker boots and another black T-shirt that read, "Cajuns do it in the swamp."

Hearing the door close, Nic raised his eyes, and his gut tightened at the sight of Hope. There was something about her that called to him; she was delicate, fair, and almost innocent in nature. His need to protect her was strong, instinctual, like whatever essence made men the protector of women was tripled when God designed Nic.

Rising from his car, he grinned when she stopped and stared at him. She may have just gotten off work, but he wasn't takin' her home until he had the answers he needed about her past, and he figured a beer, some music and laid back people was just the ticket to get her to open up to him. He'd waited long enough for answers, giving her time to adjust to their relationship and spend time with him and Nicky, but they'd been together for more than a week now and he was done waiting. He couldn't protect her if he didn't know what the hell to look for or who.

"You look dressed to go out, are we going somewhere?'

"The lady is not only beautiful, she's smart," Nic grinned and then grabbed her at the waist and pulled her in closer. He leaned down and said, "Hey, sugar," before his lips teased her own. When she was thoroughly dazed, he pulled back, grabbed her hand, walked her the few feet to his car, and deposited her inside. When he got in, he turned to Hope and told her, "Time to talk," then watched as she blanched and then nodded her head. He wanted to laugh at her reaction, but she looked like a woman being sent to the gas chamber. He knew whatever had her running was serious, and he wasn't waiting another day. He needed her to be honest with him so he could keep her safe.

When Nic didn't take the right that led them back to the condo, Hope kept her mouth shut. She'd hoped he was kidding when he said they were going out, but now she was too busy running circles in her head about what she should tell him to care. She was putting him and everyone she cared about here in danger by staying, she knew that, and if she were smart, she'd try to leave again until it was safe to come back. But, the nauseous feeling she got in her gut any time she thought about leaving him, always stopped her dead in her tracks, and she felt as helpless to run this time, as she did from her husband. Love was holding her captive it seemed.

After ten minutes of driving Nic crossed the Crescent City Bridge, and made his way down to Vallette Street until it deadened at Patterson Drive. The levee, keeping the Mississippi river from flooding the surrounding neighborhood, was in front of them, but Nic turned left and headed one block down to Old Point Bar. The bar sat on the corner; it was no frills, small and jumping to the lively beat of a band playing Cajun music. People were milling around outside, and the band was setup in the vacant lot next to the bar where people were dancing as well. She was surprised he'd brought her here for a serious talk; it seemed loud, too crowded. Then she thought about having a drink, being around lively music as she told him what she could and figured it was as good as place as any to lie.

Hope had made a decision while Nic drove; she couldn't tell him everything, not yet. The truth would come out eventually; she knew that, but she couldn't tell him everything now. He'd hate her, look at her with disgust, and it would open wounds that seemed to be closing a little bit each day for him. She had to protect him from her ugly past as long as she could until he wasn't so raw from losing Chelsea. 'Cause that's what you do when you love someone, you protect them, shield them.

She hadn't done that when she was pregnant, she should have protected her son and run then, but she didn't. She wouldn't make that mistake again, she would protect Nic, let him heal, and when she thought he was ready, she'd tell him the truth, the whole ugly truth, and pray when she did, he'd forgive her.

Nic found parking a block up, and when they exited the car, he came to her side and helped her out. Then he draped his arm around her neck as they walked down the sidewalk, pinning her to his side. They had to push through throngs of people to get to the bar, and when they did, he ordered two beers. The bar was small and rustic but appealing, and Hope wished they were here for any other reason than they were. Once they were served, Nic pulled her outside and across the street so they could sit on the levee and listen to the music but still hear each other talk. Once seated, Hope took a drink of her beer while her heart pounded; she wasn't good at lying and Nic had figured that out the night she tried to leave. She prayed she could pull this off and figured if she stayed, as close to the truth as she could, maybe she'd get away with it.

"Ok, sugar, tell me everything. No secrets, no lies, I can't help you if I don't know what's going on."

Hope inhaled, let it out and then started.

"My husband and his brother were into illegal business transactions. I found out, went to the police and had to leave town for my own protection. Once the police make arrests, I'll be safe."

"What kind of illegal business?"

"Import export." Nic watched her face and saw the fear. She didn't want him to know, so he figured he'd give her that, what they were transporting wasn't important.

"Did you work for them?"

"No, I, uh, found paperwork on his desk."

"And now you're afraid that they will harm you?"

"Yeah, the whole family can be, um, unpredictable." Nic knew what unpredictable meant, and he wanted to hit someone.

"Name," Nic growled, his emotions getting the best of him.

"What?"

"What's your husband's name?"

"I, a, I'm not married anymore."

"Then what's your ex-husband's name? I can't keep you safe if I don't know who to look for."

Sighing, because she hadn't thought about how to answer this question, she pulled out her wallet and a picture of her husband and his brother she had tucked away in case she needed it. Pulling it out, she handed it to Nic and watched while he studied the photo of the two men.

"Which one?"

Hope pointed to John, and Nic's eyes focused on the bastard, memorizing every detail of the coward, wanting him right in front of him so he could beat him just like he'd done to Hope. He handed the picture back to her and said "His name?"

"John Delaney," she lied and hoped that would buy her some time.

"That it? Nothing else? Just you need to stay hidden until they are arrested?"

"It's why I'm hiding, yes."

Nic watched her eyes, and he could tell she was holding back something. He'd have to work on breaking down her walls, but for now, he had enough information to keep her safe.

"So tell me, sugar, where are your parents, your family in all this?"

"They were killed in car accident, along with my brother."

"Jesus, I'm sorry," Nic whispered as he drew her into his side.

"It was a long time ago, Nic, I'm fine."

"Sugar, no amount of time lessens the loss, it just makes it bearable. You have me, Rose and Big Daddy now, no need to go it alone. We'll keep an eye out; no one will get near you I promise you that."

Resting her head on his shoulder, she wondered if he would forgive her someday for her lies. She hoped so, but even knowing she might lose him once he found out, she'd take that chance. He forced her to stay, made her believe that she could have a life, something beautiful, to dream again. For that, she would do her best to help him heal, give him the love he needed to move forward while she watched over their shoulders, and kept them both safe.

They sat there on the levee listening to the music, drinking beer and just being. When the song changed to a ragtime Cajun song, Nic jumped up grabbed her by the hands and said, "Dance with me angel."

"Here? On the levee?" Nic shook his head and grinned, then pulled her up to her feet and then bent at the waist, threw her over his shoulder again and marched towards the crowd.

"Darlin' Cajun music must be experienced in large crowds to be appreciate it."

"Nic, I can walk," Hope laughed.

"Yeah, but why spoil my view?" Nic answered back and swatted her sweet ass.

Nic made his way through the crowd to the sounds of hooting as other men slapped him on the back for capturing a woman. He grinned while he listened to Hope laughing and begging to be put down. Once he got to the dance floor, he put her on her feet, pulled her close, then started moving to the beat, swinging Hope out, and then back to him while she smiled. He hadn't felt this lighthearted in over a year, and as he looked at Hope, he was convinced she was an angel sent from heaven to help him heal his broken heart.

As the music died and a slower song began, he pulled her to him, and buried his head in her neck. Hope wrapped her arms around his waist and felt his heart beating hard against her chest. She tried to absorb his strength, his goodness; tried to feel clean, as if being close to him would cleanse her of her sins. When Nic pulled back, she looked up at him and this time when he leaned down to kiss her she didn't hold back, she allowed him to descend. When he was an inch from her lips, he took his eyes off her mouth and whispered, "I won't bite, sugar," and then winked, touched her mouth with his and kissed her gently as they swayed.

As they danced, focused on each other, they were unaware of the blue eyes that followed their every move, every touch, and every kiss. Kat stood in the crowd watching Nic's face as he danced and knew she was in trouble. That was the face he gave her when they were younger, the face he gave her when he'd courted her. Feeling her nails dig into her hands, she released her fists and headed back to her car. She had to think, come up with a plan before it was too late. Though, in the back of her mind, she knew it already was. She wanted to send Hope back to whatever hole she crawled out of, but how?

Settling herself behind the wheel of her Mercedes, she sat there tapping her hand on the wheel. If she couldn't get Nic's attention while that woman was around, she knew who could. She'd send Nicky to his dad's early this week, which would keep Hope out of his bed. Then all she had to do was come up with reasons to spend as much time as possible with the two of them. He'd remember what it was like to be a family and stop this silly love affair with the waitress or cook or whatever it was, she did for a living.

As she reached for her keys, she caught site of Nic and Hope as they made their way around the corner of the bar. Nic was nuzzling her hair; his arm wrapped protectively around her neck and shoulders, and Kat was frozen in place as she watched. He stopped next to his car, and pushed Hope against the side settling between her legs as his hands came up to capture her face. Nic leaned in, and Hope opened her mouth inviting him to take what he wanted from her. As the kiss grew more passionate, he leaned her back against the hood of the car and Kat watched as he rubbed himself on Hope, crotch against crotch and her heart rate accelerated.

How she could sit there and watch her husband, and he *was* her husband, no silly piece of paper would tell her otherwise, was beyond her. She likened it to being caught in a daze by something that your eyes couldn't interpret, something beautiful or heinous that you couldn't turn from in shock. But there she sat as Nic all but made love on the hood of his car, his hand going under her top, Hope's back arching at his touch, neither one of them aware, nor did they seem to care that they could be seen. Disgusted with their display, she turned her eyes and waited until she finally heard his car doors open and then close. Once they'd driven off, she sat there a little while longer as she recovered. Needing to get home to a sleeping Nicky, she started her car, determined more than ever to put a stop to this affair, and then pulled out without looking and hit a passing car. *Well, wasn't this just her night? Dangit-all!*

Fourteen

Nic woke the next morning before Hope. She was tangled in his arms, head to his chest, legs mixed with his as he leaned in and breathed in her scent. She was naked; he'd all but ripped off her clothes once they walked through his door. Both had been in a hurry to undress, their lips barely leaving the others as they fought with their clothes. He'd picked her up, her legs wrapped around his waist, and then he'd walked down the hall stumbling into the wall, so he'd used it to press into her body as he made love to her mouth. They'd both fought for dominance, but once he'd placed her on the bed, she'd rolled and climbed on top of him, kissing him, grabbing his hands and putting them over his head.

"Lay back and relax," she'd whispered in his ear, and his cock had jumped at her words. Her silken hair, a veil around them, she'd kissed him once more nipping his lips and then his chin as she made her way down his body. Her nails had scored his chest, and then her tongue kissed the pain away. Moving further down, his breath had escaped him when her warm hand and even warmer mouth had closed around his shaft.

Just the memory of how soft her mouth was on him, the way she teased him, her tongue rimming his crest, drawing a growl from his chest as his hands had fisted the sheet, had him hard again.

When she took him to the back of her throat, he knew he

wouldn't last much longer. Knifing up, he'd flipped her on her back as she'd gasped, and then slid inside her seating himself fully and then held as they both caught their breath, groaning as he stretched her, and she'd clamped down hard around his cock.

Cupping her face with one hand, he'd watched her expression as he'd pulled out slowly, drawing out the pleasure both received. Hope had moaned softly and tried to close her eyes, but he'd barked, "Eye's on me." When he'd almost left her body, he'd slammed back in and watched as she gasped and then shuddered around him. Resting his forehead to hers, he continued this, slowly pulling out and then pounding back in until she was panting. The exquisite bonding of their bodies, the heat, and the passion, all built to a frenzy as Nic found her neck and bit down where her shoulder met her neck. They exploded together in a release so powerful, Nic barely heard Hope calling out his name for the blood thundering through his head. Then he'd grunted in triumph at the sound of his name on her lips.

He'd roared *"Mine"* in his head as he'd filled her body and vowed no one would harm her, or give her another day's worry as long as he had breath in his lungs. He protected what was his at all costs, and the word "kill" even entered his thoughts.

He knew she was holding back, thought maybe even protecting him from the ugly truth of her past. Why, he didn't know, but he didn't care what she'd done to survive; all that mattered was that she was done with it and in his arms where he intended to keep her for a very, very long time. He didn't know why he had such a strong reaction to her; he had from the moment he laid eyes on her. All he knew was since she entered his life a month ago, something had shifted in his core, and for the first time in over a year, he slept through the night.

Nuzzling her neck, he cupped her ass and ground himself into her leg waking her. Hope's eyes slowly opened, and when she saw his dark soulful eyes staring back with hunger she reached between his legs and grabbed him, moving her hand up and down as his lips found hers. He rolled into her, keeping his arms braced, so her hand had room to work its magic. The sexual cloud that had settled over them, as their hunger for each other began to rise, was broken by the sound of his front door opening and Nicky shouting, "Dad!"

"What the fuck?" Nic growled in frustration. He looked at the clock, knew Nicky should be on his way to school, and if he was here, there was only one way he got here—Kat.

"Be out in a minute, bud," Nic shouted before his son threw open his bedroom door and saw more than Nic needed him to see. Then Hope started to panic whispering "Oh, my god," trying to get out of the bed before Nicky saw more of *her* than she wanted. They hadn't slept together with Nicky under his roof; he'd gone to her at night and returned a few hours later. He wasn't a kid so to speak, but Nic didn't want him to see Hope this way. When Hope tried to escape the bed he grabbed her around the waist, pulled her back to him, kissing her neck and telling her, "Stay here; I'll find out what is going on."

Rolling from the bed, Nic pulled on jeans from his dirty clothes hamper, barely buttoning them, and stalked out of the room bare chested as Hope watched. Hope was trying to decide what to do, but the sight of him in nothing but his jeans had short-circuited her brain, so she laid there while he left the room. When he was gone, she sat up and looked for her clothes until it dawned on her their clothes were in a trail from the front door to the hall. Mortified Nicky would see them she threw the bed sheets over her head and tried to die on the spot. The thought of Nicky finding her bra hanging from a light—not that is was, she was pretty sure it was on the kitchen counter—was too much to bear. She wondered if God would grant her a peaceful death when the humiliation of the moment Nicky found it, overcame her body.

Nic had his eyes on Kat as he came down the hall, and she'd at least had the good grace to turn her eyes from him, when she saw how pissed he was at her unannounced arrival. He'd lay money on the fact she'd done it on purpose.

After watching Hope kiss Nic, she'd played the martyr at dinner. Giving him looks like he'd betrayed her, torn their family apart by moving on with his life. He hadn't spoken directly with her since that night, just dropped Nicky off at the end of his week, and drove away without a word to her.

As he entered the room, he caught Nicky looking at the floor, his eyes landed on the tangle of clothes he, and Hope had left. He wanted to shake Kat for putting him in this position, but when Nicky's head came up, and his eyes looked down the hall and then back to the clothes, he smiled. Yes, he'd definitely missed the moment when his son stepped over the threshold into manhood.

When he'd stayed with Nic, and Hope had hung out with them, they'd behaved themselves, only brief touches and no kissing. Even though he'd kissed Hope at the bar, he didn't want to shove his relationship in his son's face in case it upset him in any way. As far as Nicky was concerned, Nic and Hope were just good friends so to speak, taking it slow in his eyes, getting used to each other. He had no doubt his son was well versed on the details of sex, but he didn't need it thrown in his face, and that wouldn't have happened if Kat had called before dropping in.

When he reached them, he bent down, snagged their clothes off the floor, and when he saw Hope's lacy bra on the kitchen counter, he dropped the clothes on top to cover it. Kat raised one of her sharply plucked eyebrows at him in response, and he narrowed his eyes in warning.

"What's going on?" Nic asked Kat.

"Well, I knew with Nicky leaving in a week's time you wouldn't get to spend much time with him while he's at your parents, so I thought I'd let him stay with you until he leaves." Nic was shocked she'd be that considerate, and immediately went on the defensive waiting for the punch line—he didn't have to wait long. "And since it *is* technically my week, I figured we could just share him and eat our meals together; spend the evenings together just like old times. Doesn't that sound wonderful, sugar? Our family back together again." *There it was*, Nic thought, another desperate attempt to win him back, but this time using their son to do it.

"Outside," he growled then looked at Nicky and said, "Stay here, we'll be back in five." Rounding his son, he grabbed Kat's arm and pulled her with him to the front door.

While Nic dealt with Kat, Hope had gotten out of bed, found one of Nic's dress shirts, and pulled it on. She needed her clothes, but wanted to wait until the coast was clear. Listening through the bedroom door, she heard Nic's loud voice say "Outside," and then the front door open and then close. With her heart hammering in her chest, she cracked the door open a tiny bit, listened, heard no voices and crept down the hall. Peaking around the corner, she saw no one in the living room or kitchen, and the condo was quiet. Her clothes were on the kitchen counter, and she sprinted to them so she could get back to the bedroom before being caught. As she grabbed them, she heard a noise and looked left, catching Nicky bent at the waist and his head in the fridge. He looked up, their eyes met, and she froze. Her eyes were glued to his as her cheeks turned red, and she silently prayed to God to kill her now. Nicky stared back at her, and she watched as his lip twitched like his fathers and then smiled a huge Nic like smile.

"I, uh, I think I'm gonna go die now."

Nicky's smile got bigger, and he rolled his eyes "Like I don't know my dad is a babe magnet, he has lots of friends."

"What?"

"His struggle is real,"

"His struggle?"

"Fightin' off all the babes who are after him." Hope's eyes widened, what she didn't do was head back to his room to put clothes on, an error she would regret.

"He has lots of friends?"

Nicky figured if Hope thought that he was a hot item, she would be impressed that she'd caught him, so he lied, "Oh, sure, dozens of them." He watched as Hope's face paled and then she ducked it, clearing her throat.

"Well, that's good he has so many, uh, friends, I'll just, um, head back to my condo, nice seeing you again, Nicky."

For some reason Nicky got the impression she wasn't impressed, in fact, he got a sick feeling that he may have screwed up. He watched Hope hesitate, then with the bar blocking his view, she bent at the waist pulled her jeans on from the night before, grabbed her purse, shoved her top, bra and panties inside, found her shoes, and stalked to the front door.

"Hope wait!" Nicky panicked as she reached for the doorknob. She didn't look at him; she wrenched the door open and found his dad and mom on the landing, his mother crying and his dad holding her.

Nic was sick to death of Kat's antics, and when he told her so, she had thrown herself in his arms, crying crocodile tears, and using their dead daughter as a reason to keep him close. When his door flew open, and Hope stepped out, pain evident on her face, he tried to peel Kat off him so he could stop Hope as she flew down the steps. Nicky came flying out after her saying, "Stop; I can explain," and Nic was done.

He got untangled from Kat, turned to Nicky and asked, "What

happened?"

"I told her your struggle was real with the babes."

"In English," he barked.

"That you have babes chasing after you and have lots of friends. I thought she'd be impressed that she'd caught you, but she seemed upset."

Nic sighed and hung his head to reel in his temper and after a moment he raised his head and in a firm, yet loving tone replied, "No more lies, no more hiding shit, and do me a favor, don't help me with the *"babes,"* as you call them, I've got this covered."

Then Nic whipped around to deal with Kat in time to see her smirking in victory at the little scene that just played out, and he made a decision. He didn't give a fuck if it upset her, if she hadn't pulled this shit none of this would have happened. He turned back to Nic and asked, "You want a family day huntin' crawfish?"

"What about school?"

"Figure they can do without you for one day."

"Awesome, what Bayou?"

"Honey Island?"

"Sweet, I can be ready in ten," Nicky shouted and then ran back into the condo.

"Can we stop by the house so I can change?" Kat replied behind him. Thrilled her plan was working. Nic turned around; anger etched on his face and on a low growl explained, "Kat, you crossed me one too many times. I'm takin' my boy and my woman crawfishin' you can go spend that alimony I pay you each month on your fuckin' nails."

After that parting shot, Nic stormed into his condo, packed his gear and he and Nicky went downstairs and knocked on Hope's door. When she answered, obviously recovered and moved from upset to angry, she presented them both with a pissed off face. Nicky wasted no time admitting to his lie and blurted out, "Dad doesn't have friends over, I was tryin' to make you comfortable, and thought if you thought that Dad was a catch you would like him. I'm sorry; I think you're great just so you know."

Hope being Hope melted at his words and forgave him on the spot. "Your dad is a catch that's why I was upset. Thank you for telling me the truth."

That fiasco behind them, Nic put his hand to Hope's stomach and pushed her back so they could enter her condo. Once in, he instructed her to, "Get your old clothes on we're goin' crawfishin." Then he figured since the cat was out of the bag, and Nicky didn't care; he smacked her on the ass, kissed her on the neck, and then mumbled in her ear, "After we eat tonight I'm having you for dessert."

Hope choked on a laugh as she made her way down the hall wondering what the hell crawfishing was and if it required her to handle them. She may serve them, but she always insisted that Big Daddy handle them—those beady black eyes gave her the willies.

Fifteen

It's hard to explain a Louisiana bayou. The winding the water takes as you go deeper into the prehistoric environment. Cypress trees tall and foreboding, their moss covered limbs blocking the sun in places, lending an eerie feel to their surroundings. The greens of vine flowers that covered some of the trees, even the green covered water was a sight to see. The quiet at times, like the wildlife, plants and trees themselves knew you were there, interrupting their tranquil world. Alligators lying in wait, Herons, perched on rotten stumps, their necks curved towards the sun. Snakes and turtles cresting the surface of the water and then ducking back down as you passed, all were foreign and in some cases a scary world to Hope, but nonetheless beautiful in their own right. She could see how a person could get lost out there, turned around, but also lost in a different way, lost in your own mind. The tranquility of the place lends itself to solving world hunger, stopping wars, or even coming up with a recipe for the perfect gumbo to appease Big Daddy and his quest for perfection.

The roar of the propeller broke Hope from her thoughts, as water lilies rocked in the water as they sped past towards some secret crawfish hole. Nic and Nicky swore it was the best spot for miles, and with the season's end approaching, they were determined to get one last big catch. Nic's airboat was loaded with mesh traps, a small cooler with fresh meat and hotdogs guaranteed to attract a crawfish within smelling distance. All was in the front of the flat-bottomed airboat, as Nicky and Hope sat in the middle while Nic drove high above them in the driver's seat. They were thirty minutes outside of New Orleans at a place called Honey Island, where Nic had a truck and airboat he kept in a storage unit for just such outings with his son. They'd driven down in his car and pulled out the boat, then put in near the swamp tours and watched as the large tour boats filled with people. They'd passed houses and shacks built on stilts with boats tethered to porches that sat right on the water. Nic had called them swamp people, those who lived there year round, and some had been on their porches and waved as they sped past towards their fishing spot.

When Nic came to a bend in the river, he took a right off the main waterway to a narrower inlet. After several hundred yards, he killed the motor, and they drifted onto a bank of solid ground as Nicky jumped out to stop the boat from floating back out. Thankfully, it was sunny where he'd parked, the mosquitoes were forming in the shade waiting to attack Hope and Nic didn't want her porcelain skin marred by bug bites. Stepping out of the back, his shrimp boots on to protect his legs, Nic leaned in without a word and yanked Hope out of the boat and carried her onto the bank placing her on the solid ground, and she sunk to the tops of her feet.

Solid ground in the bayou isn't exactly solid, more like squishy mud, and she'd been caught off guard. She didn't say a word to him at first as he put her down, stealing a brief kiss before heading back to the boat to retrieve the traps. For some reason, he liked carrying her places, but she felt like a child when he did it.

"I could have walked you know."

"And deprive me of the satisfaction of carrying you?" Nic replied over his shoulder as he handed Nicky a trap.

"You're a caveman you know that, right?" Nic winked at her as his only answer and continued unloading.

Hope looked around, saw a fallen tree nearby, and decided to sit while she watched the two Beuve men set about baiting, then wading out into the shallows, dropping the mesh traps into the water and then wading back to the so-called bank. When they both came out of the water and stood before her, she knew if she ever wondered what Nic looked like as a kid, she only had to look to Nicky. Even their walk was the same. Now they were standing in front of her, with their hands on their hips, both smiling the same smile and about to laugh.

"What?"

"I hate to tell you this, sugar, but you're sittin' on poison ivy."

Hope jumped from the log to see a green waxy looking vine covering the surface. She'd worn jeans out of habit, but she wasn't sure she hadn't touched it. Nic grabbed her arm, and Nicky snickered as he followed behind them. Hope heard it, turned her head and stuck out her tongue turning the snicker into a laugh. Nic stopped near a bag, pulled out liquid soap and ordered, "Wash your hands and don't touch your face." When she finished, Nic hoisted the bag back into the boat, turned and without a word picked her up again and placed her in the boat. Then he climbed back in as Nicky shoved them of the bank, climbing in the front, and Hope was confused.

"Why are we leaving?"

"Gotta let them soak for a few hours," Nicky answered.

"We'll take a tour of the area, grab some lunch at the "Poor Man's Shack" and then come back after the crawfish has had time to fill the trap," Nic added as he leaned in and kissed her one more time for good measure. Now that he could show more affection in front of Nicky, he intended to at every opportunity.

Grabbing a pole out of storage in the front of the boat, Nicky turned the nose of the boat towards the water, as Nic fired up the propeller. The loud thunder of the engine sent birds flying into the air as Nic gunned the engine and moved them back the way they'd came. Once on the river, Nic opened up the throttle, and they went flying on top of the water. After a mile or so, they came to an area with tall grass and Nic turned the boat out of the river and flew across the wetlands. Birds went flying again, and Nicky pointed to an alligator hidden amongst the reeds catching some sun. Twenty feet or so off the right side, Hope saw an animal that looked like a beaver and Nicky hollered, "Swamp rat," to her questioning eyes. Further up, in a crop of trees, she saw a huge nest at the top of the tree line and was about to ask what kind of bird had a nest that large when a bald eagle landed with some animal in its mouth to feed their young.

It was amazing the different topography in a bayou, wide rivers, narrow inlets, and wetlands teaming with wildlife all within miles of each other. All her life she had this vision of the swamp being just that, a swamp, dark, creepy and mysterious, but their outing today had opened her eyes to the beauty of the place.

Time passed quickly and soon Nic was heading back down the river towards the inlet where they'd set their traps. When he passed the little cove, she looked up at Nic, and he shouted "Lunch." Further down, he took a right off the river and made his way slowly around fallen trees, past other boats tethered with men eating sandwiches, until a large shack came into view. There was an old man on his deck manning a smoker, and a sign on his dock that said, "Don't ask and I won't tell, BBQ sandwich and chips $5."

Hope raised her brows at Nic, and he grinned. Determined not to *ask* for fear she would find out, Hope said nothing. Nic cut the engine and glided his boat alongside the porch, and then reached out a hand to shake the old man's and said "Where y'at, Virgil."

"Awrite'," Virgil replied and then said, "T'ree?"

"Three will do, and throw in some Zapp's."

Virgil leaned over and opened a cooler at his feet; he pulled out three foiled covered sandwiches, three bags of plain Zapp's potato chips and handed them to Nicky. Nic pulled out his wallet and handed the man double what the price said, and Hope smiled at his generosity to the old man. The man obviously wasn't one for conversation, because he took Nic's money, gave them a salute, and then turned back to his smoker as Nic pushed off the deck and started the boat to head back towards the river. Nic took them back to their fishing spot, and they stayed in the boat while they ate. Slowly unwrapping the sandwich Nicky had handed her, Hope sniffed it and then watched as Nicky took a large bite and then smiled at her.

"Do I want to know?" she asked the boat at large.

"Nope," Nic laughed and then bit into his own sandwich winking at her.

Pulling the soft, spongy bread apart, Hope looked at the meat, it didn't look like snake or alligator, and when she sniffed it, it smelled like pork. Not wanting to be a girl and refuse to eat it, she mentally made the sign of the cross and took a bite. Surprisingly, it tasted like pork, but a bit gamey and tough. Nic handed her a bottle of water from the cooler, and she opened her bag of chips while she kept eating the sandwich. It was peaceful as they ate, while Nicky asked questions about mundane stuff until he turned the conversation to Hope.

"So, T-Hope, where are you from?" Without thinking, she answered and could have kicked herself.

"Nevada."

"Is your family there?" he continued.

"Um, no, they died when I was a kid," she again answered without thinking, and hoped Nicky wouldn't ask any more questions about her past. It wasn't that she was ashamed of growing up in foster care; it just sounded so pitiful, and she hated the looks she got when people found out. Not to mention, there were some who thought if she grew up in the system, she was somehow uneducated, or in some cases a bad person, who'd do anything to survive.

When Nic cleared his throat but said nothing, she knew he was holding back. Then Nicky, being his father's son, meaning he wasn't dumb, said, "If you didn't have parents who raised you?"

"A very nice older couple that took in kids who needed homes raised me." She wouldn't tell him that the Johnson's had been wonderful, but so old they couldn't keep her and the other kids for very long, or that once they turned the kids back over to the state, it had been one bad home after another.

"Like grandparents?" he asked.

"Just like grandparents," she replied.

Deciding it was time to change the subject, not wanting Hope upset by any more questions Nicky might ask, Nic cleared his throat again as he thought about tiny Hope in the care of strangers. He'd heard some of the horror stories about kids in foster care, and he prayed to God that wasn't Hope's story. He'd add that to the list of things he needed to get her to open up about, but patience was something he was sure he would need to have where she was concerned. As far as he could tell, her life had been one bad thing after another, and he intended to rectify that as soon as possible.

After clearing his throat to break the flow of conversation, he nudged Nicky on the shoulder saying, "Time to get the traps." He then turned to Hope and ordered, "You stay in the boat while we wade out and get them."

"I need to, um, use a bush," she answered back, and Nic looked around to see where she could go. About fifty feet inland were a group of bushes she could make it to without any help, so he pointed to them.

"Use those bushes, I'll wait here and keep an eye out, shout if you need me," and then he smiled and finished with a crooked grin, "And watch out for poison ivy."

Rolling her eyes, Hope stood, and Nic helped her off the boat handing her some napkins. She looked at them and felt her face grow warm with embarrassment. She said "Thanks," and then stomped her way carefully through the swampy mud towards the bushes, mortified they were just sitting there watching her go pee.

Hope rounded the bushes, pulled down her jeans and started to squat when she heard a grunting noise behind her. She turned around, and saw what looked like baby hogs about ten feet away grazing on the grass. In awe at seeing wild hogs, she watched them for a moment and then squatted again to do her business. As she stood and pulled up her jeans, she heard a guttural cry from a larger hog and turned to see one the size of a German Sheppard heading straight for her. Its mouth was open, large canine teeth like spears aimed right at her and Hope screamed "NIC," as she started running in the direction of the boat.

Nic heard the hogs cry right before Hope screamed, and his stomach hit his throat. Not missing a beat, he jumped into the boat, grabbed the rifle he had stored in the front, and jumped out of the boat moving as fast as he could through the mud and water. Hogs were fast, faster than humans were, and they could be lethal if provoked. Nic knew she couldn't outrun it; her only chance was to climb high.

"Angel! Tree, NOW!" Nic shouted and then drew aim on the hog.

Hope followed his instructions, headed to a Cypress with lower limbs, and jumped reaching for the branch. The hog grabbed a hold of her pant leg as she hung there trying to pull her back down. Nic put the crosshairs of his rifle on the huge beast and squeezed the trigger aiming for its head. Blood went flying as the hog stumbled back and then went down, its legs convulsing as it took its last breath.

Hope, still hanging onto the tree limb, watched the hog drop and then lost her grip and fell to the ground. Nicky shouted, "Hope," as he ran past his dad and Nic followed. When they reached her, she was sitting up looking over her shoulder at the hog, pissed as hell.

"You okay?" Nicky asked.

"Yeah, but that stupid pig put a hole in my jeans, and these were my favorite dang-it."

Nic barked out a laugh and then helped her stand, pulling plant life from her hair as she looked at her soggy jeans covered in mud. He looked her over, making sure she was unharmed except for her jeans of course, and then moved to the hog. He guessed it weighed close to a hundred and fifty pounds and figured Virgil could use another meat source besides swamp rat.

After wrapping the hog in a tarp, somehow getting it and the onion bags full of crawfish onto the boat, the traps secured and Hope in her seat, Nicky shoved them off once again. They headed back to the river as the sun started setting on the bayou. In his youth, Nic had thought there was nothing prettier than the sun setting while you watched from a boat. He was wrong. As the sun lowered indicating another day was done, the glow it put on the water seemed to throw an ethereal halo around Hope's face. If he hadn't already thought she was an angel sent from heaven, he would have been convinced at that moment.

Sixteen

The incessant ringing of Hope's doorbell woke her the next morning. Tired from her day in the sun and heat, Nic had told her "Shower then bed, sugar," when he'd woken her in the car once, they arrived back in New Orleans. She'd fallen asleep during the drive back, a full day exhausting her. When she'd woken, finding her head on Nicky's shoulder, his dark eyes smiling back at her blue ones, she'd just nodded, kissed Nicky on the cheek, Nic on the lips, and stumbled with Nic's help into her condo waving good night to both. Now it was morning, barely, and someone was ringing her bell, repeatedly.

Throwing the covers back, mumbling, "Coming, where's the fire?" she made her way to the front door and opened it, expecting to find Nic. What she found were a pair of blue eyes, similar to her own, with professionally arched brows that had been done in a neutral palate. Kat, not waiting for an invitation, dressed to kill in another wrap dress of light blue that highlighted her eyes and compliment her blonde hair, pushed through Hope's door as if she owned the place. She took in Hope's appearance from head to toe, and her lip curled. Unlike Kat's perfect ensemble, Hope was in another T-shirt. She'd taken a shower, barely combed out her hair, and then thrown on a clean shirt, moisturized and fallen face first into the pillow. Hope had neither curly hair nor straight, but if she went to bed with it wet, her extra thick hair would be a tumbled mess. Some might call it sex hair; Hope just called it a pain in her ass.

After her careful examination of Hope and her attire, Kat launched into why she was on her doorstep, though Hope was not the least bit surprised by her explanation.

"I think you and I should get a few things straight," was Kat's opening line and hearing that, Hope moved into the kitchen to start a pot of coffee. She would need plenty of caffeine to deal with Nic's ex this early.

"You want coffee while you explain what we need to get straight?"

"You're just a replacement," Kat blurted out and Hope stopped and looked over her shoulder at the woman.

"For?"

"Why me of course . . . Sugar, Nic and I may have a few silly problems but I'm his wife, and once he gets over his little snit he'll come back to me. So, woman to woman, I'd hate to see you get hurt."

"A few silly problems?" Hope choked out. "Last I heard he divorced you over those silly problems," she reminded Kat.

"In the south we call that a technicality. The important thing for you to know is that I want us back together, Nicky wants us back together and when Nic is done having his fun with a pale comparison of the woman he loves, you'll be forgotten like yesterday's news."

"And what makes you think I'm a pale comparison?" She knew the woman was trying to rattle her, lay the groundwork for doubts that Hope wasn't woman enough for a man like Nic. She wasn't doing a half-bad job of it except for one thing; she'd seen firsthand Nic was done with her. His trust broken Nic wouldn't easily forgive, Hope was sure of that, and it was then she realized how her own situation might end with the same results.

"Why just look at you, sugar. Blonde hair, blue eyes, it's like looking in the mirror. Though, your style of dress is, of course," she sniffed in indignation at Hope's attire and continued "Different."

Switching the pot to on, Hope turned around and looked at Kat. Long blonde hair, blue eyes, but much taller than Hope's own five foot two. She was sleek, polished, the type of woman a man like Nic would have as his wife. Then she thought about Kat out on a boat with Nic, trudging through the mud of the bayou, being chased by wild hogs or eating mystery meat sandwiches and couldn't see her with Nic. The man she had married had changed over time, changed due to heartbreak and death, and the man who'd emerged had a sense of how delicate life was and seemed to have a need to live it fully while he was here. He might have a thing for blondes, but she doubted that hair and eye color were what kept him around. Nic had a need to protect people, but also feel loved above all others by his woman, and Hope had a need to be protected, cherished, while she gave her whole heart to someone. They complemented each other, giving each what the other needed, and that was the draw for both of them. They'd found each other at a time that both needed what the other had to give.

Pausing before answering, Hope looked one last time at Nic's past and realized she had nothing to worry about from this woman. Nic was hers as long as she didn't screw it up all on her own.

"I appreciate your stopping by and imparting your heartfelt concern for my well-being."

"It sounds like a "but" is coming," Kat snapped.

"The lady is not only beautiful, she's smart," Hope bit out, her own anger increasing at having been confronted by this woman. A woman, she might add, who'd had it all in the palm of her hands, and let it slip through her fingers because she was selfish.

Kat narrowed her eyes, the cordial, almost friendly woman she'd portrayed disappeared, and the true Kat made an appearance.

"You're a common waitress with no breeding. Nic will have his fill, get his rocks off with you and then, sugar, he will return to the *true* love of his life. Enjoy what time you have with *my* husband, but when he dumps you for a superior model; don't say I didn't warn you." With that parting shot Kat marched to the door, her head held high as she opened it, walked through it, and slammed it behind her. Then she wobbled on her feet as she made her way to her car. She was sure she could rattle the bimbo's cage, get her to back down, but if anything, Kat had watched her resolve strengthen as she explained to her that Nic would dump her. It may be eight in the morning, but Kat needed a drink, and her momma—Momma Monroe would know exactly how to handle this tart.

***

For the second time that morning, Hope's doorbell rang. Only this time she was sure it wasn't Kat. She had no doubt the woman would be back, but after a long shower and two cups of coffee in her system, Hope was smart enough to look through the peephole this time before opening the door.

Nic smiled as he entered; a bag from a local bakery in his hand and Hope crossed her fingers he'd brought her beignets again. She wasn't disappointed.

"I come bearing pastries, angel. Tell me you have coffee, and we can run away together."

"Tempting, but Rose would find us and then you'd have some explaining to do."

"As scary as the old woman can be I'd take my chances," Nic

147

crooned as he lowered his mouth and kissed Hope for the first time that day. It had been ten hours since he'd touched her lips, and he decided it was about ten hours too long.

"You just want me for my coffee, admit it," Hope whispered against his lips. He thought about that for a second; her coffee was infinitely more desirable than his, so he agreed.

"Sugar, you found me out. It's not your body, your mind or your gumbo I want, it's your coffee. Now, fill me up woman and make haste."

"Ogre," Hope laughed.

"Wench," Nic answered back then swatted her ass as she made her way to her kitchen. Nic followed and pulled out a plate for the pastries as Hope filled two cups. When she made her way back to him, he grabbed her arm, pulled her to the couch, and made her sit. Turning to give her his full attention, he put his arm across the back of the couch and then took her hand in his, tangling her fingers with his own.

"Tell me about your childhood," Nic asked, not waiting for the right time. He wanted to know more about her past, and was tired of waiting for her to tell him on her own.

Hope was caught off guard by his question, but relieved when he'd asked about her childhood instead of her husband. She knew he wanted more information, but she was afraid he would walk away if she told him the truth. He'd breathed life into her this past month and after thirty-eight years of just existing, ten of those living in fear, she was afraid of losing him.

"I was twelve when my parents died. My mother, father and brother were coming back from a ball game, and they ran a red light. A large truck struck them, and it flipped the car killing all of them. I had stayed the night at a friend's house and wasn't with them." Nic's face softened and he curled his hand around her neck squeezing it for support as she continued.

"I was able to stay at my same school, so I didn't lose my friends when I went into foster care. The Johnson's were older, already had four kids to take care of, but they made room for me, and I lived there for two years until they grew too old to care for us."

"And after that?" Nic asked. Hope didn't look at his eyes when she answered. She didn't want to see his pity; it was what it was and she'd had twelve years with loving parents and then two more years with kind elderly people. She was luckier than most in foster care, and she knew it.

"I bounced around from home to home."

"Because they couldn't find a permanent home?"

"More or less," Hope hedged hoping he'd accept that as her answer.

Nic could see her wall go up; there was something she didn't want to talk about, but he needed her to trust him. He squeezed her neck again, and she looked at him as he whispered, "Tell me, sugar." He watched her eyes close, and then she took a deep breath and nodded.

"Sometimes they were abusive, and I'd leave, go to a friend's house and then social services would take me back. After I'd run enough times, they'd find a new place for me."

"Abusive how?" Nic bit out, trying to control his reaction.

Hope looked away then took another deep breath and told him, "Fists sometimes, sexually, or they'd want a slave to do all their housework."

"Christ," Nic swore under his breath, and then pulled her into his arms. Hope laid her head on his chest as he ran his finger through her hair. She hadn't thought about those times in a while, and in comparison to what the last ten years had been like, they were a walk-in-the-park.

"What happened when you turned eighteen?" Nic asked still

holding on to Hope.

"I packed my bags, was given some money that the state had been holding for me from my parent's estate and found an apartment, a roommate and never looked back."

"And then you met your husband?" He felt Hope tense, but he held on. He wanted it out in the open, all of it. She couldn't move forward until she told him everything, and he needed to know what that bastard had done.

"No, it was ten years before I met him."

"Where did you meet him?"

"It doesn't matter; it's all in the past, and I'd rather not talk about it," Hope told him as she pulled back from his embrace.

She watched Nic's face growing angry at her refusal to talk about the past, but she couldn't tell him, not yet. She stood from the couch to get some distance from him and to pull herself together. Moving to the window, trying to think of something to change the topic, Kat came to mind. She wasn't going to tell him about her morning visitor, but if Kat could save her hide right now, she would take it.

"Hope, dammit, talk to me," Nic told her back as he walked up behind her.

"Kat came for a visit this morning," she blurted out as she turned to face him, and then watched his shock and then anger at what she'd said sink in.

"And you're just now telling me this?"

"Yes, I just remembered to tell you," she lied.

"Anything else you just remembered to tell me?" he bit out in frustration. Hope bit her lips to avoid answering the question and Nic saw the move, narrowed his eyes at her and then crossed his arms looking formidable. "You ever gonna let me in?" Nic asked when she didn't answer, and he watched as her face paled.

"I'm trying," Hope answered honestly and they stood there at an impasse, staring each other down. Nic gave in this time, but he wouldn't the next—he wanted answers.

"You gonna share about Kat?" He tried to gentle his words, he could see she was trying, had revealed a lot already, so he'd give her more time to come to him before he backed her into a corner and demanded it. You can't build a relationship on secrets or lies, and he wasn't sure what she was keeping from him, but something told him it was a little bit of both. He needed her to trust him with her past so he could protect her from it. He didn't want another situation like the one he had with Chelsea; he wasn't going to lose one more person he cared about because of secrets.

"She wanted me to know that she wanted you back," Hope finally replied and he watched her face and gauged her expression for the truth. He figured that was the gist of it, though he had no doubt that Kat had said more than she wanted Nic back.

"I don't give a shit what she wants, it's not gonna happen."

"Even if Nicky wanted it?" Hope heard herself ask. That was the one point that Kat had brought up that caused her concern. He loved his son and would do anything for him, but would he tie himself to a woman he didn't respect?

"He doesn't, he knows what she did, but even if he did, I wouldn't. There's been too much water pass under that bridge, and the fact is, I don't love her or trust her. All I see now when I look at her is a selfish woman who put her own needs above those of her family."

Nic moved closer, leaned his forehead against Hope's and whispered "Loving someone means you put them first and put yourself last. You trust them with your heart; you trust them with your life, and you fucking trust them to guard your heart with their life . . . Will you, Hope?" Nic asked and then leaned in and brushed a gentle kiss across her lips.

"Will I what?"

"Will you trust me with your heart?" he replied and then watched as her confusion lifted and tears filled her eyes.

Hope buried her head in his neck drinking in his strength and prayed to God that he'd feel the same way once John was arrested, and she told him the truth. Because she knew with every fiber of her being, it would kill her if he walked away.

***

Hope's thoughts were heavy with guilt, so she'd ventured out after Nic left for his office, and tried to hide herself in the crowd of Bourbon Street. Normally people watching would take her mind off her troubles, but it seemed everywhere she went she saw someone or something that reminded her of her lies. No, lies weren't exactly right. Sleight of hand was all she had done so far. She hadn't told Nic anything about her husband and his brother that wasn't true, except his name. She couldn't keep him safe if he had John's real name and she knew he would fish for information. If John caught wind anyone was looking into him; it could get dangerous fast. As for the other secret, well, she couldn't tell him one without the other, and until John was behind bars, she couldn't risk Nic finding out. She was protecting him; that's what she kept telling herself even though she knew that was partly a lie. She was protecting her own heart as much as Nic's life. He'd asked her to trust him with her heart, and she did. The problem was; she just didn't know if he'd want to protect it once he found out what she did. If she couldn't even forgive herself, how was he supposed to?

As she continued to walk something bright caught her eye, and she turned her head in time to see the fortuneteller from last month standing in her shop door watching her walk past. She was across the street this time, so she couldn't snag Hope's arm and pull her in, but her eyes stayed on Hope until the hair on the back of her neck rose.

Like some unseen force, Hope found herself walking across the street in front of a car, its tires locking to avoid hitting her. When she reached the other side, Hope turned and looked at the wild, raven haired woman and tried to turn away from her, but couldn't. As Hope stood there staring, Madame LeFarr stuck out her hand, and Hope watched as her own hand came up and took hold of her outstretched hand and then she followed her inside.

Seventeen

The tourists were crowding the sidewalks of Bourbon Street, but not so thick, that Nic wouldn't know Hope when he saw her. He was exiting a sandwich shop when he caught sight of her leaving the same tarot card shop he'd seen her at a month before. He tried to cross the street and catch her, but he lost her in the crowd once he made it to the other side. As he passed the shop, he saw the same woman from a month before standing in the doorway. She was looking in the same direction Hope had gone, and it struck Nic both times this had happened the woman seemed distressed.

He didn't believe in magic spells or voodoo, but something was bringing Hope back to this shop, and each time she rushed off the woman seemed concerned. Going with his gut, wondering if maybe they were friends and Hope had opened up to this woman, he opened the door and stepped inside.

Dressed, as she had been the first time he'd seen her, in bright colors made out of fabric that was thin, he opened his mouth to ask her about Hope, but she cut him off.

"She is protecting you."

Nic narrowed his eyes, looked around the shop and then turned his eyes back to the woman.

"Who is protecting me?"

"Hope."

"You and Hope are friends?"

"No, though she is charming."

"What else has she told you?" Nic asked hoping he might gain some insight into what he was dealing with for once.

"She won't tell me anything the cards read her future. The spirits guide me, and they are telling me she's in danger, hiding, protecting someone, and that love is close, a great love that she could drown in if she doesn't destroy it before it has time to ignite." Forgetting he didn't believe in this shit, Nic found himself asking, "How will she destroy it?"

"The cards didn't say, just that she was at a crossroads, and she needed to tread carefully."

"And she didn't tell you anything about her troubles?"

"No, I never ask, it clouds the reading when I know. I told her to think of a question she wanted answered and the cards give her what she needed to know."

"The cards tell her?"

"The cards and the spirits. There was a particularly chatty one today, a girl who couldn't stop talking about lies."

"Whose lies?" he again asked for an explanation. This charlatan may want to play it off that she got her information from ghosts, but Nic figured Hope had said something and he wanted to know what that was.

"She didn't say, just that lies would break it apart. She kept referring to herself as *tit ange*, does that make sense?" Like he'd been kicked in the gut Nic inhaled, and then anger rolled off him in waves.

"I don't know what kinda of game you're playing, but stay away from Hope," Nic growled shaken for a moment but not about to stand for this shit one more minute.

Closing her eyes, Madame LeFarr tuned in to the spirits then opened her mouth and whispered, "*Je t'aime*, Papa, I don't hate you." Nic responded immediately by grabbing her by the arms and seething, his rage off the chart, "Don't you fuckin' say another word," then he moved her back an inch releasing his hold and held her eyes. When he was satisfied she wouldn't test him, he turned and exited the shop.

Heart pounding, the knot he hadn't had in weeks was back, and he wanted a fuckin' drink more than he wanted anything. Taking the long way back to his office to calm down, he'd made his mind up he'd had enough. Closing the door on the outer offices, he fired up his computer and waited while it booted up. Nic rolled up his sleeves; his mind drifting between Hope, the fortuneteller and the bullshit she'd just laid on him.

When google opened, he typed in John Delaney, Nevada, and waited for the results. If Hope won't come clean about this guy then he'd find out what he needed to know so he could protect her. With dozens of names pulling up, he narrowed the search by adding Hope's name to the mix hoping a marriage license would pop up in vital records. Nothing. He tried variations of the name John, tried using the last name Delaney and trucking companies, and still came up with nothing. The longer he searched; the shorter his fuse became. "Lies would tear them apart," the Fortuneteller had said, but he brushed them off as a dramatic production to milk him of his money. She was good; he'd give her that much, but most Cajuns call their daughters *tit ange,* so that was not a stretch. What shook him was being called Papa and the apology for saying she hated him. Chelsea would feel guilty for that day at the rehab clinic, he knew that, and those words had kicked him in the gut.

"Parlor tricks," he mumbled to himself and shut down his computer. One thing she got right though, he hated lies, had lived with the results of them for the past three years, and he's done with them. Hope was gonna tell him the truth, and she was gonna do it soon, but right now he had work to do, and he'd wasted enough time on this wild goose chase.

***

Hope was late for work that evening, she'd been rattled again by Madame LeFarr, and lost track of time as she walked the streets to clear her head. Then when she'd gone home to change, she could swear someone had been in her condo. She didn't have much, but it seemed disturbed, like someone had been looking for something, and that had rattled her even more. She looked through everything and nothing was missing, but her things seemed like they'd been handled and neatly put back, almost too neatly. A cold chill had settled around her, and she'd almost called Nic at his office but thought better of it. If she didn't bring John up then she could avoid talking about her past. Besides, she didn't think John would go through her stuff; he'd sit down, wait for her to come home and then beat the shit out of her. It crossed her mind that Nic might have searched her things out of frustration, but that didn't seem like something he'd do. She didn't have anything that would trace her back to Nevada except her driver's license and it was where she'd left it in her backpack. After panicking, she'd come to the conclusion she was seeing things, but remained on alert as she made her way to the bar for her shift.

Entering through the back to avoid any questions Rose and Abby might have, she threw her bag into her locker and made her way to the kitchen.

"Look who da' dog done drug in," Big Daddy shouted when she stopped at her station.

"Sorry, I lost track of time," Hope replied and grabbed the basket of vegetables to wash and prepare for the evening dinner crowd.

"What's on your mind, T-Hope?" Big Daddy asked as she rinsed potatoes for the boil.

"Not a thing, just focusing on the potatoes."

"You don't say? *Cher*, you know Big Daddy got big shouldah's he do, so lay on me your troubles."

Hope stopped scrubbing and looked at the man. He was the closest thing to a father she'd had since she was twelve. His sincerity got to her, and she found her mouth opening without her permission.

"Do you think if someone keeps the truth for a good reason that they deserve forgiveness? Or is a lie of any type an unforgivable offense?"

"We talkin' 'bout your past?" Hope held his eyes and then lowered hers and nodded. "We talkin' about Nic and your past?" She nodded again but didn't look at him. She was afraid of what she might see.

"*Cher,* any man a real man, he gets passed a lie told out of love he do."

"He didn't forgive Kat," Hope mumbled but he heard her just the same.

"Dat' woman did not lie for love, she betray her whole family she did, and for no reason but she full of shee-it and her own importance."

"Do you think Nic will see the difference?"

"If it comes from you, yes. You listen to Big Daddy; don't let your past dictate your future. You hear what I sayin'? No man, woman or child, is perfect, we all do da' best we can. Da' important 'ting to remembah' is this, love can bridge any gap as long as it's built on trust."

"Okay," Hope replied feeling better but not by much. She knew she loved Nic, might have fallen in love with him when he stood between her and the drunk, but what she wasn't sure about was how he felt about her. He was guarded because of his past with Kat, so she knew he wouldn't leap into a relationship with her without being wary. Had Nic had enough time to feel something for her other than lust and his need to protect her? Unfortunately, Big Daddy was right—she was out of time. Nic wanted answers and if he got them from someone other than her, he would be hard to reach. Whether she was ready or not, she had to come clean, and she had to do it tonight.

The dinner rush seemed to drag that night, yet, at the same time flew by. Hope teetered on panic most of the evening and annoyance that the orders kept coming. Now that she'd made the decision to tell Nic, she wanted to get it over with and face the music. Better to find out now, that he couldn't handle the truth, than month's down the road when losing him would kill her just as surely as if he plunged a knife into her heart.

When she left for the evening, she was a little concerned that Nic wasn't waiting for her. Since she'd moved in below him, except for the week they avoided each other, he'd been here when she got off work and driven her home. Tonight he hadn't come to the bar or called to say he couldn't make it. Abby and her husband had given her a ride home, and she was heading towards her door when she saw there were no lights on in the upstairs unit. Nic wasn't home. Unlocking her own door, Hope pushed it open, flipped the light on, and let out a scream when she found Nic leaning against her kitchen counter. He had a blank look on his face and was holding a sheet of paper, he didn't smile when he looked at her, didn't come to her and kiss her, he just stood there staring at her and Hope knew he'd found out.

"Nic?" she whispered.

"Don't," he barked out, anger written all over his face.

"Don't what?"

"I don't want you to say anything."

Nodding, watching his face as he stared at her, eyes blank and cold as they ran up and down her body. When his eyes came back to her own, the tears welled while she waited for his recriminations to start. He lowered his eyes to the sheet of paper and started reading out loud.

"Last Thursday police were called to the home of David G. Cummings, owner of Cumming's trucking. When they arrived, they found the body of Mr. Cummings on the kitchen floor, cause of death due to a knife wound inflicted by the deceased man's wife, Jessica H. Cummings. Mrs. Cummings called 911 after an altercation that left her husband dead and Mrs. Cummings with two broken ribs, multiple contusions and a fractured wrist.

Both Mr. Cummings and his brother were under investigation for drug trafficking when his death occurred, and police have since informed the press that Mrs. Cummings was instrumental in acquiring evidence that is expected to lead to the arrest of her brother-in-law John D. Cummings.

Hospital records indicate that Mrs. Cummings has been treated multiple times over the past ten years for various injuries reported as accidents. One such incident ended the life of her unborn child in 2009. Medical officials refused to comment on whether or not any of the previous injuries were caused from abuse, but did say Mrs. Cummings is resting comfortably and is expected to make a full recovery. It is unknown if her involvement with the investigation caused her husband's attack and police aren't commenting at this time."

"You killed your husband?" He asked with no emotion.

"Yes."

"He and his brother are drug dealers and you stayed married to him for ten years?"

"Yes," she replied. He didn't want excuses he wanted the truth, and then he was done with her. She wouldn't prolong his pain and her own. She would answer his questions and then let him walk out of her life.

"Are you really in danger?"

"Yes."

"From John your dead husband or John the brother-in-law?" Nic asked sarcastically.

"My brother-in-law."

"The paper says you had a history of abuse that you miscarried, that he beat you till you lost your son?" He seethed his hands balling into fists, "And yet you stayed married to him?"

"Yes."

Nic said nothing for a moment trying to reconcile the angel in front of him with the woman from the article. She knew they sold drugs, and she stayed married to him. His gut rolled at the idea.

"Did you help them sell drugs to innocent children like my daughter?" he roared.

"NO!"

"But you knew and you stayed. Was it the money?" he asked with disgust.

"No," Hope whispered, it was because she was weak, afraid, but it didn't matter now.

"And the baby, your son? You never once told me about your loss. You consoled me, told me you didn't know how I felt. Was any of that real? Was anything you've told me since we met the fuckin truth?" Nic shouted his rage building that he'd been this much a fool.

"Yes," Hope replied but her voice broke. Now that he knew everything, and she saw it from his perspective, there was no doubt in her mind that he hated her.

"Any other lies you need to tell me?" Nic bit out, still no emotion on his face, only blank, cold resolution that the woman he'd cared about wasn't who he thought she was and that nearly broke her.

"No," she choked out still holding his eyes. She wouldn't be a coward like she'd been for ten years.

"Nice to meet you finally, Mrs. Cummings. Welcome to New Orleans where fools and ghouls wander the streets."

He moved suddenly, walked past her, and when he reached her door, he threw a punch at the wall, his hand going all the way through it and he thundered, "FUCK," as he left Hope standing in the kitchen. She didn't chase him, didn't beg him to stay. He was done with her, and he deserved better than to have her causing a scene on his front lawn. With movements better suited to a zombie, she turned and closed the front door locking it and securing the chain.

Moving to the bedroom, she crawled into the bed with her clothes on, pulled the covers over her head and laid there until the sun rose, and the birds chirped announcing a new day had arrived, and still she didn't move. Only when her bladder required it did Hope get up, and when she was finished, she crawled right back into the bed and pulled the covers back over her head. Sleep finally claimed her, though it wasn't restful, it was filled with images of dark soulful eyes laughing, angry, hungry, but mostly they were blank. They were the eyes of a man who'd been lied to, cheated on and who'd buried a daughter he'd loved. They were the eyes of a man who was done.

Eighteen

It's funny how a day can change the course of one's life. The weight that had been hanging around Hope's neck for the past month was gone, but the emptiness she felt was far worse than any noose around her neck.

The sun's bright rays shown through the blinds, lighting her room with a brightness she'd taken for granted until she opened her eyes, and for a moment watched as they skipped across the floor in a magical dance. She wanted to look at those rays as a symbol that her life would be brighter now, since she had nothing to hide, but her reality wasn't as warm as those dancing sunbeams. A gray day with angry clouds would have better suited the mess she'd made of her life, of Nic's life. Deciding she could lie there as a martyr would; feeling sorry for herself and the mess that she alone had brought down on her life, or, she could get up, clean up and do something to lessen Nic's pain.

She should have trusted him to listen and understand what she had been through and why she hadn't left, but she didn't, and now she needed to accept the consequences of her actions. Nic had been honest with her, caring, understanding, and she still hadn't let him see the real Hope. She was so damn selfish; she could barely look at herself. It was time to move on and leave Nic and those she cared about to their lives. Let them heal from her deception and move forward, while she tried to live with the guilt.

Trying to shake off her despair, Hope walked to the bathroom and turned on the shower, then moved to the closet and pulled out her bags to pack. She needed to call the train station, find out what states they went to and then decide a course of action. Picking up the brochure, she'd held onto when she first arrived, Hope scanned it for departure times. When the words blurred as tears welled in her eyes, she dropped the brochure and buried her face in her hands. For the first time since Nic walked out the door, she let sorrow consume her, and she fell to the floor as a guttural cry spilled from her throat. She cried for the pain she'd caused, the pain she'd endured, and the happiness she could have had if she'd just trusted Nic with her heart like he'd asked. She continued to lie on the floor as her sobs turned to hiccup's, but still she couldn't move. Exhaustion and mental fatigue set in eventually, and as the shower ran, Hope drifted off into blissful darkness.

***

"Why da' food so slow?" Maman Rose hollered through the window to the kitchen.

"We short old woman, I cookin' fast as I can," Big Daddy shouted back. He didn't have time to talk; he had plates backing up on him.

"Did dat' no account Jasper not show?"

"*Non*, T-Hope," he replied, worry etched on his face.

"Dere' sometin' I should know 'bout?"

"She not call me old woman, I don't know her everah' move."

"But you know sometin' I see it in your face."

Big Daddy threw his towel down, stalked across the kitchen to the window, and leaned in so only her ears would hear.

"She was gonna tell Nic last night of her trouble and she was worried he'd not forgive her for keepin' da' truth from him."

"And you just now tell me dis'?" Rose shouted.

"I not loose in da' lips, it her b'nez to tell!" he replied and then turned back to his station as he heard Rose shout behind him.

"I will feed Nic to da' alligatah' if he broke my girl I will."

Big Daddy nodded he'd heard Rose and then added, "Stand in line, Rosie, Big Daddy get first crack."

***

"*Cher*?" Hope opened her eyes to see Rose standing over her. Confused, she looked around and realized she was on the floor, and the shower was still running.

"*Cher*, you okay?"

She tried to take a deep breath and answer her, but it came out like sob, then the tears came again, and the next thing she knew she was in Rose's arms as the big woman rocked her back and forth.

"You told Nic?" Hope nodded and held on to Rose as she replied, "Dat' man gonna be da' death of me he will."

Rose moved Hope to the bed, had her sit, and then put her hands to Hope's face telling her "He a stubborn man he is, but he a good man and he will get ovah' what it is you done."

"No, he won't, I lied to him, and I kept important things from him, things he should have known before starting anything with me. He deserves better than that, and you know it."

"And you don't? . . . What you do dat' so bad, kill someone?" Hope blanched when she finished, and Rose's eyes grew huge.

"Who you kill?" she whispered.

"My husband," Hope whispered back.

"He lay his hand on you?"

"Yes."

"More dan' once?"

"Yes."

"Den' he got what he deserve. I'd kill him myself for laying a hand on my T-Hope I would."

"There's more than just that, Rose," Hope continued and then stood from the bed, walked to the shower and turned it off. When she emerged from the bathroom, she took Rose's hand and led her down the hall to the kitchen. When Hope saw the front door was still chained she asked Rose, "How did you get in?"

"Back door, Nic need a better lock, I broke-in in under two minutes I did." Nodding her head, knowing she wouldn't tell Nic anything, she found the article Nic had dropped and handed it to Rose.

She watched as Rose read the article, her face reacting to what she was reading. When Rose was finished, she laid it down on the counter and then drew Hope back into her arms and cried.

Hope stiffened in her arms, confused why she was crying. Hugging the woman back, she asked her "Why are you crying?" Rose pulled back, leveled wet eyes on Hope, and answered in disbelief.

"What you mean why I cry? You suffered for years; he took your *tit ange* from you, forced you to live in hell he did and kept you beaten down till you had to kill him to be free."

"I should have been stronger, I should have left."

"He shouldah' been a man and treat you wit' a gentle hand not his fist, don't you take his blame, *Cher*."

"We were both to blame, Rose. I should have left when I found out I was pregnant, protected my son, but I didn't. It took me two years to get the nerve to hand over evidence to the police 'cause I was scared they would kill me, all while kids like Chelsea were dying. I'm as much to blame as he is, if not more."

"How in da' world do you come up wit' dat'? Did dat' bastard try and fill your head wit' dat' garbage?"

"No, I knew it when I was living it. I was weak, scared; only thinking of myself. Nic saw it as soon as he read the article, knew what a coward I was."

"Dat' is horse poop. Nic may have been upset, but he not blame you for what others do. You give him time, *Cher*, he will come round' he will." Hope took a deep breath and nodded. She wasn't going to argue with Rose; she wasn't here when Nic left, she didn't see his face, his reaction. He was done. "Good, now, you take a shower and eat sometin,' but I expect you back at work tomorrah,' yes? Nic will come to his senses he will, and everah'ting will be all right." Hope nodded and then hugged Rose, her heart breaking a little at the thought of leaving this woman behind.

Rose moved to the door, and when she saw the hole in the wall Nic had left, she turned to Hope and smiled.

"Dat' man care deeply for you. He put his hand tru' da' wall 'cause he could not put his fist on da' man who hurt you. You give him time, *Cher,* I promise he will come back."

Hope remembered the sound of the sheetrock caving in as his hand burst through it, and then his angry "FUCK" as he left. For half a moment, she wondered if Rose was right, but steeled herself against hope. She smiled at Rose and then opened the door for her. Rose walked through it and then turned and stared back at Hope, reading her. Before she turned to leave, she leaned in, kissed her forehead, and said, "What does not kill us makes us stronger, yes. You just hold on till he calms down, *Cher* . . . Promise me?" Hope bit her lips and nodded, figured another lie after so many didn't matter at this point.

Rose climbed into her big SUV and knew she was on borrowed time. T-Hope had the look of someone already gone, and if she didn't reach Nic soon and talk some sense into the man, she would leave and never come back. She'd hunt his ass down, and he'd better listen to her if he knew what was good for him, 'cause if he didn't, she'd let Big Daddy fricassee his ass and serve him up for dinner.

She drove to his office, and he wasn't there, he'd called in saying he was taking a personal day. She went back to his house and pounded on his door, but no one answered and his car was gone. She called Big Daddy and asked him if he knew any other bars he went to and then drove to one close to his house, but no Nic. She wondered if he had driven to Baton Rouge to visit his family, but didn't have their contact information and she sure as hell wasn't calling Kat to get the number.

Parking on a side street, Rose tried to put herself in Nic's shoes. *Where in the hell would that stubborn Cajun go?* Hope killing her bastard husband was not what would bother him; it was the drugs and her baby dying. That would get to him the most Rose figured, open wounds that hadn't begun to heal. She could well imagine he'd turned around what he'd read and all but crucified Hope. He needed a big dose of Rose reality to fix his stupid, stubborn ass. Frustrated, Rose looked around the street trying to come up with some sort of idea of where she could find him. *Either he doesn't want to be found, and he's hiding where she'll never find him, like the swamp, or he's somewhere no one would think to look.*

Rose thought for a minute more, and then an idea popped into her head. Starting her car, she headed out of the French Quarter and headed uptown until she found the neighborhood where Kat lived. Pulling down the street of huge homes that Nic had designed, she passed Kat's house but no Nic. At least she didn't have to worry he'd been a fool and gone running back to that cow to get over his sorrows, but it still didn't solve her problem. *Where in the hell is Nic?*

Rose thought about everything Nic had been through and what

he'd learned about Hope, and another thought occurred to her as she pulled back out of the neighborhood. If he was dealing with Hope's past and how it intermingled with his own, then the most logical place he would go broke her heart . . . *Chelsea.*

***

What few belongings Hope still had from her former life were packed into two bags. She'd left them at her front door while she scrubbed the bathroom, vacuumed the floors and washed any dishes she had used. She was running on empty, no food in her stomach, no coffee in her system, and the headache from lack of caffeine and crying was slowing her down. She needed to finish the cleaning and get to The Bayou and collect her wages, say goodbye to everyone and then get to the train station. But, before she did that, she had to say goodbye to Nic.

Pulling out some paper that she'd kept from a hotel, she sat at the kitchen counter on the old stool Nic had put in the condo for her, and began to write the words that she hoped would be enough to say how sorry she was. She tried to figure out how to tell Nic, without sounding desperate, that the month she had spent with him meant more to her than anything she experienced so far in her thirty-eight years. How his kindness, protectiveness had meant the world to her and even though she had hurt him, she let him know she would never forget him or Nicky and that she wished them all the happiness they deserved in this life. By the time she'd ended the letter, her tears had left stains on the paper, and some of the ink had smeared. Signing it simply with her name, no terms of endearment to anger him, she kissed the letter and placed it inside an envelope. She would leave it at the bar with Rose to give to Nic once she was gone, and felt he was ready to read her words. When she finished, she stuck the letter in her pack, checked all the rooms one last time, then pulled the key off her key ring, and placed in on the kitchen counter for Nic to find. She took one last look at the condo, the happiest home she'd had since her parents had died and then opened the door and walked out.

Nineteen

Rose's instincts were on the money, Nic was seated on a marble bench next to the mausoleum that held Chelsea's body. Arms resting on his thighs, a cigarette between his two fingers as he blew a stream of smoke out his nose. He only smoked when he was upset, and Rose figured this was as good a reason as any to partake in an occasional smoke.

He saw her coming and said nothing, just looked her in the eyes as he took another drag from his cigarette. When she reached the bench, she sat down, put her purse on the ground and then sat back and sighed.

"Whatever you came here to say, say it," he mumbled not looking at her; his eyes towards the ground waiting for whatever she would lay on him.

"You a stubborn man, Nic Beuve." He scoffed at her but didn't argue he knew he was stubborn.

"And you're a nosy woman."

"How else I gonna know what happens in my bar?"

"You're not here to talk about your bar, did she call you?"

"Oh, no, not dat' girl, she more stubborn dan' you."

"Then why are you here?"

"Cause you makin' da' biggest mistake of your life if you let dat' woman go."

"I'm not talkin about it Rose," Nic grumbled and drew more smoke into his lungs.

"Oh, I know you bettah' dan' dat'. You may not talk, but you damn sure will listen."

"Then get it over with, I've got shit to do," Nic growled not ready to get into this with anyone.

"You can be an ass you know dat'?" Rose waited for a reply but got none, so she decided to give him both barrels.

"Woman grows up in foster care, nasty b'nez dat' but grow up she did. Survived it only to be tied to a man who used his hands for pain rathah' dan' pleasure. He had her so scared to leave she don't even when baby comin.' Den' he beat her and she lose da' baby and what will she has left to live. You followin' me, Nic?" Rose watched as Nic's jaw tightened, and his fist clenched. She had his attention, but would he listen?

"Aftah' he bring her so low she don't care weddah' she live or die, she finds out he runnin' drugs on top of everah'ting else he put her tru.' Now, I don't know about you, but I tinkin' if a woman gets beat long enough and hard enough, at some point she gonna shut down and not let anyone in, yes?"

She watched Nic close his eyes but still he held his tongue, and she figured that was good, he wasn't' arguing the point, just fighting it in his head.

"Dat' woman has lived a nightmare, den' to save her own life she had to kill da' monster who strip her dignity. She risked her life to give police enough to arrest da' only family she has and no one, not one person is even lookin' for dat' woman or care she is gone. She was so isolated in da' fear she had no one till she come here."

"Enough," Nic growled and stood from the bench.

"Enough?" Rose hissed. "Enough what, Nic? Enough truth dat' da' woman is no saint? Dat' she make a mistake like we all do. Dat' she was scared for her life, scared her past would come here and hurt you?" Rose spit out and watched his face fall. "I 'tink she has paid dat' debt don't you? Any sin she may have committed ain't as great as what she been tru' . . . So, tell me, what you gonna do Nic? You gonna be just like dat' bastard who beat her when she was down, or are *you* gonna be da' man who saves her from hell?"

"*Mon Dieu*, you don't pull punches."

"Not when it comes to love."

"No one said anything about love," Nic argued, but she could see in his eyes he was lying. "I cared about the woman I thought she was, I don't know who the fuck she is now," he hissed then he shook his head and mumbled, "I need time to sort this shit out."

Rose stood, grabbed her purse and threw it over her shoulder glaring at Nic, then made the parting shot to end all parting shots, determined to light a fire under his ass 'cause they were running out of time.

"You do dat' Nic, you take all da' time you need to decide if da' woman I had to pick up off da' floor dis' mornin', so full of sorrow dat' she could not stand, is worth your time and attention." Then she turned on her heels, and left him to his pride to digest what she had just said. Though the whispered "Fuck" she heard behind her told her Nic was the man she knew he was. Prideful to a fault, protective to a fault, and above all else, a very smart man. She figured it would take him about an hour to change his tune, if it took longer—she was losing her touch.

As Rose walked away, and Nic followed her with his eyes, the force of her parting shot burned into his mind. He could see Hope clearly lying on the floor, crying, and the knot in his chest tightened.

"Fuck." He closed his eyes and remembered her face as he shot question after question at her the night before, her expression a portrait of pain and sorrow, her eyes filled with tears that she wouldn't let fall.

"*Mon Dieu*," he realized what a bastard he'd been.

After a long day at the office, the encounter with the fortuneteller, and no results searching for her bastard husband he'd been in a foul mood and gone home to change before heading out for dinner. When he arrived home, he'd found an envelope with no name stuck in his door. When he'd opened it and read the article inside, confused at first, until he'd gotten to the part where it mentioned the dead man was the owner of a trucking company. He'd frozen in place, his heart pounding, and he'd started over.

Nic closed his eyes when thought back to how quickly his anger had escalated into rage reading about that bastard, knowing how badly he had abused Hope. So badly, her only recourse to save her life was to stab him, and his heart knotted thinking about how scared she must have been.

He hadn't been angry with her at first until he'd continued to read the article and found out that import export was code for drug trafficking. Then all the anger he'd been holding onto for those who pushed drugs onto kids let loose. How could the woman he knew, the gentle, fiery, sexy and angelic to the point of perfection, that he'd met and fallen for in four short weeks, stayed married to that man?

Then he'd read that she'd been pregnant, that he'd beaten the life out of their child, and his rage increased tenfold. He wanted his hands around that bastard's neck so he could kill him himself for laying a hand on Hope, and for killing an innocent child. What had struck him the hardest; not once, in the more than four weeks since he'd met her, had she mentioned she'd lost a child. She'd consoled him, told him his pain was justified, but never said, "I know how you feel I lost a child too." How does a person lose a child and not mention the loss? That stuck in his gut worse than anything he'd read. It made her seem cold, uncaring, and coupled with the other information, she changed from an angelic woman who needed protection, to a cold and calculated bitch, just like Kat.

By the time Hope had gotten home from work, his mind had been twisting and turning for three hours. He'd turned her into a monster, and he the fool who fell for her tricks. However, in the light of day and cold, hard facts by a nosy Cajun, Nic was beginning to think that the only person who'd turned him into a fool was he and Kat.

Hope had told no one her past, told no one her real name, though he suspected the H. in her full name was for Hope. That being said, if she told no one, then how in the hell did that article make it to his door? Those who knew them liked them, liked that they were together. Unless one of them was harboring a malicious side, the only person who thought they stood to gain anything by coming between the two of them was Kat.

Looking back at his daughter's resting place, for some reason, he felt the need to tell her, "*Tu me manques je t'aime*. Papa knows you don't hate him, angel." A soft breeze settled over him and a sense of calm hit him as he sat there and considered all that had happened. Closing his eyes and picturing his daughter's face, her blue eyes sparkling as she played some practical joke on her papa, the word "hurry" whispered through his head. Taking a deep breath, he rose from the bench with a clearer head and decided he had a few questions for his ex-wife. If she was the one who'd left the article, then she'd somehow found out Hope's identity. Kat could be a bitch when she wanted something, and he wouldn't put it past her to call that sonofabitch in Nevada. Hope wouldn't be safe until he was behind bars, and whether they worked this out or not, he didn't want her running because that bastard knew where she was, so before he could reach out to

Hope, he wanted to make sure she was safe.

***

Kat wasn't home when Nic got to her house, so he pulled in the drive and decided to wait. This was too important to put off; he needed to know if Kat left the article. 'Cause if it wasn't, he needed to find out quickly who did, Hope was in danger until he nipped this in the bud. Kat was vindictive enough and it was just her style to leave the article and then sit back and watch the fireworks. She'd have to be close to know if it worked, Nic figured and then he wondered if she'd been in the street watching him exit Hope's condo in a rage.

As if she could sense he was looking for her, she pulled into the driveway not long after him, and it crossed his mind she could have been following him, watching him at the cemetery.

Exiting her car, she produced a huge smile for him as he got out of his own and waited for her to come to him. She was dressed to kill as always, but there seemed to be a bounce in her step as she walked towards him.

"Hey there, sugar, what a nice surprise," Kat told Nic.

"Kat, you gotta minute?"

"For you, I've got the rest of my life," she purred and tried to kiss his lips, but he turned his head to avoid them. Stepping to the side Nic started walking towards the front door as Kat followed, her high-heeled shoes clipping the sidewalk as she hurried behind him. Nic unlocked the door, then stood back, and let her pass before him. Kat's hand brushed his stomach as she passed him, and she smiled sweetly at him, acting coy, demure.

"So what did ya wanna see me about, sugar? Nicky isn't here he's at soccer practice."

Nic didn't mince words he jumped right in and asked, "Did you leave me that article about Hope?”

“Article?” she lied and Nic saw the recognition in her eyes.

“Yeah, Kat, the article about Hope being attacked and almost killed by her husband.” He saw a flash of anger in her eyes, and he knew she had left it. Kat had expected him to read the story and not see an abused woman, but a murderer.

He looked towards her office where she kept her computer and started walking towards the door. Kat rushed forward asking, “What are you doing?”

“Getting the truth for once,” Nic replied and then opened the door and pushed past Kat.

On her desk was a sheet of paper with the name Jessica H. Cummings, Nevada and Nic picked it up and showed it to her, his jaw clenching in anger.

“It was for your own good, Nic. The woman is around our son, and you needed to know she was a killer.”

“Hope was attacked by a man who repeatedly beat her for ten years, she’s no killer,” Nic shouted.

“The same husband who sold drugs? Are you gonna stand there and tell me that she didn’t know, that she is innocent of everything? Come on, sugar, you're not that stupid.”

“I’m not gonna tell you anything. You’re gonna listen to me, and you listen good,” Nic ordered and then walked up to Kat using his size to intimidate his ex-wife. “She risked her life to get evidence to the police. That bastard would love to know where she is, and you have a bug up your ass thinking she is competition. I know you, and if you have any thoughts about making a phone call, I will sue you for full custody of Nicky. Do you understand what I’m saying?”

“You’d choose that drug dealer’s wife over your own family?”

“I’d choose Hope over *you* any day of the week,” Nic roared, “Now; do you understand what I’m saying? If John Cummings so much as sniffs in her direction, so help me God, you will wish you'd never picked up that phone."

Kat's face paled, and her hand came up to her throat. She looked around the room, stalling, trying to come up with anything she could use as a defense against his threat and came up empty. So, she changed tactics. Kat looked back at Nic and announced, "You let that woman near my son, and I'll sue *you* for full custody."

"That threat won't work and you know it. After what you pulled, with the connections I have in this town and the houses I've designed for sitting judges, I can make one phone call, and Nicky will be gone tonight," Nic threatened back.

"You wouldn't," Kat whispered.

"Kat, the way I'm feeling right now you don't want to test that, I promise you."

"She's a common bar maid, a drug dealer's wife—"

Nic cut her off on a shout, "There is nothin' common about Hope." Then it hit him like a lightning bolt, swift and powerful, how he felt about Hope, and it all sank in. *Jesus, what had he done?*

Urgency to leave and find Hope washed over him, and he looked at Kat and bit out, "Are we clear? You'll keep your fuckin mouth shut, or I swear to Christ I'll make a phone call, you hear me, Kat?" Nic ordered tired of her games.

She didn't respond to his question; Kat looked caught in some trance, like she couldn't' quite believe what she was hearing. Done with her, Nic walked passed her heading for the front door as Kat called out, "Nic." He ignored her as he rushed to his car and got in, squealing his tires to get back to the condo and talk to Hope.

When he arrived, he pounded on the door shouting, "Hope," and when she didn't answer, he tried the doorknob and found it unlocked. He walked in, saw her key on the kitchen counter and ran down the hall to the bedroom. Gone. She was gone.

"Sonofabitch," Nic yelled and ran back to his car heading for The Bayou.

He reached it after a long five minutes with traffic clogging the roads. If he'd been looking at passing cars, he might have seen Hope in the back of a cab, unshed tears in her eyes as she headed towards the train station, but he was too busy cussing himself and the idiots in front of him.

Double-parking in front of the bar, Nic rushed in, passed Henri at the bar and threw open the door to the kitchen. He found Rose and Big Daddy huddled together; a cell phone in each one's hand looking worried.

"Where is she?' Nic shouted.

"You stupid, Cajun, sonofabitch, what take you so long?"

"Rose," Nic rumbled low in his throat, silencing her, "Where the fuck is Hope?"

"She gone, I try to stop her, but she say she gonna leave wit' or wit'out money, so I gave her what I owe her, and she leave. Headed to da' train station she is. Here she left dis' note for you," Rose cried out and then handed him a letter. Nic opened it with shaking hands and read her tear-covered words that gutted him, leaving no doubt in his mind that he was the biggest fool that ever lived.

Nic,

Sorry, isn't a big enough word for how I feel. No word can cover the depths of my regret. Just know that even though I lied, I did because I cared too much. I hurt you and I wished to God I hadn't. I was scared to open up and then I was scared if I did, I would lose you. You've given me more love in the past month than I've had since my parents died, and I will always remember New Orleans as a time of hope for unrequited dreams.

Take care of Nicky, tell him I'm sorry I had to leave without saying goodbye, but I think it's best for all concerned.

No more lies, Nic, you know everything except one thing. You were the best thing that's ever happened to me in my whole life, and I hope that someday you'll find someone who makes you as happy as I was for a few short weeks. You deserve that and more."

Hope~

Nic finished reading then swallowed the knot in his throat and mumbled "Oh, *mon coeur*, I'm gonna put you over my knee when I find you."

Twenty

Dreams, simple things everyone has; dreams of riches, fame, love and family, or creating a perfect batch of gumbo. Some work hard to attain them, and some have them dropped in their laps and don't appreciate them. Then there are some, no matter how hard they try, who can't find a way to reach them. They drown in the sorrow of those unrealized dreams as they fight to grasp hold, only to have their fingertips brush them, giving them a sense of what it feels like to hold them in their hand. But, like anything in this life, if you don't grab hold with a firm grip, what you try to hold onto will slip through your fingers if you don't stay focused. Nic should have tightened his grip when he had hold. Should have seen what was in the palm of his hand, the beauty he possessed. Because just like the dreams Hope had of gentle hands to hold her, children to fill her heart while surrounded by family and friends who cared. Nic's dream of a future filled with a woman he loved passionately—were slipping through his fingers with each tick of the clock.

Rushing from the Bar with Big Daddy in tow, they piled into his car still double-parked out front. Hope was ahead by thirty minutes, and he had no idea what train she was boarding. He was prepared to bribe every ticket agent until he found the one who sold Hope her ticket.

As he drove swiftly through the streets, cars honking as he cut them off, Hope was purchasing a ticket for New York, final destination, Canada. She hoped to hide there from John until he was brought to trial and sentenced.

She made her way through the turnstiles, her eyes down to avoid the stares she was sure were there. She'd held her emotions in check all the way to the train station, but as she purchased her ticket, the realization that she was indeed leaving choked her and the tears she held at bay won out.

If Nic had seen those tears as he made his way faster still to the station, he would have ripped his own heart out at the sight. But, he was too busy cursing his own stupidity for doubting that the woman he'd held in his arms, made love to with a passion he hadn't felt in years, was anything but the angel he knew she was, and if he didn't reach her in time, he feared he'd never find her.

As Hope made her way to the train that would take her from the first place she'd felt safe, cared for, genuinely happy since her parent died, Nic was stuck at an intersection two blocks from the station. A collision between a car and truck had traffic at a standstill. Frustration mounting, Nic barked, "Fuck it," and opened his door and told Big Daddy, "I'm running the last two blocks, meet me at the station when you can get through." Then he took off running, his eyes on the train station as he jumped curbs, rounded stopped cars and threw his hands out to stop vehicles as he ran through a green light, not wasting a second to stop.

Hope handed her ticket to the conductor, and when the man smiled at her and saw the pain and tears in her eyes he asked, "You okay, miss?" Nodding, and then she shook her head no, she sucked in a breath and then answered, "I really enjoyed my time here and hate to leave." The conductor laid a hand on her shoulder and leaned in telling her "The magic that is New Orleans stays with you your whole life. You come back soon and fill up again with Cajun dreams."

Biting her lips to keep from breaking down, his words hitting too close to the heart of the matter, she nodded and then climbed the steps and made her way to her seat. She stored her bags underneath her seat, sat down, put her head to the window, and closed her eyes to block out the pain as Nic finally reached the station.

Running to the ticket counter he stepped in front of a large man who was next in line and ignored that man's "Hey, back of the line," as he leaned in and asked, "Blonde woman, petite, looks like an angel, did she buy a ticket from you?" The man behind the counter shook his head, and Nic moved down the line to the next agent and repeated the same question over and over until he found a woman who said, "Yes, sad woman, I was worried about her."

"What train?"

"We aren't supposed to give— "

"Her name is Hope. I screwed up and if I don't stop her, she'll never know." The older woman looked over her shoulder then clicked on her keyboard. "She bought a ticket for New York, and it leaves," then she looked at the clock on the wall and said, "Now, platform four."

Without so much as a thank you to the woman, Nic bolted away from the ticket counter, jumped the turnstile, and bumped and pushed his way down the hall to get to the train.

As Hope heard the conductor announce the departure, she took a deep breath and said her quiet goodbyes. Nic's dark soulful eyes smiling back at her, Rose's boisterous laugh, Big Daddy's fatherly advice, all forefront in her mind as she heard the train's engine begin to throttle. A knot formed in her throat, and the tears began to fall as Nic rushed to the platform shouting, "Hope."

She didn't hear his call; the windows were thick and the engine loud. He ran down the side of the train, looking through the windows at the passengers, searching for her blonde hair.

As the train started to pull forward, Nic shouted, "Stop the train," to a conductor standing on the platform but the man shook his head. Nic kept moving forward running faster than the train as it pulled forward slowly to leave the station. He caught sight of blonde hair a car ahead and sprinted to the window and saw Hope with her eyes closed; head pressed against it. He shouted, but she didn't hear him, so drew his fist back and punched the window hard.

Hope, eyes closed, her heart in pieces jumped when something hit her window, and she turned to see Nic running next to the train shouting at her. She froze at first; convinced her mind was playing tricks on her, and then mouthed "Nic?"

When Hope turned and looked at Nic, finally seeing him, he knew he didn't have time to say anything, but "Get off the fuckin train, NOW." He watched as her eyes grew wide, and she hesitated for an instant as he ran out of platform, and the train continued down the track. He stood there as car after car moved past him, but he kept his eyes on the train praying to God that she understood him.

Just as he thought she was gone, Hope emerged at the back of the train, and Nic ran to the edge and shouted, "Jump!"

Hope hesitated, then took a deep breath and launched herself onto the platform landing on her hands and knees, but only for a second. Nic scooped her up, and the minute she felt his arms around her the floodgates opened. She buried her head in his neck, and then wrapped her legs around his waist holding on tight, afraid to let him go. He'd come for her, like a white knight in a fairy tale; he'd come for her and was holding her in his arms, his mouth at her ear whispering, "*Mon coeur je t'aim.*"

Nic buried his head deeper in her neck, the realization he'd almost been too late seized him and he hissed, "Fuck, I almost lost you, I'm such an ass."

They stood there; Hope wrapped around Nic like a monkey, her sobs in his ear as he tried to put into words how much of a fool he was and that he loved her. He fuckin' loved her, and he hadn't known it until he'd stared into the eyes of a woman he thought he'd loved when he married her. He hadn't known what real soul-fulfilling love was, until he'd almost thrown it away because of his stupid pride. It doesn't take years to fall in love when a person is your other half. Your heart recognizes them, sees them for what they are the minute you cross paths. The trick to finding them is to listen to your heart not your head.

"You came," Hope whispered in his throat, amazed that he'd come after her, felt deep down that he hated her, and she was so confused.

"Always, angel, like I said, I'd rather cut my hand off than let you leave."

Hope didn't let go, didn't' want to let go, she kept her arms and legs around him as he walked down the platform so he could get his woman home and apologize in private. No eyes or ears to keep him from saying exactly what needed to be said.

"Nic?" Hope whispered in his ear.

"Yeah, baby?"

"Did you just tell me you love me in French?"

"Oui, ma doux amour," he whispered back and then stopped, let her feet hit the ground and then raised his hands to cup her face. He wiped the tears from her eyes, kissed her forehead, her cheeks, and then her nose. He ran his thumb across her bottom lip and watched as her tongue snaked out and tasted his finger. He leaned down, nipped her bottom lip, both hands in her hair as he captured her mouth and poured his love into the kiss.

Hope whimpered as his tongue tangled with hers, still in shock that he'd come for her. When he wrapped an arm around her back lifting her off the floor so he could plaster her to his body, he deepened their kiss. The kiss felt like a new beginning like a door had opened, and together they were walking through it with no more secrets between them. It was a branding, a coming together as one and any hesitation she had about why he'd come after her were washed away when he mumbled against her lips.

"God gave me three gifts in this life; one he took too soon, one that makes me proud each day and one I never saw coming until she stumbled into my life and woke me up. I won't take them for granted another day, and I'll fight like hell to keep them safe," Nic vowed then pulled back and said in all seriousness. "But, if you ever take off like that again I will put you over my knee till you can't sit for a week."

"What?"

"Learn quickly, sugar . . . I will love you, fight with you, die for you, but I will also put your sweet ass over my knee if you run from me."

"You wouldn't?" Hope asked shocked, and maybe a little turned on.

"Oh, sugar, you wanna find out, try me and see what happens. Fair warning though, if you like it, I'll find another way to punish you for running."

"That train is looking better and better to me," Hope announced.

"They have cars with beds, you wanna test me, have at it. I'll make do with close quarters."

"How come you never showed me this side before?"

"You were too busy looking over your shoulder to see what was right in front of you."

"What was right in front of me?"

"Your future, angel, all six foot two inches of him," Nic explained then brushed his lips across hers until she opened her mouth. Nic drank in the taste of her until he wanted to bury himself deep, and show her what it meant to be well and truly loved by a man who used his hands for pleasure, not pain.

***

"Nic," Hope gasped as his lips brushed against her silky thigh. Then he gave her what she wanted when his mouth found her core. He ran his tongue through her folds finding the tiny bundle of nerves and he flicked her with his tongue. Her back arched off the bed; her hands yanked his head down to her pulsing center, needing relief, and he grinned at her.

He'd built her into a frenzy, his hands teasing her, his fingers finding a rhythm as he plunged deep inside her finding that spot that turns a fire into an inferno. He'd curled up his finger, tapped that spot that made her fly and she exploded on his hand, riding it hard. Nic watched the beauty that was Hope as she climaxed, and he felt the wetness drench his hand. She was so responsive to him, like she was made for him alone. Moving up her body, trailing kisses and nipping each nipple as he moved between her spread legs, she was waiting for him to anchor himself deep inside her silken heat, to bring them both to a climax that signaled the beginning of the rest of their lives.

With patience, he didn't have; Nic gave her what she needed. A gentle hand to give her pleasure, words of love to heal her heart, and finally his body to show her that a man, powerful in size, could give her nothing but pleasure be it with hand, mouth or cock.

Running a finger down her folds and feeling the wetness he'd created, he growled in possessiveness. Grabbing his shaft and centering it at her entrance, he pushed in as Hope gasped from the feeling of fullness. Nic hissed at the heat, then sank in and held. He buried his mouth in her neck and bit down as he pulled out and plunged back in.

"Oh, God," Hope whimpered as she bent her head back, the feel of Nic's teeth digging into her neck caused her core to spasm. Nipping his way to her ear, he drove in deep again, sinking into her sweet, hot flesh as he groaned, "This is mine, this body, this heart."

"Yes," Hope answered, her breathy word causing his cock to swell even more.

"I'll keep you safe," Nic grunted as his own release built quickly. "No man will lay a hand on you again, do you hear me?"

"Nic, please," she begged needing more, more pounding, more everything until he shattered what was left of any walls she kept around her. At her plea, he pulled back, rammed in hard, and repeated it over and over until they were both moaning.

His pounding sparked a blaze that erupted for them both on his final thrust. She shouted his name as he buried himself to the root and pulsed inside her, emptying himself into her warm, silken flesh. Gasping for air, stuck together with sweat and sex Nic rolled to his back, bringing Hope with him and tucked her into his body. They both lay there catching their breath, the air heavy with their scent. Nic rolled up, grabbed a towel from his chair and cleaned them both, too tired for a shower. Then he grabbed the bed sheets and pulled them over their bodies. Running his hand down her side until he found her sweet ass, he squeezed it and then kissed her head as she burrowed into his side, relaxed, satiated and exhausted. He whispered "No more pain, sugar, we put the past behind us and move forward together, you with me?"

"I'm with you, Nic," Hope whispered into his chest.

Contentment he hadn't known in a while consumed him, and he felt his eyelids grow heavy, as Hope lay tucked into his side. Hope's breathing slowed, and Nic knew she'd fallen asleep, exhausted from the last two days. Wrapping her tighter into his body, he closed his eyes secure in the knowledge that Hope was completely his and safe.

As sleep set in, Nic decided he'd worry about John Cummings and his threat to their happiness tomorrow. Tonight, he would hold his woman, wake her later and show her again how he felt, and then in the morning, he'd get beignets and eat those off her as well. But, for now, he'd sleep the sleep of a man whose dreams were fulfilled by reaching out and grabbing hold with both hands and not letting go.

Twenty-One

When Hope opened her eyes the next morning, the sun shining, warm, strong arms wrapped around her, she smiled. For the first time in forever, she smiled a smile of true happiness. Hopeless was the best way to describe how she'd felt until God gave her this second chance, one she'd been looking for her whole life. Coming to New Orleans on a whim, Hope now knew was God directing her to Nic.

Ten years she'd lived on eggshells, each year taking a little more of who she was; she'd been outgoing once, mouthy even. A trait she hadn't fully lost and a source of anger for David. When he wasn't acting like she was priceless and the love of his life, he was moody and explosive. He could go months without an outburst, but the constant wondering when he would lose control again took its toll. She'd withdrawn to avoid his anger, but every once in a while the old Hope would come out, defiant, tired of being scared. Since she'd been in New Orleans, she felt the old Hope reemerging again, and it was freeing. Guarded at first, a trait she'd brought with her from Nevada, she kept people out. Fortunately, they'd ignored the hand she'd put up and scaled her walls, smashing holes into them. Now she was lying in the arms of a man who loved her, whom she loved, and with time and God's grace, she knew she could begin to heal.

Nic was spooning Hope, her head laying on his arm, his other arm wrapped protectively around her waist, his leg draped over hers, securing her to his body. In all the years she'd been married, not even in the beginning when she'd thought he'd been her Prince, had she felt this loved, this protected, this connected. Not wanting to waste another minute of her life, she tangled her fingers with his on top of his hand and then brought it up to her breast.

Even in his sleep, Nic responded to her body, knew instinctively what to do as if he'd been programmed to sense her needs and moods from the first time he'd kissed her. Nic wrapped his hand around her breast, his mouth and nose nuzzling her neck slowly as his mind cleared the fog of sleep.

Hope reached between them, found his hardening shaft and brushed her thumb across its crest as she heard Nic inhale sharply, his hand tightening around her breast. Rubbing her hand up and down his length as it hardened further in her hand, Nic groaned in her neck as his arm pinned by her head reached around and captured her nipple with his fingers. Thumb and forefinger claimed her hard peak and he pinched and tugged as his other hand reached between her legs. He found her wet folds and inserted two fingers inside as she mewled and moved against his hand. Still holding his length, she increased the speed of her hand as he moaned driving his hips into her ass as the pressure built.

Nic felt her core tighten around his fingers as his cock swelled larger in her hand, and he bit down on her neck, needing to anchor her, claim her like a wolf claims his mate. When he felt the blood rush to his cock, he applied his thumb to the bundle of nerves at the apex of her sex, and rolled it as they both were both consumed by their passion. Grunting out his release as Hope whimpered her own; he claimed her lips, feasting on them as the aftershocks rocked through their bodies. Releasing her mouth, Nic rose up, kissed the hollow of her neck then kissed each of her breasts, flicking his tongue over the nipples he'd ignored.

"I neglected these," Nic told her breasts. "I'll make it up to you later," he whispered as Hope giggled.

"See that you do," Hope insisted, enjoying the playfulness between them.

Nic rolled to his back trying to take Hope with him, and she pulled back.

"What?"

"Thanks to you I'm a mess, I'm hitting the shower." Reaching for her shirt before he could stop her, it was then Hope remembered she had no other clothes.

"Shit, I left my bags on the train." Nic grinned at her dilemma and threw his hands behind his head.

"That's ok; you can live in my house naked, sugar," Nic chuckled, his grin wide, his brows wiggling.

"And when Nicky stays with you?" Hope reminded him. Nic's face fell a bit, and he rolled towards her responding, "Good point, I don't need my son as competition for your affection."

"Pfft, no competition, he'd win hands down," Hope laughed and then smacked Nic's ass as she tried to exit the bed. He grabbed her at the waist and hauled her back to his chest nibbling on her neck. There was something about the spot where her shoulder met her neck that he couldn't get enough of, so why deny himself?

"How 'bout we shower and then I'll take you shopping for clothes," Nic whispered flicking his tongue against her ear.

Hope loved his mouth on her neck, so she didn't respond at first because, well, it was Nic, and he was talented with his mouth.

"I, oh," Hope stuttered as his hands came to her breasts, his open palms rubbing the nipples in circles, giving them the attention they deserved.

"Sugar?" Nic whispered in her ear. "How 'bout we finish this discussion in the shower, preferably while you're against the wall."

"Works for me," Hope agreed, as her head fell against his shoulder, the topic of conversation forgotten for more important issues.

***

When Nic said go shopping for clothes, what he really meant was Rose would take her shopping for clothes. Nic's a man; he paid the bills, he doesn't shop for that shit. He gladly handed over his credit card to Rose saying, "Whatever she wants." Rose being Rose took that literally and dragged Hope through all the French Quarter boutiques.

"Hemline," for the discerning fashionista; "Feet First," fun & stylish handbags, footwear and accessories. "Grace Note," (Hope's favorite), fun vintage clothing and accessories where she found killer jeans that fit her like a glove. But, she thought Nic's favorite would be "Minou Minou" where she picked up a sexy little coffee colored, baby doll nightgown, with lace across the breasts that left nothing to the imagination. The silk caressed her curves, taking her angelic looks so far away from heavenly that Rose feared Nic might have a heart attack when she wore it. Not that she figured it would stay on that long.

Hope had been insistent about paying to the point of anger, but Rose told her "No, *Cher*, you belong to Nic now; he takes good care of his woman."

"Just because we're together doesn't mean he has to buy my clothes," Hope had argued, but Rose had just taken the stack of stylish tops and jeans she'd tried on, and put them all on the counter.

"Trust me, he won't give a hoot what you say, he gonna take

good care of you and 'dat is all you need to know."

"He can't afford to buy my things and take care of Kat and Nicky," Hope argued trying to put the clothes back. Rose pushed them towards the personal shopper, as the woman watched them argue, and said, "Nic come from old money, he got more dan' enough to go round. His daddy in Sugarcane, big plantation up Baton Rouge way, and Nic his only heir."

"But—"

"Listen to me, T-Hope . . . A man like Nic, he a real man, not like dat' man you married who kept you under his thumb. Nic will take care of you; you will want for 'notin, not one 'ting, you hear me?"

"I don't want his money, Rose; I was married to a man who put money above everything. I'd be happy in a shack without a penny to my name if Nic were with me."

"You gonna give him everah'ting you have to give?'

"Of course, I'd do anything for Nic."

"Den' how dat' different' from what he doin' right now by buyin' you what you need?" Hope narrowed her eyes at the old woman, and Rose smiled knowing she had won.

As they paid, Hope's new clothes were packed in fancy boxes with tissue paper and tied with pink and purple ribbon. It was a far cry from the thrift store purchases she made in the last few months. As she signed the receipt, still debating if she could let Nic pay for her clothes, she felt the hair on the back of her neck rise just before she heard, "I see you wasted no time spending my husband's money."

Rose and Hope spun around at the same time, and Rose's hackles went up.

"Well, look what da' dog drug in, da' Kat-woman herself. Careful, Kitty-Kat, Nic won't take kindly to you upsettin' his woman."

"Rose, always a pleasure to see you, though, you're hard to miss, sugar," Kat hissed and Hope saw red.

Rose being a big woman didn't care about Kat's claws. She loved her womanly curves; they spoke of a good life filled with children and heaps of food that filled her soul so she could give it back to others. Yeah, Rose was a big woman, but her Roscoe loved it. Still does. Several nights a week, too.

Hope could handle the insults she threw her way, could ignore Kat's implication she wanted Nic for his money. What she couldn't abide was Kat's insults towards Rose, and since she was on a short fuse from the last two days, she let Kat have it.

"You can say what you want to me I could care less what you think. Nic wants me in his life, so that's where I'm staying. But, you ever disrespect Maman Rose again, and it's on."

Kat squared off with Hope and seethed back, "You're nothin' but a no account whore who thinks she can weasel her way into *my* husband's bed and spend his money. He'll wake up real quick, sugar, and when he does, I'll be waiting with open arms."

"Seriously?" Hope asked. "You are not to be believed. You hide behind your breeding and your sense of self-importance. What makes you think people will just forgive you and turn a blind eye to your actions? Nic has moved on, and you need to accept it."

"I have close to twenty years' experience with Nic that tells me you are nothing but a temporary play thing. *I* am his wife; *I* am his soul mate, the love of his life, and he will remember that. You may think you've won, but trust me, I always get what I want, always."

"Oh, *sugar*," Hope replied in her best southern drawl, "I think you're forgetting just who walked out on whom." Then she leaned in and asked Kat-woman, "Were you insane, or just selfish? I really want to know. All that is Nic and you threw him away for a roll in the hay?" Then shaking her head Hope finished with "You had it all, the love of a good man, beautiful children and just like a spoiled child you wanted more, you're not only weak you're pathetic."

Hope and Kat stood there, neither one wanting to back down. The air was thick with angry energy until Kat curled her lip in anger but had nothing to say in defense. Looking Hope up and down, she sniffed in disgust at what she saw before her and then turned on her heels to leave the shop. Both Hope and Rose watched as she her swung her hips, flipping her golden locks, and then pulled open the door and sashayed down the street.

"Dat' woman gives da' sisterhood a bad name she do," Rose announced as her eyes followed Kat.

"The struggle is real," Hope deadpanned and Rose turned to Hope, a smile on her face and both women laughed.

***

"What are you doing?" Nic asked Hope as she hung her new clothes in the closet of the downstairs condo. Nic had come home from work to a note saying she was at her place, and he'd marched downstairs.

"Putting my clothes away. Can you hand me that bag on the bed?"

"Sugar, I can see what you're doing, what I want to know is why you're doin' it here?"

Hope turned to Nic, confusion on her face. Then she paled a bit. *Did he not want her to move back into the condo?*

"I, well, do you want me to move?"

"Angel," Nic growled.

"I'm sorry, I just thought . . . I'll pack my things and look for another place in the morning."

Nic rolled his eyes to the ceiling praying for patience and then grabbed her as she tried to move past him.

"You aren't movin' anywhere but upstairs."

"Upstairs?" Hope asked shocked.

"Upstairs, with me, now pack your shit and let's get changed and head out for dinner."

"Nic, I can't move in with you it's too soon."

"Do you love me?"

"Nic—"

"Do you love me, Hope," he demanded, giving her a squeeze to get her full attention.

Hope's breath hitched as she stared at him. Yes, she loved him, so much it scared her to speak the words. But, as Nic stood there demanding to know, the vulnerable look on his face as he waited for her answer, she melted. Nodding her head because she couldn't deny him anything, she whispered, "Yes, I love you more than anything."

Nic closed his eyes as Hope whispered she loved him. He'd been so busy trying to make up for the pain he'd caused her that it hadn't occurred to him until just then that she might not love him back. Lowering his head to hers, keeping his eyes trained on her sky-blue pools, he answered "Then get your ass upstairs, baby, 'cause I'm hungry and from the looks of those bags it's gonna take you a while to sort this shit out."

"That wasn't very romantic, Nic. I'm standing in your arms handing you my heart, and you tell me to get my ass upstairs?"

"I'll rephrase it then," Nic mumbled as he brushed a kiss against her lips. "I love you and want you in my bed every night, now, get your *sweet* ass upstairs before I haul you to the floor and show you just how much you mean to me."

"Better," Hope breathed out on a whisper sending a jolt of arousal through him.

"Oh, sugar, you ain't seen nothin' yet," he whispered back and then claimed her mouth, her body and her heart.

As they lay amongst the clothes that seemed to scatter during their closet romp, Nic picked up a skimpy dress and raised his eyebrows.

"You don't actually think I'll let you outside in this dress?"

"What's wrong with it," Hope demanded, snatching the dark purple with plunging neckline dress from his hand. It was perfect for dinners out Hope thought, and Rose said Nic would love it.

"Oh, the list is long, but the most important one is I'd end the night in a fight with anyone who looked at you."

"You're cute when you go all macho manly "this is *my* woman" hands off," Hope giggled.

"Angel," Nic interrupted her giggling and rolling his naked body onto hers.

"What?" she laughed.

"Your tits in that dress would stop a Mardi Gras parade."

"You're ridiculous," she chuckled.

"I'm a man, same thing," he explained and then moved down her body, pulled a pink hard nipple into his mouth, and again gave her breasts the attention they deserved. Needless to say, they never made it out to dinner that night.

***

One week later . . .

"You are not buying me a car," Hope informed Nic as she made breakfast that morning. He was nuts, certifiable even if he thought for one minute that she would allow him to buy her a car.

Nic just sipped his coffee as he opened the paper and grumbled, "I can and I will."

"Nic, I don't need a car, I can walk to work from here."

"Yeah, sugar, you can, but what if I need you to pick Nicky up for me, or you need to go uptown or a million other places," Nic explained, shocked she had a problem with him buying her a car. She was his woman for Christ sake; did she think he'd make her ride the trolley or take a taxi to buy groceries?

"Then I'll get a loan and buy my own car," Hope retorted her hands on her hips trying to convey just how serious she was in this matter. He was not buying her a car.

***

"I can't believe I let you use sex to get your way," Hope complained the whole way from the Jeep dealership.

"A man's gotta do what he's gotta do to get his woman to toe the line," Nic chuckled and then grinned as he took a right on Frenchman's street heading towards The Bayou.

They were currently in Hope's new, all white, and loaded to the max Jeep Wrangler Sahara—with leather seats and tow package of course, Nic had insisted.

Hope had made the mistake of A.) Challenging the man and B.) Expressing her love of all things Jeep when she'd said she would buy her own car. Two hours and multiple orgasms later, Nic had coerced her into letting him buy her a car.

"You've been holding out on me, by the way," Hope complained.

"Sugar, in the game of life a man's gotta have a few tricks up his sleeves."

"Interesting, so if I wanted to get my way then all I'd have to do is show you how flexible I am?"

"Flexible?"

"Very, very flexible," Hope breathed out like a 1-800 phone sex operator and then finished with "I've been studying yoga for ten years to deal with stress, *sugar* . . . Does downward dog mean anything to you?"

Nic's grin fell and his eyes heated, "That just earned you a cell phone," he bit out as he pulled into the employee parking lot and parked.

"Wait that wasn't supposed to happen," Hope cried out.

"Then you shouldn't have mentioned the positions I can get you in," Nic chuckled as he grabbed her neck and pulled her to his mouth, "Downward dog tonight, sugar."

"I've got a big mouth," Hope sighed.

"And you use it well."

"Don't be crass."

"Don't be cute," Nic mumbled and then kissed her before letting her go and exiting the Jeep.

Hope got out, slammed the door, and looked at her all white, to die for Jeep and grinned.

"See ya, snowflake."

"Jesus, you named your Jeep?" Nic laughed as he hooked his arm around Hope's neck and walked her to the back of the bar while pocketing her keys. Hope watched the keys disappear and frowned.

"Are you ever gonna let me drive her?"

"Tomorrow, after you've earned it yoga master," Nic grinned and then opened the door and walked her in while she stared daggers at him.

Before heading to the front of the bar, Nic kissed her sweetly, ran his nose down the side of her own and then whispered, "Make me something fiery, angel, just like you."

Twenty-Two

The honeymoon period is beautiful to watch, Rose thought as her eyes followed Hope as she brought a meal to Nic at the bar. It had been more than two weeks since she'd jumped from that train and every day they grew closer and closer. The shadows they both carried in their eyes seemed almost gone, and the playfulness between them made Rose's heart swell with happiness. She'd come to love Hope like a daughter and Nic was already like her son. She'd never met two people who deserved to be happy and in love more than those two.

She knew there would be good times and bad times, you don't go through what they had and come out unscathed. But, Nic was a strong man, and he could bear Hope's troubles easily on his shoulders. Hope, she had come to find out, was tough as nails. Abused, scared to leave, lost her baby and had to sleep next to a man she despised. There weren't many women who could bear that and not be irrevocably damaged, yet in her own way, Rose knew that she was. But, Hope was made of sterner stuff, had adapted the best she could to what life threw at her, and managed to survive with a good sense of self still within her. She figured there would be days that it would sneak up on Hope. Seeing a little boy playing or when a man raised his voice, but our life experiences make us who we are, mold us, shape our perspective and since you can't run from your past, you move forward. The key to overcoming past tragedies is to move on with your life, be productive, live life to the fullest, not bury yourself in the pain. What better way to thumb your nose at someone who tried to destroy you than to say, "Look at me, I'm still standing," and Hope was doing just that!

She confided in Rose, told her she still felt guilty for her son's death, but placed the blame for the rest where it belonged, square on the shoulders of her dead husband. She'd told Nic the ugly details of her husband's death, and he'd shared the emotional moment when he'd seen his daughter laid out on the table in the morgue. Talking about your pain with someone who knows how it feels is the first step in healing, and who better to share it with than someone you love and can understand, she figured.

Rose looked around the bar, saw they had a light crowd and since she was so happy at that moment for her friends, decided they needed an impromptu party to celebrate love conquering all.

"Big Daddy!" Rose shouted through the kitchen pass-thru.

"Comin' old woman, where da' fire?"

When he reached the window, Rose smiled, and hooted, "Grab your scrub-board it Zydeco time."

Big Daddy hooted back and turned to Roscoe, Rose's husband, who'd made an uncommon appearance at the bar and shouted, "Rosie in da' mood for a partay,' grab your accordion old man and let's rock da' house."

"Well, all right," Roscoe agreed and moved to Rose's office where she kept one of his piano-accordions for just such emergencies.

Rose turned around smiling after watching the two men get their instruments and shouted, "Time to get to da' ass shakin,' Abby, move dem' tables and make Maman a dance floor."

Hoots and hollers could be heard around the bar as Abby and the other waitresses began moving customers to booths and stacking the tables in the corner. Big Daddy and Roscoe came out and stood at the wall while Rose pulled out her harmonica and blew it.

"Listen to Maman y'all," Rose shouted, "Dis' here a celebration of life. We can no change da' past, but we sure as hell can enjoy da' 'futcha. *Laissez le bon temps rouler,* let's bring dis' house down, yes?"

Roscoe squeezed the piano accordion in and out, as his fingers flew across keyboard. Big Daddy ran a spoon down the front of his scrub-board keeping the beat with Roscoe, as Rose blew her heart out on the harmonica.

Hope, still standing at the bar watching all this play out, started laughing at the sight before her. Customer's jumped up, swinging to the beat of Zydeco La Louisianne as others hooted and clapped to the beat. Nic stood, reached across, lifted Hope over the bar, and led her to the dance floor as the song played loud.

Swinging Hope out and then back to him Nic showed her how to do the two-step again as Rose watched and figured God was smiling down on the sight.

They played "*Ma Tit Fille*" "*Parley-nous a boire*" and "Zydeco Gris-Gris" all while Nic kept Hope close as he led her around the dance floor.

After an hour or more of dancing, the trio of musicians called it an evening, but turned on the overhead music keeping the atmosphere alive and everyone dancing. Rose and Roscoe moved to the bar, popped open a bottle of beer, and then touched their bottles together as they watched Nic and Hope sway to a slower Cajun song.

"Rosie, you done good. Those two remind me of you and me not too long ago," Roscoe told his wife and then he kissed her cheek.

"What you mean remind you of not too long ago?" Rose asked raising her eyebrows.

"All right, woman, I only meant— "

"Roscoe, you love me and you know you do."

Roscoe grabbed his wife by the hips and pulled her into him nuzzling her neck. "My Rosie is the love of my life, my sunshine, my Mississippi Queen," he murmured in her ear, and not for the first time in their forty plus years together, Rose shivered at his touch.

Rose wrapped her arms around her husband, laid her head on his chest, and listened to the sound of his heartbeat. She loved Roscoe fiercely, and when he touched her, he made her feel twenty again. As she stood there in the warmth of his embrace, her eyes moved to the window, and she stiffened when she caught sight of Kat standing in the window, watching Nic and Hope as fury sparked in her eyes. Rose pulled back from Roscoe and looked in Nic's direction. When his eyes landed on hers, she jerked her head towards the window. Nic's face showed confusion until he looked and saw Kat for himself. She didn't move from the window when he caught her staring, didn't even try to hide the contempt she had while watching Nic and Hope dance. Nic grabbed Hope's hand and led her off the dance floor taking her to Rose and Roscoe.

"Stay here," Nic ordered and Hope watched confused as he walked to the door, wondering where he was going until she saw Kat in the window, both arms crossed under her large breasts looking like she could spit nails.

Rose kept a hand on her shoulder and tightened it when she felt Hope try to move towards the door. Nic looked back at her as he opened the door and shook his head when he saw the look on her face. Rolling her eyes at him, he bit his lips together to keep from laughing at her expression and then slowly shook his head again. Nic wondered if she'd ever fuckin' listen to him without some sort of argument, verbal or non-verbal. Sighing, 'cause he was pretty sure the answer to that was no, he decided right then he didn't care, she was so fuckin cute when riled up he'd let it slide.

Back to the matter at hand, getting rid of Kat, he pushed through the door and met her on the sidewalk.

"You need something?"

"You bought that tramp a car?" Kat hissed.

Nic sucked air through his nose and tried to censure his reaction. When she got a bug up her ass, like now, nothin' he said got through so he bit out, "Watch your mouth."

"I can't believe you're letting that slut play you like this. She's only after your money, sugar, you need to wake up and see her for who she truly is," Kat shouted.

"I'm giving you fair warning, Kat, watch what you say or I'm done." Nic growled low.

Kat moved forward and put her hands to his face, trying to reach him like she used to when they were married. Nic's head jerked back and then he stepped back, not wanting her hands on him in any way.

"Baby, please," Kat begged, "Forget this woman and come back to me and Nicky, we need you."

"Nicky has me, always. But I'd sooner die than let Hope go."

"You don't mean that," Kat panicked reaching for him again.

Nic grabbed her hands and pushed them down, needing her to finally fuckin' get that they were done.

"I've never meant anything more, I love her with everything I am," Nic answered, and watched as her face paled for a moment and then grew angry again.

"You'd choose a woman who threatened the mother of your child?" Nic's face showed confusion and Kat jumped on it. "I was minding my own business and she threatened me like a common street thug. Ask Rose, she was there, ask her if your precious

Hope threatened to take a hand to me if I so much as looked her way again."

Nic looked through the window at Rose and Hope and figured she wasn't lying. He didn't give a shit if Hope had threatened Kat, what he did give a shit about was she had kept it from him. This whole scene could have been avoided if she'd just told him and he'd have dealt with Kat himself.

"You believe me, don't you sugar?"

"Oh, I believe you. I believe you got in her face and she pushed back, that I absolutely believe," Nic gritted out then watched Kat explode.

"She's a whore, worse than a whore she's a gold-digging, murdering, drug pushing piece of shit," Kat screeched her control going from calm to out of control like a hair-trigger and Nic moved into her, getting right in her face.

"Shut your fuckin' mouth," Nic thundered, his voice holding a lethal edge. "I'm done with your shit; you stay away from Hope do you hear me? You so much as look her direction your monthly manicures are gone. She sees you on the street your fuckin' car is gone. She breaks a nail because you upset her and I will sue for custody, do you understand me? Whatever fuckin' game you think you're playing, it ends today. Except for Nicky, you don't exist for me. I don't know what happened to the woman I married all those years ago, but, you, Kat, are so far from that Georgia Peach that it turns my stomach to even call you my ex-wife."

Kat stepped back when Nic was done, put her hands to her hair and grabbed hold, like she was hanging on by a thread.

"I don't understand? This doesn't make any sense," Kat mumbled in shock, trying to wrap her head around the fact that he'd choose some whore over her.

Watching Kat battle some inner dialog, he didn't care if she figured it out or not, he was done being jacked around by this woman. Looking through the window while he waited for Kat to clue in, Nic watched Hope walk to the bar and take the phone from Henri's hand. She put the phone to her ear, said something to the caller, and then her face fell and the color drained from her cheeks. "Shit," Nic muttered and turned back to the door as Kat tried to stop him. He shrugged off her hand, and forgot she existed as he headed to the bar, eyes on Hope as she started the tremble. When he reached her, he grabbed the phone from her hand and asked, "Who's speaking?"

"This is Detective King with the Reno police department, who's this?"

"Nic Beuve, Hope's man, why are you calling?"

"We asked Mrs. Cummings to keep in touch with us in case we had news or needed to alert her to John Cummings location. I called to inform her that as of two days ago, he'd skipped town."

"Fuck," Nic hissed and grabbed Hope around the waist and drew her to him.

"That would be my reaction if Mrs. Cummings were my woman, so keep her safe."

"Won't let her out of my sight, you can count on it."

"Have her keep in touch so we know where she is at all times and I'll call her cell if we have any news."

"I don't want her upset anymore, you need to relay whereabouts you can do that through me," Nic barked at the detective, then rattled off his number, and then disconnected with "Later."

Hope had buried her head in his chest, and when he hung up, he wrapped both his arms around her and held on tight.

"He won't get near you," Nic vowed in her ear and she held on tighter.

"He's gonna find me and then all of you will be in danger," Hope whispered, scared out of her mind. She should have left on that train to keep them all safe from John.

"He's not gonna touch you, I'd kill him before he did." Hope was too lost in her thoughts to hear him and tried to pull away.

"I should leave, he can't find me if I keep running," Hope told no one particular and Nic tightened his arms, tried to hold on to her as she pushed hard to escape. "I need to leave to keep you safe," Hope cried out, struggling against him, "I need to leave, let me go," she shouted and Nic pulled her back, locked his arm around her and pulled her into the kitchen and away from prying eyes.

He took her to Rose's office and shut the door, then sat down on the couch and pulled her into his lap. She buried her head in his neck and sobbed as Nic envisioned his hands around John Cummings neck.

The calm before the storm, Nic thought as Hope cried in his arms. He knew once she had time to digest everything, she'd be pissed, and he needed her pissed. Scared she would run, pissed she would fight. He needed her to stand beside him and fight for their future, not run scared trying to keep him safe.

Slowly her sobs turned to hiccups and he felt her arms go limp. Rose came in as he held her, bringing her purse and sagely advice. When she saw Hope had fallen asleep from exhaustion, Rose whispered, "You hold on tight to her, you hear me? She stubborn when she 'tink she protectin' you. Dis' man will not take any more from *tit ange* do you hear what I sayin'? Don't you let her pull away from you, fight her everah' step, yeah?"

"Yeah, I hear you Rosie." He'd sleep with one eye open if he had to, to keep her safe and save her from herself.

Standing with Hope in his arms, she woke slightly when he moved and she snuggled into him mumbling, "What did Kat-woman want?" Nic chuckled; no doubt she'd learned that phrase from Rose. He wanted to argue with her about not telling him about her encounter with Kat, but figured that was water under the bridge considering John was on the loose. Then it occurred to him he needed her pissed and fighting mad. It didn't matter whom she was pissed at, just as long as she was something other than scared.

"She wanted me to know she thought you were a whore and that you threatened her," Nic told her, thanking his ex for finally giving him something besides a headache.

"I'm sorry, she said what?" Hope asked her voice suddenly less sleepy and turning angry.

"It's not important, angel, go back to sleep."

"Not important? Did you just say she called me a whore and you don't think that's important?" Hope bit out.

Nic set her on her feet and she glared at him. He was so relieved to see her pissed he pulled her in his arms and kissed her while Rose stood by and laughed.

Pushing back from Nic, Hope shouted, "How dare she call me a whore. She sleeps with every Tom, Dick and Harry and calls me a— is she still here?" Hope asked Rose over Nic's shoulder.

"I not notice, *Cher*, you want me to look?"

"I'll do it myself," Hope answered and then broke Nic's hold and marched out of the room.

Nic watched her leave and then turned to Rose. "Kat's gone isn't she?"

"Mebbe', mebbe' not. If she still here I'll pop da' popcorn and watch—you like butter on yours?"

Nic rolled his eyes for patience, then to be on the safe side chased after his woman. Though, the thought of Hope tearing into Kat did put a smile on his face.

"And though she be but little, she is fierce," Nic whispered Shakespeare's words, and thought the man was thinking of a woman just like Hope when he wrote them.

Twenty-Three

The last week after Detective King called was a slippery slope of emotions. One minute Hope was in tears, the next she was angry. Nic spent most of that time trying to keep her off balance. He figured if she had too much to focus on she couldn't stay stuck in her head worrying about John Cummings. He'd called and been briefed by the Detective again, and they had no idea where Cummings was or if he even knew where Hope was living now. Which meant he could be right outside the door or in Canada. The not knowing would eat Hope alive, and Nic knew he needed to do something to take her mind off Cummings, and he couldn't think of a better place to go to feel loved and secure than his childhood home.

"Up, out of the bed and get packed," Nic told Hope as he threw back the covers from the bed. Hope rolled over, squinting her eyes at him and then rolled back. "I'm tired, I want to sleep."

"You can sleep in the car; we're going to Baton Rouge to see Nicky at the summer house. My parents have been dying to meet you for weeks, and I miss my son."

Hope rolled to her back quickly, and Nic didn't miss the look of apprehension on her face.

"Your parents?"

"Yeah, sugar, now get a move on."

"What if they don't like me?"

"Angel—"

"Oh, my God, what if they hate me?"

"Sugar—"

"I don't have a thing to wear!" Hope shouted.

Nic grabbed her by the ankles, and pulled her to the end of the bed while she squeaked. He lifted her from the bed, placed her on her feet and chuckled while he walked her to the shower.

"One thing I've learned about women, baby, you'll never have the perfect outfit," then he smacked her sweet ass, turned on the shower and got busy relaxing her for the trip.

***

The Beuve's summer home on the banks of the Tickfaw River was a charming cottage that had two stories and a wrap-around porch. There was a dock stretching out onto the river and surprisingly a pool even though the river was at their back door. Nic's mother preferred to see what she swam with, he'd explained, and Hope decided she agreed with his mother when she remembered the alligators that sunned themselves on the banks. There was a boathouse for their speedboat and houseboat. Nic said they had two because you never know when you'd want to go fast or take it slow and lazy, and it all sat on a full acre. This was so your neighbors weren't right up your ass— as Nic put it.

His mother and father were waiting on the steps of their large covered porch when they arrived. Large porches were a necessity in Louisiana to keep the sun at bay. Most houses had them and were frequently utilized on long summer nights while they drank ice tea and welcomed in the night. When Nic parked the car, they both descended the steps with smiles on their faces, waving to both her and Nic. When his parent's faces melted into loving looks of acceptance, Hope forgot about being nervous and smiled at them both, her worries about the perfect outfit just a memory when she saw smiling back at her.

Nic's dad, Nicholas Sr., was as tall as his son was, but with more gray hair than black. His face, an older version of Nic's, had aged to perfection with just the right amount of laugh lines on his face. Strong cheekbones, heavy brows, and full lips told Hope he'd been a heartbreaker in his youth. He was lean, but not too lean, and the way he curled his wife around the shoulders, tucking her into his side, said his eyes never wandered in all the years they'd been married. And who would even look at another woman when you had one as beautiful and gracious as Tilly on your arm?

Taller than Hope, most were, she was blonde as well with blue eyes and a cupid's mouth. She had a full, shapely figure that she'd kept in shape most of her sixty-five years, but just enough softness and curves that you knew her husband enjoyed her. She was dressed in a cool summer sundress, of pastel-green, and rhinestone encrusted flip-flops. Her hair was swept up in a messy up-do and Hope could tell by looking at her relaxed outfit she could care less what Hope had worn. She was the essence of a southern woman who could give a rat's ass about the latest fashion and more about being comfortable while looking feminine—Hope loved her at first sight.

Nicky tried to act cool when they arrived, he'd smiled and waved but didn't rush forward to hug his dad. He gave Hope a grin, and she smiled at him and nudged him in the shoulder. Nic Sr. was the first to address Hope, and he did it in southern style. He walked up to her, grabbed her by the shoulders, drawing her in for a big bear hug.

"We've been beggin' Nic to bring you up here ever since we heard about you, sugar," he crooned like a riverboat gambler, and Clark Gable came to mind from the movie "Gone with the Wind."

"It's a pleasure to meet you, too," Hope answered back. Nic Sr. then shifted her to Tilly who smiled brightly and gave her a genteel hug.

"Just look at you, why, you're as pretty as any southern belle I've ever met."

"She's got piss and vinegar like one too," Nic chuckled and then tucked Hope under his arm as he leaned in and kissed his mother's cheek, "You look especially pretty today, mother. Have you been drinking from the fountain of youth again?"

"Of course, it's called Cajun Lemonade. Y'all take a seat on the back porch, and I'll fetch you both a tall glass."

"I'll get their bags," Nic Sr. called out as he rounded the back of her Jeep. "Nice car son, kinda girlie for you though."

"It's Hope's dad, she lets me drive it when she's in a good mood."

"What he means is he never lets me drive it, so I'm confused as to why he bought it," Hope laughed and then realized what she said.

Tilly looked at her son and then asked, "You bought it for her?"

Feeling the color drain from her face, Hope started to apologize and tell them he forced her to buy it, but before she could say anything Tilly wrapped an arm around her and said, "Oh, sugar, you and I have got to have a conversation about how to handle Beuve men." Then she shouted over her shoulder, "Y'all go fish or somethin.' Hope and I have some photo albums to sort through."

***

Two hours later and five photo albums sorted through, Tilly turned to Hope as they laughed over a picture of Nic dressed as a girl for Halloween and asked, "Do you love him?" Hope was taken off guard by the question and choked on her Cajun lemonade. As she sputtered, Tilly grabbed a napkin and handed it to her chuckling "Subtle isn't one of my strong suits, sugar, sorry about that."

Hope wiped her mouth and took a deep breath then turning to Nic's mother told her, "Yes, I do, more and more each day." The smile that crossed Tilly's mouth spoke of a mother's love for her son having found the right woman to love. She beamed and grabbed Hope's hands and advised, "Then you need to put him in his place from time to time. Don't let my son walk roughshod over you. He's like his father, likes to run everything. You let him think he does, but in the back of your mind remember behind every great man is the woman steering the ship."

"Yes, ma'am," Hope smiled, and Tilly scoffed, "My mother is ma'am, you can call me Tilly."

Right on cue, the men and Nicky came in from the sun, carrying catfish they'd caught in the river. The dark gray fish with whiskers hung from a fish stringer, and Nic's dad plopped them down in the kitchen sink on their way into the great room where Tilly and Hope were sitting. Both men came to the back of the couch, and both women looked up as they lowered their heads and kissed them sweetly on the lips. When both Nic's pulled back, smiling sweetly at their women, Hope and Tilly sighed. Young or old, newly coupled or forty-four years married, when a hot guy kisses you, you swoon.

"We havin' a fish fry for dinner, sugar?" Tilly asked her husband. Nic Sr. brushed her cheek once with the back of his hand before turning back to the kitchen.

"That we are, Tilly darling,' that we are." The sound of a fish hitting the counter caught Tilly's attention, and she told her husband, "You make a mess, you clean it up."

"Sugar— "

"No you don't, Nicholas Beuve, my hands smelt for a week last time."

"I'll clean up if you gut them dad. Wouldn't want momma or Hope's hands in those guts anyway," Nic called out to his father.

At that announcement, Tilly leaned in whispering, "My hands didn't smell, but really, the guts are just not appealing in the least." Nic heard his mother and turned, smiled at her and then winked as he made his way to the kitchen.

After dinner, they all retired to the back porch. Nicky set up a game of dominoes, and they relaxed with drinks as the crickets began their nightly calls. Frogs soon joined them and in the distance, a loud splash from the water indicated an alligator was hunting for his next meal. Croaking calls from a Heron as she fed her young added to the magical evening of just being and it was heavenly.

No worries, no deadlines, just family, the sounds of the river and Hope snuggled in next to Nic. If there ever was a perfect day, Hope figured this had to be close to it. Nic was right she needed to relax and not worry so much. He'd notified the police the alarms were always on when they were home, and as Nic had said, John could be in Canada enjoying the fruits of his illegal labor. Nic was running his fingers up and down her arm as she laid her head on his chest. Tilly watched them both, a small smile on her face as Nic Sr. was explaining the rules of dominoes again to Nicky. The sun had lowered in the sky, and Hope decided she'd never seen a more beautiful sunset, when the silence of the night was interrupted by the sound of shoes on the steps of the porch.

"Well isn't this just a cozy sight," Kat remarked sarcastically as she took in the occupants of the porch. "*My* son, *my* husband, and the *whore*. Oh, my apologies, I didn't see Sister Theresa and Saint Nicholas over there," she finished with disdain.

"Momma?" Nicky stuttered, alarmed at his mother words and her appearance. Normally well-kept Kat looked different in a T-shirt and shorts, with no makeup on her face. Tilly stood immediately and put herself between Nicky and Kat, her anger apparent, as she hissed, "Not in front of Nicky."

"I don't hide my feelings from my son," Kat shouted, "If this is the type of company he'll be keeping while in your home, I'll just take him home."

Nic had stood and tried to enter the fray, but his mother had put up her hand to stop him, and like all good sons, he didn't dare cross his momma.

"We have every right to have whomever we want in our home, and that includes you. That being said, you've overstayed your welcome, and I suggest you head on back to New Orleans on your broomstick."

"Nicky, get in the house," Nic barked out, his tone breaking Nicky from his deer in the headlights trance, as he watched his mother and grandmother face-off. He moved quickly to the door, but looked back over his shoulder at his parents, one last time, before walking inside and closing the door. Nic turned back to his mother and told her "I'll handle this. You go inside and look after Nicky." His mother crossed her arms and raised her brows, holding her position. She wasn't moving an inch, and he knew it. Sighing, he turned to Kat and grabbed her arm marching her down the porch and around the house. She struggled the whole way as Tilly, Hope and Nic Sr. stood there and watched, all three in different degrees of shock and anger.

Hope looked back at the house and wondered if she should go to Nicky. He wasn't a baby anymore, and his mother being upset at her presence might make him unpredictable, and with no experience with kids, Hope bit her lips unsure what to do. Should she leave it to Nic or try to explain the situation herself? She was just about to turn to the door, and attempt to console him, when Nic's mother broke the silence.

"That woman is a bitch."

"Now, sugar," Nic Sr. replied with a chuckle in his voice.

"I'd use another word for her, but ladies don't talk like that in polite company."

Nic Sr.'s chuckle became a laugh, and he wrapped his arm around her shoulders and pulled her into his chest. Hope let out a giggle, and then threw her hand over her mouth as the giggle became a laugh, as well.

The sound of screeching tires alerted them to the fact that Kat had left, and when Nic rounded the corner, he found his parents and his woman in varying degrees of laughter. Shaking his head, he looked to the heavens and wondered not for the first time if it was just him, or was everyone in his life nuts. He came up the steps, moved past the lunatics, and entered the house calling out to his son.

"Nicky, we're goin' out on the boat. Grab your shoes and life vest."

Nicky came around the corner, a wary look on his face and Nic told him, "She's gone. Your momma's just dealing with some stuff right now. She didn't mean what she said."

"Why'd she call Hope a bad name?" Nic sighed 'cause he couldn't tell his son the truth without hurting him. So, he kneeled down and told him, "Even adults have bad days and say things they shouldn't. Your mother is a good woman and so is Hope, but sometimes people just don't like everyone they meet."

Nicky rolled his eyes and broke it down for his dad.

"What you really mean is mom is jealous of Hope, and she called her a bad name to be mean." Nic's lip twitched and again he realized his son was too sharp for his own good.

"Yeah, somthin' like that." Nicky nodded and then shook his

head as he went to get his shoes, and his mumbled "Grownups, jeez," made Nic chuckle as he headed back to the porch.

"Is he okay?" Hope asked with concern in her voice as he pulled her under his arm.

"He's a kid, they bounce back quickly. You ready for your first sunset and night under the stars?"

"Sounds great, but what about Kat?"

"She's heading back to New Orleans. She won't be coming back if that's what you're asking."

"Good, I'm uninviting her when Nicky's here, I'm not putting up with that behavior again." Tilly replied and then asked "We gonna take Nicky out on the boat and shoot fireworks?"

"We got any?" Nic asked his father.

"Always," Nic Sr. replied as if that question was an affront to his manhood.

"Then load'em up, Dad, time to blow something up."

Nic Sr. rubbed his hands together in excitement and Hope heard Tilly mumble, "I'd like to blow *someone* up." Nic snapped "Mom," in warning, afraid Nicky would overhear.

"Blow her all the way back to OZ," Tilly kept on and Nic Sr. barked out "Enough, you made your point *espésces de téte dure.*"

Tilly bit her lips and looked at Hope and Hope bit her lips to keep from laughing. There was no doubt about it; Hope didn't see good things in her future when it came to handling a Beuve man. If Tilly could be silenced, there was no hope for her.

Twenty-Four

South Louisiana is humid most days, add in ninety plus degrees and it's humid and hot like a steam bath. Hope was experiencing her first heat wave since arriving in Louisiana on the sidewalks of Louisiana State University or better known as LSU. "Geaux Tigers!" was everywhere on the campus of the university Nic had attended and his father before him.

Nic and Nic Sr. had decided that a day trip to Baton Rouge, the city of Nic's birth, and the city that housed the great university, were the order of the day before she and Nic headed back to New Orleans. Though the campus was practically dead, college students were home on their much-needed summer break, Hope could feel the energy of the university.

They took pictures in front of Mike the Tiger's habitat, though the LSU mascot was taking a break sunning himself, he did raise his head once and look their way. They toured the dairy store where students raise the cows and make fresh ice cream daily, and they took a walk around LSU Lake as they ate the creamy delight.

But, the biggest draw for all three Nicholas Beuve's was the football stadium. Tiger stadium, home of the LSU Tigers football team and arguably the worst place to play if you're an opposing team, was huge. Under construction, but due to be completed that summer, the stadium will hold 100,000 when construction is complete. Hope and Tilly were behind the men as they all three morphed into little kids at the sight of the construction and the coming football season.

"Dad, can we get Tiger Den seats for next season?" Nicky shouted as they walked the perimeter of the stadium.

"Only a man would think spending thousands of dollars on season tickets for football was a great idea," Tilly mumbled.

Hope bit her lips hearing that 'cause she didn't agree. Though she lost her family at twelve, she had vivid memories of watching football with her father. They, however, had been Oklahoma Sooner fans. She always thought it was odd that her father, who'd never lived in the sooner state, had bled crimson and cream. But he'd told her about how they'd had the longest winning streak ever, forty-seven straight games, from 1953-1957, and that he'd been mesmerized by that team as a kid. His enthusiasm for his adopted team had rubbed off on her, and as a tribute to her dad, she watched every game she could when they were on TV. Now *she* bled crimson and cream, and standing next to the football stadium of the team that beat her Sooners for the national title in 2003, her football hackles went up.

"Depends on the team," Hope replied.

"Indeed it does," Nic Sr. answered back and she just smiled. Though the smile said, "this team is not one of them."

"You don't like Tiger football, angel?" Nic asked shocked at the thought of his woman not liking his beloved Tigers.

"Not since 2003."

Nic's brain remembered quickly, and he grinned slowly as he asked, "Please tell me you're not a Sooner fan."

"I may not be sooner born, but I *was* sooner bred, and when I die I'll damn sure be sooner dead," Hope announced and then watched as the three men looked at her with varying degrees of "what the fuck."

"Dad," Nicky chuckled as he looked up at his father,

"Saturdays are gonna be interesting at our house."

Both big Nic's threw their heads back and laughed and Tilly and Hope both giggled at the astute kid.

"You'll learn to love the Tigers, sugar," Nic laughed as he wrapped an arm around her neck and pulled her into his side, plastering her whole body to him. Hope looked up and then grinned slyly saying "Not in this lifetime, pal. I hold a mean grudge."

Nic leaned down and whispered in her ear "I'll make it up to you when we get home." Hope melted into him, thinking about how he'd make it up to her, and figured that was a start, but he'd have to work hard before she'd forget.

After touring the campus, they made their way to "Walk-On's" for lunch. It was a hang-out of Nic's when he'd gone to school at LSU, and the food was out of this world good. Big sandwiches piled high with mountains of French fries on the side and tall glasses of sweet tea to top it off.

"I can't eat all this," Tilly exclaimed.

"Then why did you order it?" Nic Sr. replied as he bit into his own mile high sandwich.

" 'Cause it looked good."

"Then give me what you don't eat," Nic Sr. answered around a bite of food.

"You don't need to be eating all of this either," Tilly went on.

"Woman, I'll eat what I damn well please," elder Nic replied.

"Then you can get the bicarbonate of soda in the middle of the night."

"I won't need the bicarbonate of soda," he snapped at his wife.

"Sugar, you'll not only need it, you'll find out we are out of it at 2am." Staring at his wife, he cleared his throat mumbling, "We'll stop on the way home."

Tilly winked at Hope, but she was beginning to think she

needed the bicarbonate of soda already. Two bites into her sandwich and she began to break into a sweat. The combination of the heat and the greasy food had her pushing her plate away and sipping her sweet tea as the others ate. Nicky saw the move, and all but done with his own food asked "If you aren't gonna eat that, I will." Pushing her plate to him, he smiled and dug into her food. Then he finished off his grandmother's food, but he got an evil eye from his grandfather when he looked his direction.

"You keep eating like that you'll be a linebacker instead of a running back," Nic told his son.

"That would be awesome, I love tackling."

"Yeah, but you've got quick feet, and a natural ability to avoid a tackle," Nic advised.

Nicky was about to open his mouth to argue that being a tackle would be cooler, when a deep voice behind him said, "Running backs get the TD's *and* we get all the girls."

Nicky turned around, and his eyes grew wide when he took in the sight of LSU's current star running back Marshall Tucker.

"You're Marshall Tucker," Nicky shouted.

"In the flesh little man, or should I say big man seein' as you polished off three plates."

Nicky grew taller in his chair and puffed out his chest. "I play running back too," he told the LSU football God.

"I heard, you keep working on your footwork and ball control, and in a few years we'll be watching you run down Tiger field for a touchdown."

"Yes sir," Nicky breathed out in awe and then waved at the football God as he exited the building.

"Forget playing tackle, Dad, running backs get all the girls," Nicky announced and then smiled as his father and grandfather laughed.

***

Hope slept on the drive back from Baton Rouge. She was exhausted from the late night on the boat, one that had kept them both up until the early morning hours. They'd watched the glowing sun descend behind the horizon; a sight Nic figured was better than any sunset he'd seen in his life. There was just something about the bayou that made everything more intense, more alive, and he figured that was why he enjoyed those sunsets so much. Once the sun was down, they'd shot off bottle rockets and blown up tin cans while the stars twinkled in the sky. You couldn't see the stars in the city, you had to get out in that inky black water and then drift peacefully down the river to truly enjoy God's diamonds in the sky. After they'd cruised around for several hours, Nic had taken his mother, father and Nicky home, and then loaded up blankets, pillows and a basket with wine and cheese for a romantic night on the water.

Anchoring in a cove, and lowering the mosquitoes netting to keep the bugs at bay, they'd curled up on the blankets and talked, sipping wine, nibbling on cheese and then nibbling on each other.

It had been a slow seduction at first. Hope had stripped off her top as she sat across his hips, his hands kneading and tweaking her breasts and nipples as her head fell back. Her silhouette in the moons light was the most beautiful thing he'd ever seen, and his need to claim her had been swift. He'd rolled her suddenly, capturing her lips, drinking in the sweet taste of wine on her lips, as she pulled his shirt from his jeans. He'd leaned back grabbed the shirt at his collar and pulled it from his body, as Hope popped the buttons on his jeans. Reaching in, she'd wrapped her hand around his hard shaft, and he'd hissed at the warmth of her touch. Needing more of him, she'd pulled his jeans down to his hips, then leaned forward and took him in her mouth as he tangled his hands in her hair, grunting as he hit the back of her throat.

"Jesus, your mouth," Nic groaned as she pulled off his hard cock and nipped his crest.

After that he was done.

Reaching down he'd ripped the shorts from her body, pulled her knees out from under her, and flipped her onto her knees spearing into her with one grunting thrust. Hope gasped as he stretched her, set her sensitive nerves on fire, as he grabbed her hips and pound into her repeatedly. The more he thrust, the more she moaned, and when he didn't think he could take a moment longer, he'd reached forward and pulled her back to his front. With an arm around her chest, so he could anchor her to his cock, he drove in brutally, put his thumb and forefinger to one of her nipples and pinched hard, not releasing it. Then he sunk his teeth into that spot on her neck that he'd claimed as his own, thrust twice more as she opened her mouth to scream his name. Her climax was so strong no words spilled from her mouth as she clenched tight around him. On a grunt of "Fuck," Nic exploded in her warm depths, his cock buried deep as he held her in place, not moving, while the heat of her milked him...

Nic turned and looked at Hope's sleeping form, the images of their passionate sex the night before, still fresh in his mind. It shocked him how much he craved her, wanted her, and loved her in such a short amount of time. A little over a month had passed since that night in the garden, and it felt like he'd known her forever. He was that comfortable and in tune with her, and sensed her moods and how to comfort her as if he'd been married to her for years. She'd fit right in with his parents too, like she'd known them for forever, and both his parents had loved her on the spot.

When God closes one door, he opens another his mother had always said, and as near as he could see, this was God's way of opening another door for them both. He knew they both had issues to overcome, Hope more than him, but he figured they could overcome just about anything together.

Turning onto Royal, Nic pulled in front of his condo and turned off the Jeep. Hope's tiny body was resting against the door, so he leaned in and placed a kiss to her neck, waking her.

"We're home, angel," Nic whispered into her ear. Hope stretched and looked around them, surprise on her face that she'd slept the whole way.

"Bed," she mumbled as her head lolled to the side landing on his shoulder. Nic kissed her head, then got out of the Jeep, walked to her side and opened the door. She stumbled out, and he wrapped an arm around her shoulder as they walked to the stairs. When they reached the bottom, he bent down and picked her up, carrying her to the top and then placing her on her feet as he fumbled with his keys. Once inside, Hope stripped her clothes as she made her way to the bedroom, Nic chuckled at her as he picked up each article of clothing as he followed. When he rounded the door to their room, he found Hope lying face down, naked on top of the covers. Being the kind of man that he was, he decided she'd slept long enough in the car and stripped himself bare, climbed on the bed, and ended the day on a very high note.

***

Nic smoothed the hair from Hope's neck and kissed her gently as he leaned in to say goodbye. He had a million meetings scheduled for that day and had to be in the office early. Since he'd called Rose and told her he was whisking Hope off for a few days to take her mind off John Cummings, Hope had to work today, and he wouldn't see her until tonight. Wanting to see the sky-blue of her eyes before he left, he kept kissing and nipping her neck, his second favorite part of her body, until she opened her eyes.

"Hey," Hope mumbled her eyes blinking open.

"Hey yourself, sleepyhead, you feelin' ok? You seemed to be worn out.

"Yeah, just tired. All the excitement of the past few weeks is catching up with me that's all."

"I'll try and leave your body alone so you can get some sleep," Nic replied as he nipped her neck, "Tomorrow," he finished as his hand made its way up her leg.

"Don't you have work?" Hope giggled, batting at his hand.

"Mmm," he mumbled his mouth still nipping at that damn spot on her neck; it was like a siren's song calling to him whenever he got near it.

"Nic, work," Hope husked out a little turned on, but knew he needed to leave.

"Right, leaving," he whispered, and then kissed her, but she'd ended the kiss before it set fire to something he couldn't finish. Nic put his forehead to hers, closed his eyes and mumbled, "Later, angel," then he stood and walked out of the bedroom, turning once and smiling at her before she heard him exit the condo.

Leaning back and staring at the ceiling, she knew she needed to get up and take a shower so she could run errands before work. So, she crawled out of bed, and hit the shower, worrying at her lip the whole time. She'd been so happy these past two days, but this constant threat hanging over her head was making her sick. She needed John out of her life so she could protect those she loved and her second chance at happiness.

***

Knee deep in blueprints, Nic reached for his ringing cell and saw "Hope calling." Smiling at the much-needed distraction, he swiped the screen.

"You're just the distraction I needed."

"Nic," Hope shouted then rambled, "I couldn't find one of my shoes, and I went downstairs to my condo to look for it and it's destroyed."

"Your shoe is destroyed?"

"The condo. Oh, God, he's here, he's found me hasn't he?"

"Where are you?" Nic asked as he grabbed his keys heading for the door."

"Upstairs, I locked myself in when I saw the mess."

"Call 911. I'm on my way. Don't open the door to anyone but me or the police, do you understand?"

"Okay, I'm setting the alarm. I'll see you when you get here."

"See you in ten, angel," Nic replied quickly and then ended the call.

When he arrived ten minutes later, the police were there, so he stepped inside his downstairs condo and his jaw tightened at what he saw. Anything that could be had been destroyed. A crowbar he'd kept in a closet lay on the floor and used on the walls. There were so many damn holes it would be easier to tear the sheetrock off and start over. The words cunt, whore and bitch had been painted on the walls with leftover paint, and a chill ran through him. Needing to see Hope with his own eyes, he flew through the door and rushed up the stairs to find the door ajar. He pushed through the door shouting "Hope," and found the condo empty. Intense fear the likes he hadn't felt since Chelsea disappeared threatened to paralyze him until he heard Hope's soft voice on the stairs calling, "Nic are you up there?"

He was so relieved to hear her voice he didn't check himself before responding, and when he made it to the top of the stairs and looked down at her beautiful face he shouted, "I told you to stay inside till I got here." Hope's face fell for a second then she narrowed her eyes and snapped back "You told me not to answer the door to anyone but you or the police, the police got here before you, so I answered it."

As he made his way down the stairs, his heart still beating too fast, he could tell she was pissed. The officer standing next to her cleared his throat and stepped to the side as Nic got to the bottom step and looked down on her. He put both hands on his hips, she put hers on her own, and they both held the other's eyes. Shaking his head, he broke the stare first, mumbling "Stubborn woman," as his hand snaked out, grabbed her at the neck and kissed her.

"You scared the shit out of me when you weren't in the condo," Nic mumbled against her lips. Realizing he was worried when he couldn't find her, she wrapped her arms around him and buried her head in his chest.

"Sorry, I was around back with the police."

"They find anything?"

"No, but they think it's some kids who've been vandalizing in the area. They were one block over when I called and got here two minutes later."

"How'd they get in?" Hope flinched and then took a deep breath.

"I kinda forgot to close the window in the bathroom."

Nic chuckled at first and then he threw back his head and laughed. Twenty minutes ago he thought John Cummings was in town, five minutes ago he thought she was gone, so he figured laugh now or put her over his knee—but the way he was feeling it would be both.

Twenty-Five

There were days in Nic's life if he'd looked back at them and really thought about them, he'd have known there was a sign of things to come. A forewarning in his mind that told him it was going to be a life-altering day. The day Chelsea died, before he got a phone call saying that she had escaped from the rehab facility, he'd woken with tightness in his chest. He'd ignored it, waved it off as stress and gone about his day. Today was the same.

The day before the police had assured him the damage to his condo was vandalism and that kids were responsible, so he'd accepted their conclusion and let Hope drive herself to work. This morning when he woke, he'd had the same tightness in his chest as he did the day Chelsea had died and he should have listened, should have taken better precautions than he did.

Since they'd heard John had disappeared, he'd been insistent Hope not leave the condo without him except for work. He'd made her call when she left for work and call when she arrived. He'd gotten an eye roll from her, but she complied on the threat of retribution. Though, to his estimation, she enjoyed his punishment. He was thinking about that punishment with a smile on his face when his cell rang. He was trying to finish his day and get to The Bayou for a meal and visit with Hope, so he grabbed the phone without looking at the caller ID assuming it was Hope.

"Beuve," Nic answered as he stuffed papers into his briefcase.

"You got dat' girl in your bed?"

"What?" Nic answered but paused his actions as Rose repeated her question.

"You need to let Hope outta' your bed, I got food dat' needs cookin'."

"Rosie, are you saying Hope isn't at work?" Nic asked.

There was a pause on the line and then she shouted "T-Hope not wit' you?" The tightness in his chest doubled, and he absentmindedly rubbed his chest as he looked at the clock.

"She was supposed to be there at four," Nic snapped as he grabbed his keys and started walking towards the door. He'd missed the fact she hadn't called to say she was leaving for work.

"I know what time she supposed to be here, da' question is, where *is* she, *mon ami*?" Rose shouted with panic in her voice.

Nic had the phone to his ear as he hit the stairs, not wanting to wait on the elevator. He traveled down the three flights quickly, and burst through the exit to the parking lot heading to his car. Rose had yelled in his ear the whole way to the bottom, and once she stopped her rant, he told her "I'm heading to the condo to check. Call me if she shows up."

He didn't wait for a reply, just hung up on her as he lowered his large frame into his Mercedes and headed towards his home. He dialed Hope's cell, but it went straight to voicemail. Then shouted, "Fuck," as he got stuck in a traffic jam. The knot tightened more as he pulled in front of the condo, and her Jeep wasn't there. He hit redial on her number as he ran up the stairs hoping she'd left a note of some kind, but found nothing when he searched. *Where the fuck was she?* Grabbing his phone Nic called Rose back, and she answered immediately.

"Tell me you found her," Rose shouted.

"She's not at the condo."

"Call da' police."

"And tell them what? That she's late for work?"

"Tell dem' dere' a madman on da' loose and she can't be found." Nic tightened his jaw at the thought of that sonofabitch and answered, "Right, on it."

This was his fuckin fault, he should have insisted he drive her to and from work until this bastard had been apprehended, Nic thought as he dialed 911. But, just as he figured they would say, when he got through to a detective, he told Nic she had to be gone forty-eight hours for the police to deem her missing.

Nic ended the call in frustration and tried to come up with a plan as he stared at the vase of white irises Hope had bought from a florist the day before. The fragile flowers reminded him of her, delicate on the top yet a thick stalk that could hold the weight of the petals or whatever life through at it. He closed his eyes seeing their first time in the garden surrounded by the flowers. Hope's wet hair matted to her face, the curve of her breast, and the look in her eyes when he'd entered her for the first time, binding her to him. Staring at those symbols of their love, of Hope, his fear for her life turned into hate. If that sonofabitch had her, he would hunt him to the ends of the earth until he found her or kill him with his bare hands for harming her. In a moment of unadulterated rage, Nic swiped his arm across the table sending everything crashing to the floor including the vase of irises. Breathing hard, Nic stared at the flowers and picked one up, breathing in deep the flowers fragrance as he pictured Hope's face.

He knew he couldn't just stand there and wait for the police to decide she was missing, so he pulled out his phone, and found the number to Detective King of the Reno Police Department and hit send.

"You have reached Detective King, I am unable to take your call at this time, please leave a number and I'll get back with you as soon as possible."

"King, this is Nic Beuve, call me immediately, Hope's missing and I need you to light a fire under the New Orleans Police," Nic growled as he headed for his door and his car. He'd search the city himself until her found her.

As he descended his steps, a patrol car pulled in front of his condo, and he froze mid-step as an officer peeled out of his car and looked towards his building.

Nic took the rest of the stairs two at a time and met the officer at his gate.

"This the home of Nicholas Beuve?"

"Yeah, I'm Nic Beuve, are you here about Hope?"

"Sir, we found a white Jeep that seemed abandoned uptown and investigated. We found a purse in the vehicle belonging to one Jessica Cummings, and the vehicle is registered to you."

Feeling his world move off kilter at this news Nic responded with "I'll kill him," as he tried to get through the gate.

Hearing Nic's tone and his threat, the officer narrowed his eyes and demanded, "Kill who?" as he stopped Nic in his tracks with his hand to Nic's arm.

"John Cummings, Hope's brother-in-law, she handed over evidence that will send him to prison, and he wants her dead," Nic gritted out. *How the fuck had he let this happen?*

Twice he'd been unable to save someone he loved, and he wanted to rip something to shreds.

"Maybe we should go inside and discuss this," the officer calmly advised as he kept a close eye on Nic.

"I don't have time to discuss this, I need to find her, you need to find her before he kills her," Nic roared.

"I can understand your concern, sir," the officer placated as he took a step back, his hand on his service revolver, "But I'm gonna need you to calm down so we can discuss this. Now, let's go inside your home, and I'll make a call to the station and we'll see what we can do."

The officer's tone was grating on Nic. He didn't have time for this shit, and he ignored the request.

"Call Detective King with the Reno Police Department, he'll tell you all you need to know. I'm heading out to look for her."

"I'm afraid I can't let you leave until I have all the facts, sir."

"I don't have time for this shit. You want to help, take me to her Jeep so I can see it for myself."

"Is Mrs. Cummings your girlfriend?"

"No, she's my future wife," Nic bit out knowing right then he would marry her as soon as he could. "Now take me to her fucking car," Nic repeated and watched the officer read him, decided he wasn't a threat at that moment and then removed his hand from his weapon and stepped back. Nic moved through the gate, and when he moved towards his car, the officer said, "I'll drive you; I can get more information from you and move the investigation along."

Nic nodded and moved to the passenger door as the officer unlocked the doors and they both climbed in. When they arrived at an office building in uptown New Orleans, he saw Hope's Jeep and his gut tightened as they pulled beside it. When he got out, the officer ordered him not to touch anything in case of foul play, and the look Nic gave him told the officer he knew it was.

Inside were her purse, her keys and her cell phone, as if she'd tossed them in before entering the vehicle, but didn't make it. Nic looked up at the officer and caught him watching Nic's reaction. Statistics showed that when foul play was involved, it's usually the significant other who perpetrates the crime. He didn't have time for the police to suspect him he needed them focusing on Cummings.

"I'm not responsible; you need to call Detective King."

"I've given the information to the detectives in charge and they are trying to track him down as we speak."

Nic looked away praying to God that they were looking for King, and not just sitting around waiting for Nic to trip up, thinking they already had their man. He looked around the parking lot and building wondered why she was here in the first damn place, he'd told her to stay at home until it was time for work, so what was so damn important she left the safety of the condo?

"What businesses are inside the building?"

"Doctors, lawyers, a few small businesses."

"Do they have security cameras?"

"Yeah, and we asked them to review it for anything suspicious and they found nothing."

Nic's raised his brows, finding it hard to believe they had nothing on the tape. "You're telling me a woman disappears from the parking lot and the camera's caught nothing?"

"That the security could see."

"Then let me look, I know what I'm looking for."

"Can't, they volunteered to look, we need a court order to view the tapes and until we can determine foul play is involved, we can't get one."

Nic turned, leveled his anger on the police officer and ground out, "She didn't show for work, her purse and phone are in the car how much more do you need to prove she's missing?"

The officer didn't answer him, and the words *they need a body* entered his head. It would have dropped him to his knees if it hadn't angered him so fucking much.

Drilling his eyes into the officer, he dared him to say it. Fortunately, for him, the officer was smart enough to look away from Nic, but not quick enough. He was done with this shit, he needed them to look for Cummings and he needed it now, so he pulled out his phone, searched his contacts for Judge Thompson, a sitting judge he'd done a renovation for and hit send.

"Fred, Nic Beuve. I need a favor . . ."

***

Two hours later, security footage in the hands of New Orleans detectives, Nic entered the police department, and he, Detective Stevens, and Burns sat down at a computer and pulled up the security video from the parking garage. It showed Hope leaving the building, but as she got further into the parking lot, she disappeared from view. Whatever had happened to her had taken place out of view of the cameras, and it took everything he had not to throw that fucking computer across the room. By his estimation, she's been missing four hours now. The time stamp on the video said 3:30 and it was now 7:30. Nic sat there and stared at the screen. He didn't have a fucking clue what to do next but search for her. He hit replay on the video and instead of watching the surroundings, he watched Hope. She was smiling, happy, and it occurred to him this could be the last time he'd ever see her. *Dieu,* on a fuckin' thirteen-inch screen with her blonde hair blowing in the wind, as she made her way to that bright white Jeep she loved and gave girlie name. Nic felt his lip twitch when he thought about her naming the car snowflake. He'd asked her once why she'd wanted white and not a sleek color like black. Her answer, "Because it reminds me of innocence or purity." He didn't get it then, but watching her now, he got it. She'd been through so much shit in her life she wanted to be surrounded by innocence, by purity to help restore her own—to restore Hope.

Nic wanted this last image of her, he opened the disk drive and pulled out the CD, handed it to the detectives, and asked, "Can I have a copy of this?" Both detectives looked at him, then Burns, breaking the rules, made a copy of the security footage and handed it to Nic.

***

Nic searched the streets, looking in every dark corner as he headed back to the condo to check one more time for clues and any messages on his answering machine. When he arrived, he found Rose and Big Daddy waiting out front, and he said nothing to them as they all made their way up his stairs and into his condo. Nic just shook his head when Rose opened her mouth to ask if the tape showed anything. He walked over to his laptop, dropped the cd in and walked away to change clothes as they viewed the footage.

His phone rang as he was changing clothes, and he grabbed it quickly. The screen said "Detective King" and he answered it on a barked "Took you fuckin' long enough."

"Nic, I got your message to call but I was tied up. If Hope's missing it's not John Cummings, as of five o'clock Nevada time, John Cummings was behind bars."

"Say that again?" Nic replied confused.

"We took him into custody at five our time; he was caught trying to cross the border into Mexico this morning. I just got back with him an hour ago."

Nic hung up on the detective without saying goodbye and ran into the living where his computer was and moved Rose aside. Something on the tape had caught his eye when they'd watched it and tugged at his memory. He found the part where Hope had moved out of the line of sight, and then watched as the corner of a black car drove past, the right bumper smashed in. Nic ran to his desk, dug through paperwork he had and found the insurance report for damages to one of his vehicles. Katherine Beuve's Mercedes had damage to the right front bumper.

Twenty-Six

Time stands still when you think you're going to die and one of the side effects of this; the ability to pull events from the past as clearly as if they occurred the day before. Hope remembered watching football with her father, making brownies with her mother, even fighting over toys with her brother. They were all pushed to the surface as Hope watched Kat pace. Had she known when she got up that morning today might be the last day of her life, she would've kissed Nic a little sweeter, told Rose that she loved her, maybe even stopped at that French bakery and had a beignet. She'd finally had the life she'd always dreamed of, but as she watched Kat mumbling as she paced in front of her, Hope had a bad feeling all that was going the change.

When she'd tried to enter her Jeep, Kat had pulled in beside her and confronted her. She'd blamed her for tearing her family apart and wanted her to leave town. Hope had laughed of course, not reading the look in Kat's eyes. If she'd paid closer attention, she would've seen the woman was on the edge. When Hope laughed, Kat had lost it, and produced a gun from her pocket then jammed it into her ribs instructing Hope to get into Kat's car. She'd complied, afraid to fight her, and after several hours of circling the city, while Kate blamed her for everything from the breakup of her marriage to her daughter's overdose she'd driven home. Kat said she was hungry and needed somewhere she could think, to plan what to do with Hope. With the gun pointed at

237

Hope's head until they exited the car, she reminded Hope she was raised in Georgia and running would be pointless—ladies of the south had deadly aim don't ya know.

With her fingers curled tightly around the wooden arms of Kat's dining room chair, she wondered what Nic was doing. She figured he'd be frantic by now assuming that John Cummings had rolled into town and taken her. She imagined he had the police searching, unfortunately for her; they were searching for the wrong person. She closed her eyes and thought back to that morning. Nic was in his suit as she'd stood at the kitchen counter making coffee for them both. She'd remembered she needed to go to the doctor to get her birth control shot and had made a quick call for an appointment before work. She'd never gotten the chance to tell Nic about her appointment, she'd been too preoccupied with his mouth. When he'd walked into the kitchen and seen her in a short nightgown, he'd walked up behind her, pressed her into the counter as he pulled the strap off her shoulder. Then he'd buried his head in her neck as his hand came up and wrapped around her breast. It had taken her less time to get his clothes off than it had taken him to put them on, and the memory was so sweet to her now.

He'd given her so much, much more than he even knew, and she prayed she'd live to tell him. He was her white knight, like the men she read about in romance novels. She never thought they existed, was sure they were figments of some writer's imagination until he'd swooped in and forced himself into her heart, into her very soul. Now she was at the mercy of his ex-wife, and if she weren't so fucking scared she would have laughed at the irony—she was in her own romance novel gone wrong.

Hope was hungry, tired, and thirsty, and she wasn't about to ask for a thing. She kept her eyes on the gun, her tongue in her mouth, and prayed to God she could figure out what to say to this woman. Kat turned to her suddenly and looked her from top to bottom, a sneer playing across her lips.

"Whore," she hissed and Hope bit her lips in anger. Scared or not, Hope still had a temper even after all those years of being slapped around, and she had a tiny scar on her bottom lip to prove she could be flippant. So, she bit her lips harder to keep from lashing out.

Kat looked around searching for something until she spotted her purse. She moved to it and brought it to the table, laying down her gun and pulling out her checkbook and uncapping her Visconti pen.

"Name your price," Kat asked Hope, her words clipped.

"What?" Hope asked.

"You're nothing but a money grubbing two-bit slut. Name your price and I'll write a check," Kat explained but she looked on edge, desperate for a solution to her problem.

"You want to pay me to leave?"

"You're only after Nic's money," she shouted like the crazy woman she was. Hope jumped at her anger and visible hatred for her, and looked towards the gun she'd laid on the table. Hope started to lift her hand to grab it, but Kat dropped her checkbook and pen when she saw the movement and snatched the gun up, rage morphing her face into something terrifying.

"Don't move," Kat bit out aiming the gun at Hope's head, holding Hope's eyes in place as her heart pounded out of her chest. Then, as if she'd forgotten something, Kat moved away from Hope, her attempted bribery forgotten, her mental state sinking further into madness as she paced again.

Usually the poster child for the sophisticated woman, Kat looked like she hadn't bathed in days. Her hair was a tangled mess its shine gone and her clothes looked like she'd slept in them. Hope wouldn't have recognized her if they'd passed on the street, and coupled with her behavior, it terrified her. She'd never seen someone have a nervous breakdown, but she was pretty sure she was watching one unfold before her eyes. The once beautiful woman, full of attitude and her own self-importance had disappeared. What Hope was now faced with was an on the brink, out of control, sociopath. Kat didn't care that she was hurting anyone she only cared about her own needs. Unfortunately, it was clear the consequences of her past actions and losing her daughter had her on the threshold of murder.

Hope sat glued to her chair, her eyes following Kat as she became further lost in her own world. She kept talking to herself, trying to work through what she needed to do with Hope.

"I'm not gonna lose my family to a whore, she needs to go away, how do I make her go away?" Stopping for a moment, as if an idea popped into her head, she whispered, "Maybe I should call momma."

She was so busy trying to figure out how to get rid of Hope; she hadn't paid attention when Nic's Mercedes pulled into the driveway. Hope was so busy keeping an eye on the gun that she didn't see Nic walk up the steps, cross the porch and open the door. Kat and Hope both jumped when the door flew open and Nic roared, "Have you lost your fuckin' mind."

Kat was so startled when he entered, her finger already on the trigger, she squeezed it when she jumped. Hope screamed as smoke floated from the barrel of the gun and blood sprayed from Nic's chest as he flew backwards against the wall and slid down to the floor.

Like the often-dreamt nightmare when you're running down a hallway, but never reaching the end, Hope ran to Nic as a scream so shrill broke from her throat that a dog howled next door. Dropping to her knees, choking on her words, afraid to touch him afraid not to touch him, she threw herself on him screaming "Nic, oh, my God, Nic."

The pressure in Nic's chest felt like a vice grip had him in its hold, and he couldn't catch his breath. He could sense Hope; feel her hands touching him, her tears falling on his face as she kept shouting his name. He wanted to touch her, tell her he loved her, wanted to marry her, but a light in the distance kept drawing his attention away from her.

"Nic don't you close your eyes do you hear me? The ambulance is one the way . . . NIC!" he heard her shout, and he tried to focus on her voice, but that damn light kept getting brighter. He opened his eyes and looked at Hope, tried to smile one last time at her, as he heard sirens coming closer, and Kat screaming, "What have I done."

There was movement to his right, and he heard that damn Cajun accent he'd grown to love over the past seventeen years break into a caterwaul. "My boy, what have you done to my boy? Oh, sweet Jesus, don't take my boy."

He tried to lift his hand, but it wouldn't move. He blinked, as the light grew brighter still and then heard the sweet voice of his *tit ange*. "Papa," Chelsea spoke softly as she reached out her hand. Nic smiled when he saw his daughter's sweet face and finally lifted his hand to reach out to her.

Hope clung to Nic, kissing his face as Big Daddy applied pressure to the gaping wound in his chest. Rose tried to pull her off him, but she wasn't moving from his side. It was bad, she knew it was, and she was determined to fight his leaving this world.

Rose, her hands twisting repeatedly in panic, trying to make sense of how this happened, looked towards Kat. Her eyes were dead, lifeless, as she kept mumbling over and over "What have I done." Rose wailed at her "You notin' but evil, should be you lyin' on da' floor not my boy." Turning back to Nic and Hope her breath caught when she saw Nic smiling over Hope's shoulder and whispering *"Mon 'tite fille."* Rose whispered "No," and then made the sign of the cross, knew they were losing him if his Chelsea was here to welcome him home. The need to fight for him was strong, so she kneeled down beside him as the paramedics came rushing up the steps and told Nic "You not done in dis' world, you need to fight to stay here wit' Hope, wit' Nicky we cannot lose you, you hear me?"

Nic barely heard Rose's words; he was too busy staring at the shining blonde hair of his *tit ange.* As the light grew brighter, Chelsea came into better focus, and with one last labored breath, Nic heard Hope scream his name as his world went dark for an instant, and then warmth and light he'd never known in his life filled him. When his eyes opened again, he stood in the embrace of his daughter; her sweet smell hit his nose, and he remembered it like it was yesterday.

Strawberries and cream her favorite shampoo.

He folded his arms around her, holding her tight as she buried her head in his chest. After more than a year, he finally had his baby in his arms.

"Papa, I missed you so much."

"My sweet angel, papa missed you more than you know. I've got you now, and I won't let go."

"It's too soon, Papa, you have to go back."

"It's where I'm supposed to be, angel."

"Nicky still needs you," she whispered and he paused briefly thinking about his son. If he could feel any pain it would have killed him to think about Nicky being alone, then he looked at Chelsea's sweet face and knew he couldn't leave her.

"Baby, papa's not leaving you again," he responded, his need to be with her greater than his need to fight to go home and he wondered why. He loved his son, would do anything for him, but the warmth and happiness he felt standing in the light with

Chelsea seemed to override all his instincts.

"Hope needs you too, now more than ever," Chelsea told him, her bright eyes seeming wiser than he remembered. Nic closed his eyes when he thought of Hope. She'd be devastated, lost, he knew that with his entire being, but Chelsea was his daughter, and she needed him more.

"She'll have Rose," he replied but his voice broke and he felt tightness in his chest that wasn't there before. When he first arrived, he'd felt warmth, and now he was beginning to feel cold again.

He saw movement behind Chelsea and looked up to see his *grand-mére* and *grand-pére* standing there smiling at him. Laughing in surprise at seeing them both, he moved around Chelsea and wrapped them in a hug. It had been more than fifteen years since he'd seen his grandparents.

His *grand-pére*, tall and wide like all Beuve men, but with hazel eyes, slapped him on the back and then smacked him on the head as he'd done when Nic was a child and disobeyed.

"Dis,' not you time," he told Nic and instead of feeling happy to see them both, he felt sick to his stomach suddenly and an electric shock jolted his chest. His back arched in pain, and he was unable to breathe, so he grabbed his *grand-pére's* shoulder for support.

"Chelsea needs me," Nic ground out, as the pain subsided.

"Don't be a fool, she's got us," his *grand-mére*, still as feisty as he remembered and as beautiful as a spring day, shouted at him. She was tiny like Hope Nic realized, and her blonde hair had been as light as Hope's in her youth. She placed both her hands on his face and pulled him down for a kiss on the cheek. She whispered, "Time to go back," as he felt a warm hand on his shoulder, and he turned to see Chelsea, concern on her face.

"Papa, you have to go before it's too late."

Nic shook his head, determined he wouldn't let his daughter down again, but an electric shock hit him in the chest again, and he fell to his knees as he heard a distant voice begging him.

"I love you, please don't leave me."

Hope stood staring as they worked on Nic, frozen in place, watching as they pumped his chest up and down. They'd put a breathing tube down his throat, and an Ambu bag was breathing life into his body as they tried to bring him back. With each jolt of electric shock, they gave his heart, Hope jumped, and an anguished cry spilled from her lips. Big Daddy held her from behind, holding her up so she wouldn't collapse as Rose stood at her side praying to God.

Turning her eyes from the sight of Nic's strong body lying there lifeless, she saw Kat sitting in a chair surrounded by the police as they asked her questions. She had tears running down her face as she watched the paramedic's work on Nic. The sight of her tears, when she was at fault, struck a nerve with Hope and before she knew what she was doing, she tore her body from Big Daddy's embrace and launched herself at Kat.

"You did this, you killed him," she screamed as she swung her hand wide and slapped Kat across the face, bloodying her lip with her nails. Kat had been stoic until that slap, but when her head came back up she leveled a look at Hope that told her if she weren't in police custody, she would have killed Hope.

"It should be you laying on that floor," Kat calmly replied and then spat blood out of her mouth and onto Hope's shoe. A police officer stuck his arm between them and told Hope to move back. Big Daddy grabbed Hope around the shoulders and pulled her into his arms. She could see the paramedic's pick up the paddles to the defibrillator and he shocked Nic for the third time. Hope ripped herself from Big Daddy's arms, kneeled at Nic's feet, and then told him what was in her heart.

"You pulled me from the darkness, pieced me back together, and you loved me like I've never been loved in my life. You have to fight do you hear me? I need you Nic, we need you, you can't leave us," Hope begged her words choppy with emotion. "Please, Nic, please, I love you," she sobbed as one of the paramedics said, "We need to move." Big Daddy tried to pull her back, and she pulled away from him shaking her head.

"No," Hope cried out "I'm not leaving him; he has to know I love him, that I need him to fight." Big Daddy let her go, and she stood at his feet as they picked up the stabilizing board they'd placed Nic on. One tech stopped chest compressions to move him, and the other kept pumping the Ambu bag. Nic's hand fell from the gurney and Hope dashed to his side grabbing his warm hand and held on as they rolled him quickly to the ambulance. Right before they loaded him, she leaned in and whispered in his ear.

The third time the electric shock hit Nic Chelsea started fading. He struggled to stand and reached out to her, tried to keep the connection. She helped him to his feet and wrapped her arms around his waist hugging him one last time.

"It's time to go Papa," she whispered to him, and he tried to fight the pull he felt hearing Hope crying out to him.

"I don't want to leave you," he whispered back, "I failed you before."

"You never failed me, Papa. *I* failed me."

Holding her close he put his mouth to her ear and whispered "*Tu me manques,* so much it hurts," as he felt his grip on her weaken.

"*Je t'aime,* Papa," she answered back, and he tried to hold on to her but Hope's whispered voice called to him, and he let go and turned from Chelsea when he heard, "*Mon coeur je t' aime, je t' aime. You're going to be a father again, please don't leave me all alone.*"

245

Epilogue

White irises were everywhere, their scent overwhelming the room. Hope had wanted those flowers on this day; they'd reminded her of Nic, of their love. Their delicate petals, a symbol of hope, of love, of New Orleans seemed appropriate. Their sturdy stalk was Nic holding Hope up, carrying her when she'd been vulnerable, afraid—lost. The dainty petals were fragile, yet strong like Hope, and even though she'd been through hell, her very essence was one of innocence, purity, angelic like those white petals.

Rose inspected the room one more time to make sure it was ready for the reception that followed. She wanted everything to be perfect. Didn't want Hope to worry about a thing 'cause she had enough to worry about and a baby growing in her belly to take care of. Rosie turned to see Roscoe waiting for her, his dark suit making the man she'd loved all these years look even more handsome to her.

"It's time, Rosie."

"Don't know how I'm gonna get tru' dis' day," Rosie sighed. Roscoe shook his head as he made his way to his wife and then he wrapped the love of his life in his arms and put his mouth to her ear saying, "Only you would turn a weddin' into a day of mourning."

"I'm not mourning you fool, I don't know how I'm gonna get tru' dis' day wit'out crying my fool head off. Beautiful love stories always make me bawl like a crazy woman. You know dat."

"Rosie you cry at commercials."

"Dat' one wit' da' animals and da' sad song would make a serial killer cry I 'guarontee." She felt Roscoe's chest rumble with laughter as he agreed, "All right, Rosie, I admit that one gives me a knot in my throat."

"Give you more dan' a knot you old fool and you know it," Rose told him and then pulled from his arms. "Let's get dis' show on da' road . . . We got a weddin' to attend.

***

Standing in profile, Hope gazed at her baby bump as it pushed through the fabric of her wedding gown. She was six months along and baby Beuve was restless. They didn't know if it was a boy or a girl and wanted to keep it that way. Though, Hope felt sure it was a girl. Running her hand up and down her belly she whispered, "Your papa wouldn't let you come into this world without his name; we're getting married today, *tit ange*." She saw movement in her peripheral as Abby walked in carrying her bouquet, and she turned to her friend smiling.

"Nic is pacing like a caged tiger," Abby laughed as she approached Hope.

Rolling her eyes, Hope laughed with her friend. Since the kidnapping and finding out Hope was pregnant with his child, and let's not forget that he'd been shot and almost died, Nic was obsessively protective. He didn't like her out of his sight for very long, so Hope had to learn to adjust to his new over-the-top protectiveness. He'd cut back on his hours at the office to fully recover from his injuries and to be there for Nicky and Hope, not to mention dealing with the aftermath of Kat's actions. Every time Hope thought about that day, and how close they all came to losing Nic, she felt her heart race and tried to block the thoughts from her mind. She'd never been that scared, not even when she'd fought for her own life.

After the paramedics had left with Nic, Big Daddy had driven Hope and Rose to the hospital. By the time they arrived, they'd already rushed Nic into surgery and all they could do was wait and pray. Hope thanked God every day for Rose and Big Daddy's strength. Had she been there alone she would have given into her feelings of despair, but they'd both kept repeating, "Da' man is a fighter he is, don't you worry T-Hope he'll be just fine." After two hours in surgery a nurse came out and gave them an update, he was still in the operating room and holding his own, his blood pressure was good and the nurse had commented he was a fighter, that his will to live was strong. The bullet had missed his heart, nicked a lung and lodged in his back, and Hope had become ill hearing his injuries. Nic Sr. and Tilly arrived with Nicky not long after the update, all with pale faces. Nicky was a mess knowing his mother had shot his father, though it was an accident, and it had the boy clinging to his grandmother like a small child. Hope knew he would have a long road ahead of him dealing with her actions, and decided right then, no matter what happened with Nic, she would do what she could to help his mother.

Kat, in all her selfishness, had revealed a lot that day. She hadn't dealt with the loss of her marriage and most importantly, she hadn't dealt with the loss of her daughter. Grief can be a powerful thing gone unchecked, and Kat had gone on with her life not dealing with all she had lost. She'd needed a scapegoat for her own actions and Hope had been an easy target for her anger. Unfortunately for all involved, when she'd followed Hope to the doctor, seen the sample of prenatal vitamins Hope had put in her purse as they argued, she'd snapped. Hope knew what she needed was counseling, not incarceration, and if she could make that happen she would, for Nicky and for Nic.

When the nurse returned three hours later to tell them the doctor was finished and the surgery went well, they'd all cried out and then hugged each other. Big Daddy, Rose, Nicky and Tilly, even Nic Sr., had clung to each other in relief and thanked God in silent prayer for their miracle. When Nic was moved to ICU, they'd allowed visitors for fifteen minutes and Hope had insisted Tilly and Nic Sr. take Nicky in first so he could see for himself that his father was okay. But, they'd insisted she come with them, she was family in their eyes and wouldn't be left out of their family visit.

Nic, who was normally so full of life and attitude, seemed fragile to Hope when they'd walked in. He was on life-support, tubes and IV's attached to every limb it seemed, but he was alive and that's all the mattered to Hope. Tilly had rushed to his side and carefully put her mouth to his forehead as tears streamed down her face. Nicky, almost afraid to touch his father, had stood at the foot of the bed and grabbed his father's foot just to touch some part of him, as Nic Sr. had cleared his throat at the sight of his only child clinging to life.

"He needs to hear your voice," Tilly told the room and then whispered something into his ear. She then reached out her hand to Nicky and he went to her, leaned in, and spoke to his father. As he did, the heartbeat monitor registered a slight increase in Nic's pulse and Tilly smiled. Nic's father then moved to him, laid his hand on his son's shoulder and with a booming voice instructed his son to "Fight for your family, don't you leave us." Tilly had sobbed at his order and then turned to Hope, put out her hand and Hope moved to her.

"Give him a reason to fight, sugar." Tilly whispered

Hope looked at Nic, his battered and bruised body lying there, not moving, and leaned in kissed his lips and then whispered in his ear, "If it's a girl I want to name her Olivia Rose; if it's a boy, Thomas after my father if that's all right with you." At her words, the heart monitor again registered a slight increase in his heart rate and Hope smiled. She figured that was his way of saying that was just fine with him.

After two days of touch and go, Nic finally opened his eyes, and it took him all of a minute once he did to insist that damn breathing tube be removed from his throat. Three days after that, he insisted he be released, but it took him two days more to convince the doctors all he needed was rest at home with his son and Hope to recover fully. He was right. Once home, with Hope and Nicky close, he'd relaxed and let his body heal. Not that he'd had to lift a finger. Between Hope, Rose and Tilly, the man had wanted for nothing—except peace and quiet.

Once Tilly was sure her son would be okay, she'd taken Nicky back to Baton Rouge with her so Nic and Hope could have some alone time together. It was then that he'd told her about Chelsea. He wasn't sure if it had been a dream or if he'd really been with his daughter, but one thing he knew with certainty, Hope had pulled him back from wherever he'd been when she'd told him about the baby.

The next few months had been an exercise in self-control for Hope. Nic, being a man, had insisted he was fine after a week home and then began the "I don't want you out of my sight and stop lifting heavy objects or I'll put you over my knee," routine. Hope had rolled her eyes when he got like this, but understanding that Nic had lived five hours not knowing where she was, and then dealing with the legalities of what his ex-wife had done, she didn't fight him.

Kat had been charged with kidnapping and attempted murder and Nicky was devastated. Nic and Hope had spoken with the

DA, explained all that had happened in their lives the past three years, and got him to reduce the charges. Nic had hired Kat the best attorney money could buy, for Nicky's sake, and she'd been smart enough to plead guilty to a lesser sentence. Kat was then remanded to a facility for treatment and once she completed her sentence, she'll move back to Georgia where her parents can support her in her outpatient therapy, as well. The court had no problem awarding Nic full custody of Nicky, but Nic did allow supervised visits with Kat in Georgia. And by supervised he meant the whole family would travel together. On those visits, he wanted Nicky's head on a pillow he controlled at night, while he kept a close eye on his son during the day.

Two months after John Cummings was arrested trying to cross the border into Mexico, the Cartel he'd smuggled drugs for took a hit out on him. As he lay on his bunk in lockup, an unknown assailant stuck a shank into his heart, ending his miserable life. As far as the Cummings family was concerned, Hope was gone and could stay gone. No one was looking for her now.

Once Nic had all his and Hope's ducks in a row, his son under his roof permanently, he'd come home one day and loaded Hope into her Jeep and drove her out to his favorite bayou. He'd had a houseboat waiting for them when they arrived; stocked with everything they'd need for a night under the stars.

When the moon was full and Hope was naked, Nic reached into a bag, pulled out a ring with a huge diamond haloed with smaller ones, and slipped it onto her finger kissing it.

"Are you asking me to marry you?" Hope whispered looking at the ring.

"My baby isn't coming into this world without my name, so don't fight me on this," Nic warned.

"Are you marrying me because of the baby?"

"For fuck sake, sugar, I'm marrying you because I can't live without you," Nic rumbled as he rolled Hope to her back, careful not to lie on her stomach.

"Better," Hope smiled and then wrapped her arms around Nic's neck, "But your approach needs work, how about you show me your execution." Nic growled low, and then buried his head in her neck and whispered in her ear *"Ma doux amour*, you said I pulled you from the darkness, pieced you back together, but the truth is I was falling apart until you walked into my life. I'd lost part of my reason for living, and the only thing holding me together was Nicky. You gave me meaning again, restored my life to one I wanted to live. You, Hope, restored *my* hope, that this life still held something beautiful for me. Marry me my heart, my soul, my reason for living."

Breathing hard and a little shocked he had it in him, Hope whispered, "That was an eleven out of ten."

"Are you gonna answer me or leaving me hanging?"

"Oui, ma doux amour." Nic's face warmed when she said yes in his native tongue and then moved to his back taking her with him.

"You've got two months to make it happen, angel."

"That's not enough time," Hope whined.

"Two months, sugar, I mean it. I don't want you stressed in your last three months. You get two months or I'm hauling you to the justice of the peace."

Hope knew when to fight him and this wasn't one of those times. He was in protective mode again and he wouldn't budge. So, she'd grudgingly agreed to plan their wedding in two months, with the help of Rose and his mother of course.

Hope looked in the mirror one last time; her strapless off-white gown she'd ordered through a boutique in New Orleans was stunning. The hand-beaded bodice had an empire waist, and layers and layers of tulle to accommodate her baby bump. She looked like an angel, and she was more than ready to marry her prince. She'd left her hair down with loads of loose curls and tiny crystal gems here and there to give it a magical touch. Her dress had been hemmed so she wouldn't trip over it, and she'd gone with ballerina flats instead of heels so she could be comfortable during the night.

Tilly and Rose both gasped when Hope walked out of the bedroom. With her own parents gone, Rose was the closest thing she had to a mother and Tilly and Hope were becoming closer with each passing day. Big Daddy was giving Hope away and Nicky was standing in as best man. They'd wanted a small intimate wedding with only close family and friends and Rose had insisted the wedding be in her backyard. She'd pulled out all the stops, too. Twinkle lights were strung throughout trees and shrubs. A lighted trellis for the vows was in front of the water feature and a white runner down the center for Hope to walk down, with chairs on either side. The food was setup inside the house to keep the night critters at bay and a dance floor and band set near the back of the yard. The whole yard looked like something out of a fairy tale because both Nic and Hope deserved it. And when Rose decided to do something, she did it up big.

Abby, who was Hope's matron of honor, was dressed in a soft-pink, strapless gown. It too had layers of tulle and complimented Hope's gown. Her hair was up, and her long neck was graced with a strand of pearls that Hope had bought her as a gift. Abby handed Hope her bouquet of white baby roses as big Daddy knocked on the door. He poked his head inside and asked "We doin' this or what?"

Oh, yes, they were definitely doing this, even if Rose had to marry Nic and Hope herself there would be a wedding this night. Rose was about to tell Big Daddy to cool his heels when she heard Nic in the hall bellow, "Sugar, you've got one minute to get downstairs and marry me or I'm coming in and carrying you down these stairs."

"Nicholas," Tilly laughed as the room burst into laughter.

"I'm coming, sheesh," Hope called out and Nic could be heard grumbling as he descended the stairs, "Should have hauled her to the justice of the peace."

"Well, I'd say my son has waited long enough for the right woman don't you think?" Tilly announced as she wrapped Hope in a hug and then patted her baby bump. "You look beautiful, sugar. Now, go marry my son before he beats his chest and carries you off." Nodding, Hope looked around the room and smiled.

"Thank you all for everything you've done. When I came to New Orleans I never imagined this happening. I finally have a family again, one that I will cherish for the rest of my life."

"*Cher*, don't make me cry before da' ceremony," Rose wailed and then pulled Hope into a hug. "You like my daughter you is, and I'm gonna tell you what I told her on her weddin' day. Love your man wit' all your heart and the rest of it will fall into place. Dere' notin' you can't ovah'come when you put love first."

"Okay, Rose," Hope whispered and then squeezed her back, expressing her love and gratitude for her surrogate mother.

"Now, let's get you married 'cause dat' man is more dan' ready."

Big Daddy took Hope's hand and led her out the door; Abby descended the stairs first and then Hope and Big Daddy followed. Once Tilly and Rose had made their way to their seats, a Cello began playing Unaccompanied Cello Suite No. 1 by Bach as Abby made her way to the altar. When it was Hope's turn to exit the house and everyone stood, a Zydeco rang out playing the Cajun wedding march. Hope had wanted something Cajun in her wedding and thought Nic would get a kick out of the festive tune. But, when Hope made her way to the end of the runner, and she looked up at Nic, her breath caught. He wasn't smiling when he saw her; his face was the portrait of a man barely holding on to his composure. His eyes were bright with emotion looking down the aisle at Hope and as she made her way to him, his breathing became labored as he tried to keep himself in check. He lost the battle as she grew closer, and he took a few steps to close the distance between them. Then he pulled her from Big Daddy's arm, placed his hands or each side of her face and kissed her in front of God and guests.

"You're supposed to do that after we say I do," Hope whispered against his lips, but Nic bit out "Sugar, when it comes to you, I'll kiss you when and where I damn well feel the need."

Lost in his black eyes, Hope smiled as he pulled her the few feet to the altar and then looked at the priest to begin. He kept his arm around her waist during the vows, his hand low on her hip keeping her as close to him as he could. When Father Dominic had Nic place the wedding band on her hand, Nic had all but growled the words, his vow to protect her tore from his lips. Hope stuttered her way through her own, stumbling on "Till death do us part" as Nic wiped tears from her face. When they were pronounced husband and wife Nic kissed her again, but this time he did it up right. He put one arm around her waist, his other arm around her shoulders, and he held on tight as he kissed his new wife senseless. Hoots could be heard around the yard and when he finally broke the kiss, Hope muttered "Wow," as Nic wrapped his arm around her neck and asked "How long do we have to stay at this party."

"Nic," Hope warned, but he just chuckled, kissed her again, and then hustled her back down the aisle to backslaps and congratulations as he ushered her around the corner and into the house. Nic wasn't waiting hours to consummate their marriage; he wanted no loopholes for Hope to change her mind.

***

Ten tiny fingers and ten tiny toes lie between both her parents as they rested on their bed together. Olivia Rose entered the world in high fashion three months after her parents were married. Hope's water broke while driving back from a visit to Nic's parents, and Nic, ever the calm and rational man, drove swiftly to the nearest hospital and held his wife's hand as she pushed for several hours. When Hope thought she couldn't push another moment, Olivia Rose entered the world on a wail as both parents cried: Hope for the immense joy that all mothers felt gazing upon their new babies the first time. Yet, sad, wondering if her son would have had the same blonde hair. For Nic, because Olivia looked so much like Chelsea it took his breath away and that old familiar pain knotted in his chest.

As he'd held his new daughter for the first time, and she'd wrapped her hand around his finger, holding on tight, Nic vowed he'd never take for granted the blessings God had given him again.

When Olivia Rose opened her blues eyes and looked at him, he swore he heard a whispered voice say, *"Je t' aime, Papa, be happy."* Closing his eyes, he'd placed a kiss on Olivia's tiny head, and then opened them and watched as she closed her own, her tiny hand still holding his. She was content, felt secure in the knowledge that her papa would keep her safe, her momma would spoil her rotten, and her big brother would keep a very close eye on everyone's second chance.

Other books by CP Smith

Reason Series

A Reason To Breathe

A Reason To Kill

A Reason to Live

Standalone

Restoring Hope

Property OF

FRAMED

Made in the USA
Columbia, SC
19 April 2017